PINK FRONTIER

A NOVEL

BRITAIN LAUREN BOTSFORD

Paperback ISBN 979-8-9921274-2-3
Ebook ISBN 979-8-9921274-0-9

Cover Art by Juliana Ohrberg
Chapter Art by Juliana Ohrberg

britainbotsford.com

To all my lovers who took without giving.

Thank you for the inspiration.

I hate you.

I will always be the virgin-prostitute, the perverse angel, the two-faced sinister and saintly woman.

- Anaïs Nin

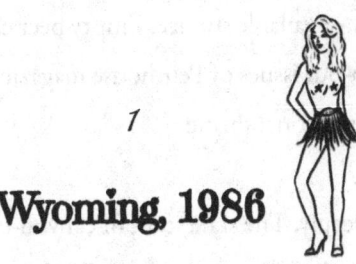

1

Wyoming, 1986

arigold "Lace" Thompson perches on her mother's kitchen counter, shoving cigarettes between her toes. The fading light of dusk pours through the tattered curtains of the cramped trailer, casting a mute glow over the chaotic interior. Dust motes twirl lazily in the golden rays, swirling through the simple heat.

One.

Her long, dirty blonde, unruly hair spills over her shoulders, giving off the impression of wild vines, barely concealing the blown-out tattoos on her shoulder blades. Elegant cursive inks the words "Stay Away" on one side. A defiant mantra. On the other, a cowboy flung skyward from a bucking horse, his outline weathered yet stubbornly alive against skin the sun couldn't bear to leave alone.

Two.

The trailer is a cacophony of neglect. A testament to the tumultuous life she's inherited. Christian memorabilia lines the walls, framed pictures of Jesus and cheesy inspirational quotes mingle with cluttered piles of junk invading any available surface. Empty beer cans, crumpled cigarette packs, and worn-out issues of Penthouse magazine form mountains of debris. An unintentional shrine.

Three.

Lace inhales deeply. The stale scent of canyon-etched cigarettes, mingling with the lingering aroma of spilled beer, forms a heady concoction in the air.

Four.

She wedges a last cigarette between her pinky toe.

Got to go through it.

She stretches into the back pocket of her worn daisy dukes, extracting a silver lighter adorned with the image of a pinup girl—a relic from a bygone era. Flicking it open with ease, she ignites a small flame illuminating the rough edges of her face. With a practiced grace, she grasps her calf, lifting her foot to her mouth, taking a long, languorous drag. Lace's eyes flutter shut as the smoke curls, momentarily escaping the confines of her reality.

Swiftly, the trailer slams open, a loud bang reverberating through the space. It crashes against the wall, rattling the chipped dishes in the sink not far from a distant storm.

The American flag, pinned as a makeshift curtain, waves in the spirit of a startled creature, responding to the sudden intrusion.

Lace doesn't flinch. Instead, she opens her eyes lazily, exhaling a thin stream of smoke through her nostrils.

Darlene Thompson sweeps in, her heels clacking sharply against the oak flooring, a sound harmonious to thunder on a clear day. Lace's mother, only forty, but the hard lines of her face and her disheveled appearance lend her the aura of someone more set in her years.

Her leopard-print bra peeks out from beneath a white wife beater struggling to contain her, while faded denim jeans, cut brutally high at her ankles, reveal a pair of towering stiletto heels that add inches to her already imposing figure. Anger radiates from her, analogous to heat waves off the asphalt, a fireball threatening to consume all in its path.

"Marigold! Didn't I fuckin' tell you no smoking in my damn house?" Darlene barks, her voice hoarse from years of smoking and shouting. She storms over to the couch, snatching pillows and blankets, hurling each one through the door and into the dirt outside.

Lace bears a familiar tightness in her chest, a sinking sensation in her gut. "Not much of a house, if you ask me," Lace snorts softly, the words slipping out before she can snatch them back.

Darlene freezes mid-throw, her back stiffening, and steadily turns to face her daughter, eyes narrowing, reminiscent of a predator zeroing in on its prey. Her lips curl into a thin, dangerous smile as she saunters across the compact kitchen, stopping mere inches from Lace, their faces nearly touching.

"If you're so grown now that you're twenty," Darlene cuts in, her voice low and venomous, "maybe you should go out and find yourself a nice chump to knock you up. Maybe then you'll appreciate the *house* you're living in."

With a mocking flourish, Darlene plucks a camel from between Lace's toes, cradling it as a trophy, each movement dripping with contempt.

Lace clenches her jaw, muscles in her neck tight. She doesn't look away, refusing to let her mother's bravado intimidate her.

Darlene grips the cigarette with a smirk, shaking her head, creating a twisted sense of satisfaction in her eyes. Lace can protest such words bite deep, sharp as a snake's fang, but they don't. She only throws it in her mental box, already overflowing. Darlene turns her attention to the lighter on the counter and lets out a laugh as she catches sight of the pinup girl. She purses her lips around the filter, inhaling deeply, savoring the smoke as it fills her lungs. Lace's eyes narrow, fury simmering barely beneath the surface.

Darlene exhales a cloud of smoke directly into Lace's face, a hazy, acrid mist stinging her eyes and filling her lungs with bitterness. Lace recoils, her heart pounding with indignation as her mother revels in the moment, a satisfied smirk spreading across her lips. With a triumphant look, Darlene turns to walk out, the door slamming behind her with a resonating finality.

Lace's entire body tenses, fists clenched tight at her sides. "My name's Lace!" she shouts after her mother, her voice shaking with fury. "And you said you only smoke Marlboros! Fuckin' hypocrite!" But Darlene is already gone, leaving Lace in the hollow quiet of the trailer.

The stubborn haze her sole companion.

As the moonlight streams through the window above her head, Lace lies in her twin-sized bed, the room closing around her as if she were a moth wrapped in a cocoon. It's a pocket-sized, claustrophobic space, with two beds pushed against opposite walls.

Jean, her younger sister, only six, sleeps peacefully on the other side. Her soft snores are the only sound breaking the suffocating silence. Toys lie strewn about, piles of clothes spilling from the single, overloaded dresser, and sun-bleached artwork prints decorate the walls.

The largest of all, a black-and-white photograph of the Las Vegas Strip, retains Lace's gaze, tugging at her thoughts. She stares at it, her heart aching for the bright lights and endless possibilities shimmering beyond her reach.

She pulls the thin sheet over her head, curling tightly beneath it. The fabric harnesses the nature of a cage, but it's her only refuge.

Some nights, I feel hollow enough that even the dust could fill me. I may disappear in the Wyoming wind if I stand still long enough.

The world outside fades, but Lace softly whispers, careful not to wake Jean, "Please, lord. Let me find my freedom."

The grass is wet with dew as Lace sloshes barefoot across the yard, each step nippy against her skin. She pins up sheets and blankets on the clothesline, the damp fabric tugging lightly against her fingers. The morning sun hangs low, barely breaking through the clouds, casting a dreary light over the neighboring trailers. The narrow strip between the trailers presses in on her, a tight, unyielding pocket of space.

Lace glances over to see Jean playing with a few neighborhood kids. They drag a plastic chatter phone through the dirt, squealing with laughter. Watching them, Lace senses a twinge of envy. When Jean pulls the string too hard, and the toy lurches forward, nearly toppling one kid, Lace snaps, "Jean, be careful, for Christ's sake!" Her voice cuts through the giggles, jarring them all. Jean freezes, wide-eyed, and Lace softens, muttering, "Just...don't hurt anyone, okay?"

Dressed in frayed blue shorts and a cropped Blondie t-shirt, Lace eyeballs at the sight of Darlene sprawled out on a gaping lawn chair. Darlene is entirely naked, as if she is sunbathing in Haulover Park instead of in their scrappy front yard. Her stomach holds a silver reflector that catches the weak sunlight; rollers are haphazardly pinned in her hair. Darlene snores lightly, utterly unaware of the world around her.

The children's laughter, the sheets flapping in the breeze, and unremarkably the cigarette burning at a snail's pace between her fingers go unnoticed. Lace jerks her head, annoyance sparking akin to a struck match. "You tryin' to give the whole block a show or just Jerry next door?"

But the dust-marked woman remains asleep, limbs slipping through the webbing. "I'm going into town," Lace states, half-hoping for a response. She bends down to steal her mother's carton of cigarettes, huffing a laugh.

Camels.

Lace trudges down the prairie edge as the sun climbs higher, turning everything bright and hard-edged. She walks with her shoulders back, chin up, as if daring the world to knock her down. Behind her, she hears the low, lazy growl of an engine, and a car rolls into view—a faded black Chevy Nova. The kind she had not long ago spotted parked outside the feed store, with patches of rust along the fender and a long, jagged crack in the windshield.

The car eases as it nears her, moving at a crawl, and Lace notices a prickling awareness of eyes on her. She glances over, and her stomach twists. It's Billy Rae Hendersen, her dad's old as dirt friend, who used to come by the trailer when she stood a kid. He leans out the window, squinting at her with an all too-familiar grin. "Well, if it ain't little Marigold," he drawls, and something in his voice makes her feel cornered, appearing as if he's got the upper hand.

Lace glares at Billy Rae as his eyes trail down her legs, deliberate and shameless, lingering in a way that makes her skin crawl. He doesn't even try to hide it; he simply grins lazily. Acting as if he's earned the right to look.

She harbors his gaze, pressing against her. Something she can't shake off.

She's learned that to be called pretty is nothing but a polite way of saying to *keep quiet and be looked at.* Somewhere along the line, far too young, her face and body stopped being hers and became an invitation for strangers to stare, a silent permission she never gave. And yet, here she is again, mirroring nothing more than a thing to be looked at, something teeny and glittering, no more than another prize for men cut from the same cloth to leer over.

Lace keeps her face steady, jaw tight. "What d'you want, Billy Rae?" she snaps, already tired of this exchange.

He chuckles, low and greasy. "Just makin' sure you're safe out here," he says, savoring each word. Comparable to a kid tasting Nerds for the first time. "Road's no place for a little thing like you. Bet your daddy wouldn't like it one bit."

Lace's anger flares torrid. "Well, Daddy's not around to care, is he?" she barks back, not hiding the bitterness in her voice. She glares at him, welcoming him to look her in the eye instead of wherever he's been staring. "And I don't need any babysittin'."

Billy Rae's grin fades, his face twitching in mild surprise. But he recovers quickly, tilting his hat as he looks at her, his smile sliding back into place, lazy and slimy. His voice cuts through the heat. "You know, you got your mama's looks," he says, his eyes dragging up and down her frame. "But I'd wager you're a little sweeter."

"Why don't you bite me, Billy," Lace cracks back, wrapping her arms around her stomach.

"Feisty," he murmurs, more to himself than to her. "You take care now, darlin'. Don't go gettin' yourself into trouble." He finally pulls away, the Chevy kicking up a cloud of dust as it rumbles down the outskirts. Lace stands there momentarily, arms clenched, watching the car disappear. Her heart pounds with anger and something she can't quite name—something she wants to shake off.

She turns and keeps walking, her steps harder and quicker, as if she can leave his voice and look behind her, miles down the fence line.

Where they belong.

2

Welcome Wagon

The relentless heat of a Wyoming June clings to Lace in the nature of a parched hide, its dry grip easing only slightly as she steps into the stale, mildewed air of the dilapidated gas station. Flickering fluorescent lights overhead illuminate all, wishing to stay hidden. Her bare black feet slap rhythmically against the cool tiles as Lace wanders through the narrow aisles. Near the counter, a snug television hums, its grainy screen showing a man in a stiff blazer and a somber expression.

Lace pauses, her hand hovering over a pack of gum, as the news reporter's voice cuts through the static, heavy with practiced solemnity.

"In the weeks following the tragedy, the tight-knit community has struggled to find answers and healing. Parents and children alike speak of nightmares and lingering fear. Some call it a miracle, others a horror. One youngster described feeling the presence of angels moments before the explosion."

Cokeville.

How could she ever forget? A man and his wife had stormed an elementary school with guns and a homemade bomb. They herded the teachers and kids into a single room. The bomb went off—something about a malfunction. People whisper about miracles—how no children died—but she can't wrap her mind around it. A lunatic strapped a homemade bomb to himself in a room packed with little bodies, and through whatever means, no child met their expected fate.

A miracle. Or maybe luck wasn't itching to bear the weight of too many young souls all at once.

Cokeville, merely two hours shy from Big Piney, uncomfortably close—too close. *That easily could've been Jean.* She imagines her sister's wide, curious eyes staring at a stranger who tells her to sit down and shut up, the comprehension of danger settling across her face. Lace's chest twists, a sharp ache spreading under her ribs. What if it had been Jean in that room, dragged into the center of some madman's crusade? Would Jean have been the kid who sang songs to keep the fear at bay, or would she have clung to her teacher, trembling?

Lace swallows hard, her mouth dry. She tries to picture herself storming through the school, tearing the doors off their hinges, and pulling Jean out before the smoke and fire could touch her. But she knows better. She wouldn't have been a hero. She'd have been stuck on the other side, helpless.

The thought makes her stomach churn. Lace's eyes drift to the television again, the reporter persistently recounting the aftermath. "A divine intervention," he says, his voice steady but detached, functioning as if he doesn't have a clue what divine intervention truly looks like.

With a heavy sigh, she trudges toward the refrigerator in the back; the door squeaking as she yanks it open. A single glass coke bottle piques her interest. She grabs it, the chill of the glass seeping into her palm. The cashier, an elderly man with a weathered face and a permanent frown etched into his features, glances up from his ancient register as she approaches. His eyes are clouded with indifference, and he barely acknowledges her presence.

"That'll be ninety-six cents, darling," he mutters, his voice gruff and disinterested.

Lace instinctively makes a grab for her bra, fishing for change, her fingers brushing against the cool metal of coins nestled between her skin and fabric. The cashier coughs, his gaze shifting over her shoulder as if searching for anything more interesting than the girl standing before him. Annoyed, Lace slaps three quarters and two pennies onto the counter, her hands resting defiantly on her hips as she waits for him to take the coins.

Instead, he stares blankly at her, offering no sign of movement. "That's seventy-seven. You need nineteen cents more, ma'am," he states flatly, his tone suggesting it was a matter of fact, not a conversation.

Lace tilts her head, irritation boiling beneath the surface. "Well, I ain't got that," she retorts, a bite to her tone as she stares him down.

The cashier pushes the coins away from him, his expression unchanging. "Well, come back when you do," he replies, as if the exchange were a mere annoyance in his mundane day.

With an exaggerated sigh, Lace snatches the coins back. "Ninety-six cents. This country is going to hell in a handbasket," she mutters under her breath. She turns sharply and storms out of the gas station. The bell above the door jingles farewell.

Stepping into the sweltering sun, the heat smashes into her. Lace squints against the brightness, her annoyance only growing as she scans the barren parking lot. A single blinking light dangles from a wire at the town's one major intersection, flicking between red and yellow.

A couple of kids ride by on rusted bikes, their laughter echoing off the boarded-up windows of the time-tested mercantile. To the left, her beaten-up school, she dropped out at fifteen for no viable reason. One day, she simply stopped showing up. No one from school came by the trailer, and Darlene never blinked twice.

Its faded brick facade looms, and the sign out front missing the letter "o" in "Home of the Broncs," now states, "H me of the Broncs." The windows are speckled with grime, and there's a faint outline of posters for school dances no one ever entirely looked forward to. A couple of stray dogs wander through the dirt lot across the street in front of the shuttered-up bowling alley, noses down as if looking for something lost.

Lace figures they won't find much except cigarette butts and empty beer cans. She remembers the nights she'd sit out behind the alley, watching the older kids sneak beers, their laughter filling the dusky veil. Something almost alive. Something she wanted to be a part of until she didn't.

Nothing ever appears to leave this place, not really. It's like it's pressing down, pinning everything here. Nothing more than a mosquito stuck to a windshield, every street and every faded building—forever stuck in the same place. The highest structure is a giant, aging billboard off to her right. It towers above the gas station, decorated with peeling paint and rusted crosses.

Its faded letters announce: "IF YOU'RE LOOKING FOR A SIGN, THIS IS IT." She stares at the billboard, its words digging into her as if trying to extract a confession.

As she rolls her eyes, she spots a man in a ridge-top cowboy hat leaning against his battered pickup truck. He's waiting for the gas pump to click off, his posture accessible but watchful. He tilts the brim of his hat toward her in a lazy acknowledgment. Ignoring his gaze, Lace clambers onto the ice machine beside the station, plopping down cross-legged.

The metal cools against the back of her thighs as she leans into it; she reaches into her pocket to slip out her lighter and pack of camels.

Closing her eyes as she inhales the smoke, trying to block out the heat and dead noise. She lets the moment settle, breathing in the faint scents of gasoline and smoke.

After a few moments of solitude, the low thump of music begins to invade her peace, growing louder and more insistent. She recognizes the voice of Jefferson Airplane, humming the tune White Rabbit. Lace cracks open one eye, squinting into the harsh light.

A red Pontiac GTO convertible speeds down the road. It skids to a stop at the pump next to the man, its engine purring with a life of its own. The car's bumper sticker intrigues her as it draws nearer *Calvin from Calvin & Hobbes* peeing on the Ford logo. A scraggly blonde hair extension hangs off the edge of the California license plate, flapping like a discarded souvenir.

Lace watches as a girl tumbles out of the car, having all the hallmarks of vibrant bursts of color against the muted backdrop of the terrain. The girl in the passenger seat vaults out without bothering to open her door. She wears pink roller blades whirling against the pavement, paired with bell bottom jeans splattered with red heart patches. A sheer tube top leaves little to the imagination, while star-shaped nipple piercings glint in the sun.

The girl gushes with energy, her laughter spilling as she rolls toward the driver's side. They exchange animated gestures, their voices lost beneath the pulsating music. Lace's gaze fixes on the passenger, captivated by her radiant confidence and carefree energy.

The driver, lounging back in her seat, props her feet on the dashboard and lazily flips through an edition of People's magazine.

Lace can make out the image of Dolly Parton following the headline, "Preppy talk from the slickest country girl ever, as she reopens her $20 million hillbilly park back home in Tennessee."

Lace leans forward, intrigued, as the passenger glides past her and into the gas station.

After a few moments, the girl returns, arms overflowing with snacks—bags of chips, candy bars, and a giant soda precariously balanced on top. One pack of chips slips from her grip, tumbling to the ground with a soft thud. Instinctively, Lace hops down from her perch, bending to pick up the fallen bag. Standing up, she finds herself face-to-face with the girl. The girl's wild, unkempt chestnut hair frames her face similar to a halo, and her piercing brown eyes, smudged with black eyeliner, widen in surprise at the sight of Lace.

"Thank you, darlin'," the girl beams, flashing a silver-toothed smile.

Lace silently hands over the bag, intrigued by this vibrant stranger.

"Where y'all headed?" she inquires, gesturing toward the driver, who now swings her legs out of the car leaning against the side, peering curiously at them.

The girl grins. "Home," she replies, her voice bright and warm.

"Where's that?" Lace presses, her curiosity igniting further.

"Town in Nevada no one knows about," the girl explains. "Me and Trish decided to take a good ole fashioned American road trip to see Yellowstone. Not much of a road trip, though. Only took us about a day, and we ran out of blow two hours in."

Lace nods, rocking back and forth on her heels. "You wanna come with?" The girl asks abruptly, her tone inviting yet urgent.

Lace freezes her mind speeds. "What?"

"Come with us," the girl says again, jerking her chin toward Trish, now back to lazily thumbing through the magazine, boredom settling in. The girl tilts her head to the side, clicking her tongue. "You've got something—what do they call it? Spunk. Reminds me of Sam Fox. I can see it. And no, it's not just because you're rockin' a massive rack."

"To Nevada? I..." Lace stutters.

"Got anyone who will miss you? Any reason to stay in this shit hole? No offense," the girl presses.

Lace takes a moment to consider, her mind flickering tantamount to candle flames in the wind. "Not really..."

"Well then, c'mon, honey. We don't got all day. It's hotter than hell out here, and I need the wind in my hair," the girl says. Lace glances down at her bare feet, the heat of the asphalt radiating beneath her. "We can go get your belongings real fast if you'd like," the girl adds, sensing Lace's hesitation. Trish perks up at their exchange. Closing her magazine with a snap. She shoots a curious look at Lace, her expression unreadable.

Lace turns to the towering billboard once more, silently praying for it to blow up in flames at this very moment. The girl follows her gaze, bursting into laughter as she attempts to point at the sign without dropping any more of her snacks. "I think God is trying to tell you something, honey," the girl quips.

Lace lets out a fleeting breath, contemplating her next move.

Should I? Maybe it's stupid, maybe it's reckless, but it's also somethin'. And I'm tired of having nothin'.

Tired of my own reflection in the trailer's bathroom mirror. Tired of the gnawing emptiness wedged beneath my ribs, a restless splinter that won't let me forget.

This could be the beginning of something—whether it blooms or burns, I can't say. I can't even put a name to it, can't even picture it, but it's there.

Wantin' somethin' you can't even see? That's a special kind of hell.

Oh, fuck it. I have to get out of here.

But before she can respond, the girl has already skated back to the car, tossing the snacks into the backseat with carefree abandon. "Shit," Lace whispers, her heart surging. In a burst of adrenaline, she jogs after them, calling out, "Wait!" The girl turns, a wide grin plastered across her face. Lace stops in front of the passenger seat, the moment stretching as she throws back a hesitant smile.

"I'm coming with y'all," she declares, her voice firm despite the tremor of uncertainty. Lace hops over the backseat door, inadvertently pushing aside the pile of snacks the girl has collected. She settles into the middle seat, her eyes landing on a cherry air freshener and a wispy dreamcatcher dangling from the rearview mirror.

The girl and Trish turn to look at her, surprise lighting up their faces. "I'm Trish," the driver says, a friendly smile breaking through her initial confusion.

"I'm Brandi," the passenger adds.

"Lace."

The two girls smile at Lace. As they pull out of the gas station, gravel crunches beneath the Pontiac's tires. Dust kicks up in a lazy cloud behind them, the midmorning sun glinting off the car's polished surface.

"So, honey, where do you live?"

Lace's heart races as she approaches her trailer. Her fingers tremble as they slip under the edge of the wind-toughened, squeaky window adjacent to her bedroom. With a firm pull, she pushes the window wider, squeezing through the narrow gap with a sense of urgency. She lands softly on the worn wooden floor, the familiar scent of stale air and aged fabric filling her nostrils. The trailer feels eerily quiet. As she stands up, Lace shakes her hair out of her eyes, trying to clear her mind of distractions.

But, from the living room, she hears her mother's voice. "Jean, c'mere, honey," Darlene says, her voice softer than usual. Lace pauses, her heart pounding as she listens. "You're my good girl, ya know that? Always stickin' by your mama." She can almost picture Jean, sleepy-eyed and clinging to their mother's side, her tiny hands wrapped around her mother's arm.

She hears a little giggle from Jean and soon after, Darlene's voice again, this time with a hint of pride. "Couldn't do this without ya, baby girl. You're my little helper, always right here where I need ya." Lace swallows hard, and there it is—the one ache in her chest, that nagging awareness. Maybe they'd be better off without her, without the girl who's constantly pushing and always wanting to run. Listening to her mom's words, she can't shake the thought she's no more than dead space around here, a wild card who doesn't belong.

For a second, she almost perceives herself as selfish. Selfish for not crawling back into bed, forgetting Brandi and Trish, and staying quiet, out of the way, like Jean. She turns in circles, taking in the cluttered room that has been her life for as long as she can remember. Her gaze lands on a worn-down leather duffle bag in the corner, the perfect size for her needs. She tosses it onto the bed and hastily gathers her belongings, shoving clothes into the bag as quietly as possible. The bag fills quickly, but as she rummages through her things, her fingers brush against something cool and smooth: a puny photograph of herself as a baby.

Time stands steady as she pauses, lightly grazing the image with her fingertips. The sight of the picture makes her glance toward Jean's empty bed, a pang of regret twisting in her chest.

What would she think? Would she understand?

Lace rifles through a nearby dresser, her heart pounding as she searches for something to say. To leave behind.

Finally, she unearths a scrap piece of paper and a pen. She uncaps the pen with her teeth, her mind rushing as the words flow from her heart.

JEAN

I'm sorry we never got much of a life together. You won't understand it now, but I pray you do in the future. I will find the dirty parts of heaven, and when I do, I will find you.

Always and forever
Lace. (formerly known as Marigold)

With a shaky breath, she folds the note neatly, tucking it under Jean's pillow—a small gesture, a whisper of hope that would linger long after she's gone. As she slips back out the window, her heart heavier than ever, weighed down with all she wishes her mom had voiced. Trish and Brandi exchange quick glances, their expressions a mix of surprise and understanding as Lace hops into the backseat, breathless and exhilarated.

"Ready?" she gasps, her chest heaving as she looks past Brandi and Trish, her eyes locking onto the ranch road line ahead.

Brandi's grin stretches as she yanks out a wrinkled, creased map, slapping it across her lap in the guise of a prize. Trish fiddles with the radio, her fingers dancing across the buttons until she finally settles on the comforting harmony of Johnny Cash's "We'll Meet Again."

"To Nevada then," Brandi declares.

As the Pontiac rolls away from the trailer, Lace lets a potent mix of fear and exhilaration swirl in her stomach. The road stretches ahead. A ribbon of possibility, promising the unknown.

She's alive for the first time in—well, forever.

Her life slipping away with each mile.

Leaning against the back seat, Lace's mind scatters, restless as the dust rising in the truck's wake. The radio purrs with a steady beat. Lace leans forward, resting her forearms on both seats. She shouts over the wind and music, "So what do y'all do?"

Trish leans her head back, her tie-dye shirt a splash of color against the fading day. "We work at a brothel out there—one of those legal sex ranches." She speaks as if sharing the plot of a favorite movie, her eyes glimmering with excitement.

"What?" Lace considers if she misheard her.

Flex Dancers?

Vexed Stancers?

Text Enhancers?

Check Branches?

No.

Lace's mind races, images flickering through her thoughts... an old film reel—romanticized notions of the Wild West, women strutting in daring outfits, and cowboys tipping their hats. "A sex ranch?" she echoes, a mix of intrigue and disbelief flashing across her face. "What the fuck does that even mean?"

Brandi leans back, a wicked smile creeping onto her lips, "It's like a playground for grown-ups, babe. People come with some real sick and twisted fantasies. Explore what gets them off. You know." Trish giggles.

Lace raises an eyebrow, "But, like, isn't that a little risky? I mean, don't you worry about the loonies out there?"

Brandi waves her hand dismissively. "Pfft! We know how to handle ourselves."

Trish adds, leaning back, "Last week, this man tied me to the ceiling fan—naked as a jaybird except for these, uh, suspenders he insisted I wear. Said it was 'cause his granddaddy was a fireman, and it was some family tradition." She pauses, savoring the gasp from Lace.

"He's down there in a cowboy hat, boots, and nothing else, hollering about how he's gonna lasso my moon, whatever the hell that means. Next thing I know, he's spinning me around like a damn Tilt-A-Whirl, and I'm just praying that fan don't come loose and send me flying through the drywall." Trish shrugs nonchalantly, lighting a Virginia slim.

"And the kicker? The bastard didn't even turn the fan on high. Had me up there wobbling like some kinda half-assed piñata. Now, when I hear a ceiling fan click on, I clench up." She smirks, flicking ash into an empty Pepsi-Cola can. "Anyway, that's why I don't trust a man who owns too many power tools."

Lace bites her lip, her curiosity growing. "So, you guys really dig it?"

Brandi and Trish collectively let out groans of agreement.

"You should really consider it, doll!" Brandi exclaims as she sticks a slim between Lace's teeth.

The horizon rolls out in waves of amber grass and sun-bleached mesas, and the distant mountains jagged close to a busted knife blade against the cloudless blue. Sagebrush dots the parched earth, and a lone hawk circles lazily overhead, its shadow flickering across the cracked red dirt.

"Maybe I will," Lace murmurs in between drags.

3

Somewhere In Utah

ace leans against the cool, cracked leather of the backseat, wide awake, her eyes tracking the faint outlines of desert scrub and distant hills. The night presses in through the car's open top, warm and heavy. Making the edges come across as if they might as well be melting into nightfall. Ahead of her, the neon glow of the "Lonestar Haven Motel - NO VACANCY" flickers in and out of focus, casting a strange pink-blue light. The lot is almost barren, with a couple of rusted sedans left to bake in the sun years ago and a busted chain-link fence leaning halfheartedly around a shimmering pool—an oil slick beneath the stars. A tattered "GOD BLESS AMERICA" banner flutters weakly in the dry breeze, clinging to a sentiment long since faded.

Trish is quick to action and kills the engine with a twist of the wrist before springing out of the driver's seat. Her cowgirl boots hit the pavement with purpose, and without a second glance, she strolls to the motel entrance. The slam echoes as she disappears into the dingy lobby. Lace stretches lazily, rolling her neck to shake off the stiffness from hours on the lonesome track.

In the passenger seat, Brandi fishes out a compact mirror, her glossy lips puckering up as she applies a fresh coat of kissing slick. The marginal ritual is a distraction. Something to pass the time as Trish works her magic inside.

Lace's gaze follows Trish through the dirty window, watching her approach the front desk with a practiced charm. Trish unwraps a piece of orange fizz candy and pops it in her mouth, leaning provocatively over the counter as the clerk—a younger man—watches her, clearly amused.

He doesn't stand a chance. Trish's fingers dance toward the wall, and a set of keys is hers in the blink of an eye. Lace snorts, shaking her head as Trish strolls back to the car, grinning like the cat that got the cream.

"C'mon, girls! Grab your junk!" Trish calls, her voice bright and playful. Lace shifts in her seat, glancing at Brandi, even now in her roller skates from God knows when, as she slips out of the car without bothering to open the door.

The wheels clatter softly as she rolls to the trunk, popping it open with a dramatic flair. Lace follows, stretching her legs as she climbs over the seat, grabbing her tattered bag from the back. It isn't much, but it's hers as the girls haul out their mismatched luggage—a bright red hardshell suitcase reading "GOING TO GRANDMA'S" and a patchwork denim duffle that has seen better days. Brandi eyes Lace's bare feet, the dirt and chipped black nail polish telling their own story. "Doll, did you not pack any shoes?" Brandi asks, incredulous, her hands on her hips, a dead ringer for an impatient mother.

Lace shrugs, wiggling her toes in the dust. "I like to be one with nature."

Brandi rolls her eyes, shaking her head as they make their way toward the soft pink door of room number four. "You won't be saying that when you step on a rusty screw and lose a foot," she mutters. The door creaks open to reveal a scene that hasn't changed since the '60s. The room is a time capsule—green shag carpet underfoot, faded floral bedspread on a queen-sized bed taking up most of the space, a single brown leather armchair in the corner, and wooden walls closing in on you. Above the bed, a mounted deer head glares out with lifeless eyes, and the musty scent of mold remains faithful to the walls. Lace's nose wrinkles at the sight.

Brandi drops her bag with a groan. "Get real. You couldn't get us a room with two beds?" she snaps, eyeing the lone bed with disdain.

Trish waves her off, already halfway to the bathroom. "Stop bein' a priss. It's just for one night." Something slips from her bra as she peels off her clothes—a tiny plastic baggie of white powder. Trish shrieks, practically giddy, as she snatches it off the floor. "Brandi! I told ya I had more blow!" Without a second thought, she dumps a line on the bathroom counter and snorts it up.

Trish strips her bottoms, revealing a tattoo of an itty-bitty, mischievous-looking cat on her hip. "That's a cute kitty," Lace says softly, her eyes drawn to the ink.

Trish glances down with a smile. "Her name's Kitty." She pauses, then bursts into laughter, as if she just remembered something wild. "Y'know, I got this done by some fella who said he was teachin' himself to tattoo."

She snorts. "He claimed he needed to practice keepin' a steady hand in missionary."

"And you went along with that?"

"Man offered half off. You think I'm saying no to a discount?"

Brandi joins the chaos, yanking off her clothes and rummaging through her bag for a zebra-print bikini. She turns to Lace, fully naked, her voice laced with faux concern. "Did you pack a bikini?"

Feeling out of place in her dusty clothes, Lace shakes her head. "No... didn't think I'd need one."

Trish dives into her bag, pulling out a Polaroid camera. She tilts her chin, trying to find the right angle, her red lips pursed in a pout that's probably practiced in the mirror a dozen times. The camera clicks, whirs, and spits out a square of film. She waves it in the air as though unveiling the Mona Lisa.

"God, look at this. I mean, *look* at this," she gushes, clinging to the developing photo at arm's length, squinting at it. "How the hell did Hugh look at me and *not* put me in Playboy? What was he thinkin'? Legs for days, hair bigger than Dolly's, and a smile that could make a preacher sin."

Brandi snorts, "That wasn't Hugh Hefner, dipstick. That was just some bald, old white guy at the county fair who told you he was."

A slap-like gasp escapes Trish's lips as she clutches the Polaroid to her chest. "You take that back right now! He said he was scouting talent for the *next centerfold*. Said I had a natural glow!"

Brandi scoffs, plucking the photo from Trish's clenched hand. "Honey, his idea of scouting talent was probably just trying to get a free feel. Did he even have a business card, or was he handing out those little calendars with the naked cowgirls on 'em?"

Trish narrows her eyes, her lip twitching. "For your information, he *did* have a card. It just... uh, looked kinda homemade. But that's what made it *authentic*." She crosses her arms with a huff. "You're just jealous Hugh saw *me* and not you."

Brandi bursts out laughing. "Yeah, I'm real jealous of your Playboy mansion. Probably his single-wide out in the boonies."

Trish snatches the Polaroid and stalks toward the mirror, muttering under her breath. "Jealousy's a mean mare, Brandi." Brandi waves Trish off.

"Lace, just wear your bra and knickers," Brandi says, winking as she slides on her bikini. "No one's here, anyway." Lace sits on the floor by her bag, chewing on her lip. She glances down at her worn clothes, a strange cocktail of self-consciousness and curiosity bubbling in her chest. Brandi crouches in front of her, her eyes softening as she cups Lace's face. "C'mon, let's shake off the dust from today. That pool's just hollerin' for us," Brandi drawls, her voice warm and inviting. Lace hesitates, her fingers brushing against the worn fabric of her bag. With a sigh, she stands, following Brandi and Trish into the night.

Lace, Trish, and Brandi float lazily in the warm water of the motel pool, their bodies cradled by the night. Above them, the sky sprawls in the shape of a canvas sprinkled with stars. Twinkling diamonds against Utah's backdrop. "So, Miss One With Nature—what's your story?"

Brandi breaks the tranquil silence, her voice slicing through the lingering heat.

Lace's peaceful exterior shifts faintly. "The desert's dry. I want to live a colorful life." The water ripples around her, reminding her of the ties she can't entirely sever.

Trish rolls over. "You got family?"

"My baby sis, Jean... and my mom," Lace replies, the words slipping out, tinged with pride yet heavy with a longing she can't shake off.

"Sounds like a pretty big life to me," Brandi muses, her eyes narrowing as she studies Lace. Lace senses their gazes, as heavy as the stars above—distant and endless, stripping her bare in the vast quiet. A door slams somewhere nearby, shattering the stillness like a falling star.

The sound echoes, jolting thick with anticipation. "Brandi, look!" Trish whispers, a thrill dancing in her voice.

"Rad." Brandi breathes, her eyes wide.

A man in his late fifties leans against a door three rooms down, half-hidden in shadow. Smoke curls from his lips. Exhaling methodically, his tired eyes lock onto the trio. Trish's excitement bubbles over, and she kicks off toward the pool's edge, her laughter floating all the way to Los Angeles.

"Hey, handsome. You look like you could use some company," she calls out, her voice dripping with flirtation. He doesn't respond with words; instead, he puffs out another cloud of smoke.

He pushes off the door, cigarette flicking from his fingers, as he snuffs it out under the steel toe of his boot. He strides toward the pool, a quiet power emanating from each step. Trish looks back at Lace and Brandi, her eyes sparkling with a devilish gleam. Ever the eager accomplice,

Brandi glides closer, her movements smooth and inviting. Lace hangs back, a mixture of curiosity and apprehension tightening her stomach.

Standing before Trish, the man leans down, his calloused hand cradling her chin. "How'd you know?" he asks, his voice a low rumble, a brooding cloud on the infinite edge—full of promise but withholding the rain.

"I'm an old soul," Trish breathes, her lips nearly brushing against his as she pushes her body halfway out of the pool.

He pulls back enough to keep their gazes locked, his attention drifting to Brandi, who swims closer, her expression sultry and inviting, and finally landing on Lace. "Are all y'all old souls?" he inquires.

"We can be," Brandi chimes, leaning into Trish, creating a tableau of allure, drawing the man's focus deeper.

A raspy and warm chuckle escapes him, intertwining with the night. "Y'all like whiskey?"

4

Paid In Full

The haunting strains of "The End" by The Doors drift from a small radio the man so kindly brought in, wrapping the dimly lit room in a sultry haze. Lace reclines in the armchair, her untouched glass of whiskey resembling liquid gold on the nightstand.

In the center of the room, Trish and Brandi sway in the role of a pair of sirens, their movements playful yet deliberate as they move provocatively in front of the man. He lounges on the edge of the queen-size bed, the crumpled sheets beneath him. With each tantalizing roll of their hips, the girls draw him closer, their laughter ringing out in sync with Jim Morrison, ensuring his gaze locks on each move.

Brandi leans into Trish, their bodies brushing against each other with electric intimacy as they peel off each other's bikinis, giggles escaping their lips. The fabric falls away, revealing their wet skin, bathed in the room's soft, mesmerizing glow. Trish crawls onto the bed with a teasing smile that could melt ice, positioning herself atop the man, her curves framing his rugged form.

He takes a long swig from the half-empty whiskey bottle, savoring the burn. As their lips meet, passion ignites, and Brandi slides onto the bed to join them, intertwining herself in a sensual embrace, their bodies moving in rhythm as if choreographed by fate.

The sight of their intimate embrace, filled with laughter and wild abandon, stirs something deep within Lace, igniting a fire she hasn't realized was there. As Trish and Brandi roll playfully on the bed, the man's gaze flicks to Lace, his expression shifting from playful to something grayer, more compelling. He leans back, brushing the girls aside with a languid grace.

"You shy or something, darlin'?" he drawls, his voice a gravelly whisper sending a shiver down her spine. Lace's heart thunders against her ribcage, the primal energy in the room overwhelming.

Caught in a web of uncertainty, a tempest brewing.

Brandi leans forward, "She's new... Lace, how 'bout you come join us?" Static from the radio blares, casting an awkward silence over the room. Lace remains rooted in her chair, nerves twisting and turning much like a live wire.

Trish tilts her head, a sly smirk drapes on her lips, her eyes glinting with challenge. "She's a virgin," she proclaims.

The man and Brandi turn their heads toward her, surprise flickering across their faces before morphing into intrigue, a predatory spark igniting in the man's gaze.

"Well, I'll be damned. I didn't know there were any more virgins left in the west," the man laughs, his tone teasing, almost mocking, as he leans back into the flat bedding, clearly enjoying the unfolding drama.

If you could even call it that.

As the heat rises in her cheeks, Lace takes a sip from her glass, the whiskey burning down her throat. "There won't be for long," she flings back, trying to mask her uncertainty with a bravado she doesn't entirely believe.

The man chuckles.

Standing at the bed's edge, the man calmly zips up his worn jeans, moving as if there is no better place than the present. Brandi and Trish lay tangled in the sheets, bodies sprawled out and basking in the afterglow. "How much I owe ya?" he asks, a lazy smirk curling at the corner of his mouth as he glances back over his shoulder. His voice cuts through the casual silence, but laced with the expectation he always gets his way. Lace's spine straightens in the armchair, alert to the conversation.

The man's hand slides into his back pocket, pulling out a worn leather money clip; the sight of several bills tucked tightly inside garners Lace's attention.

"Two hundred bucks. Three, if you wanna include Lace," Trish replies, her voice dripping with the same disregard she uses when discussing the weather.

Lace's stomach twists, the casualness of the statement slamming into her as good as a freight train. The man fishes out two crumpled hundred-dollar bills, jerking the money onto the nightstand as though it is nothing more than pennies. The cash hits the wood with a soft thud, an almost insulting gesture.

"Holier-than-thou over there didn't do anything… so two it is," he mutters, his eyes landing on Lace. For a split second, their gazes lock, and beneath his disinterested smirk, there is something else—curiosity? Whatever it is, it makes her skin crawl, leaving her with a strange, unsettling thrill. He pulls his jacket on and turns toward the door, tossing his parting words over his shoulder. A careless goodbye. "Y'all be safe out there. It's a cruel world for three pretty ladies like yourselves."

Poised across the bed in lazy contentment, Brandi gives him a playful wink. "Oh, we will, mister. Don't you worry 'bout us."

The door clicks shut behind him, sealing the space in a heavy silence. Lace's eyes drift to the nightstand, to the money scattered across it as discarded scraps, and the world tilts.

"Wait. He paid y'all?" The words slip out, disbelief curling in her voice. Lace can barely reconcile what has happened. Brandi and Trish exchange knowing glances, their laughter bubbling up.

"Honey… of course. We got something he wants, and lord knows he'll pay for it," Brandi says, her voice smooth and unapologetic. She leans back, eyes narrowing with the kind of wisdom only hard-earned experience can offer. "All women are sex workers. At least we get somethin' in return."

Lace stands frozen, staring down at the money on the nightstand.

The room is now cloaked in blackness. Lace lies at the edge of the bed, her body curling toward the door as if some invisible tether keeps her close to the escape. The oversized, worn t-shirt she wears drapes loosely around her frame, the fabric soft from years of wear. Brandi and Trish sprawl across the bed beside her, their limbs tangled, their breaths deep. They have slipped into sleep without hesitation, their bodies radiating the warmth of the night's encounter. The breeze from the AC vent stirs, and the floral curtains flutter, resembling phantom fingers, revealing a sliver of the night sky. Stars twinkle faintly above, indifferent. She takes a deep breath and stares into the midnight, trying to match the calm that has settled over the room.

But calm is a tricky thing. It surrounds her, but beneath it churns something much more turbulent. Her thoughts drift back to the money on the nightstand.

We got something he wants, and lord knows he'll pay for it.

Was that all it takes? A glance, a few words, a simple transaction? The idea of it both fascinates and frightens her. There's power in exchange—power she hasn't realized she could wield. She closes her eyes, trying to steady herself in the stillness, but her mind won't stop. What if she leans into it? Give in to the promise of easy money and the allure of control? The world has always seemed callous and mediocre—maybe this is her chance to beat it at its own game.

Yet the idea of becoming like Brandi or Trish, so casually detached, unsettles her. There's something soothing in the malevolence, a kind of safety she finds in its anonymity. But Lace knows dawn creeps around the lonesome edge and with it, more choices.

Choices she isn't sure how to make.

She sighs, letting the sound fade and blend into one with the air conditioner. For now, she will allow herself to rest. The answers can wait until morning.

5

Desert Baptism

ace stands in an unpaved lot, her hands firmly planted on her hips, tilting her head to squint at the building before her. Dressed in denim cutoffs hugging her hips, a green sleeveless cropped T-shirt emblazoned with "JUST SAY NO," exposing only a couple of inches of her midriff to the summer heat. The midday sun casts a merciless light on the large, bubblegum-pink structure, boldly proclaiming its name: "DESERT DELIGHTS RANCH." Flanked by white trim, the sign features a cartoonish pinup cowgirl, her exaggerated curves a playful promise of the place within.

Behind her, Brandi and Trish scurry around the car, frantically gathering their belongings, the sound of zippers and the rustling of fabric punctuating. As they join Lace on each side, Brandi shoves Lace's bag against her chest, causing Lace to stumble. Trish pulls a pair of red, heart-shaped sunglasses from her back pocket, sliding them onto her nose with a flourish.

Brandi pops a piece of bright pink bubblegum, the sharp snap echoing in the quiet parking lot.

"What the fuck?" Lace snorts, her brows knitting together in confusion.

"Welcome home!" Trish squeals. Before Lace can respond, Brandi and Trish each grab an arm and yank her toward the front door. Almost as if on cue, the double doors open to reveal a woman in her late fifties. She wears a black corset adorned with intricate lace detailing and a mid-length pink skirt swaying as she moves.

"Well, it's about time! Thought ya'll must've fallen right on inside that geyser!" the older woman exclaims, her voice a blend of authority and warmth. The three girls push past her and into the ranch.

"We would never dream of it, Madam Lottie," Trish calls back, teasing as they enter. Lace's eyes flicker across the sprawling foyer, grappling with the clashing colors and wild textures. Amid the chaos, a massive poster slapped carelessly beside the entrance steals her focus. The word "MENU" screams at her, demanding attention.

"The Desert Delights Ranch *sex menu*—a tantalizing selection from Nevada's finest brothel and sex resort. This list is just a spicy sample, so feel free to contact your courtesan of choice about any other naughty fantasies you dream up at The Desert Delights Ranch." Beneath, cartoon illustrations splashed in a pyramid tier fill most of the poster, each with its description:

Variety of SEX - The ol' Half and Half (oral and intercourse), or go all the way with Full Intercourse.

Variety of TWO GIRLS SEX - Girl On Girl, or a full-on Threesome.

Variety of BLOWJOBS - The Classic Blowjob, or spice it up with a Hot and Cold Blowjob.

Variety of EXOTIC MASSAGES - Go for a Breast Massage, a Happy Ending Massage, or the whole shebang with a Reciprocal Body Massage and Happy Ending.

Variety of WET-N-WILD BATH AND SHOWER - A Bubble Bath Bash or a splashy Shower Party.

Variety of FETISH SPECIALS - Couples Threesome, GFE (Girlfriend Experience), Lingerie Fetish Revue, Role Play Shenanigans, Bondage Time, Adult Toy Extravaganza, Foot Fetish Fiesta.

Brandi and Trish pull Lace deeper inside, and the place sprawls open in the fashion of some bizarre funhouse, twisting her sense of reality with each footfall. The foyer is a riot of sharp angles and vivid contrasts, each geometric shape battling for her attention. Pale pink walls stretch skyward, punctuated by creamy columns and bursts of black and white, creating a surreal harmony both lavish and disorienting.

The floor is a broken checkerboard of black-and-white tiles. If one were to look too closely, they'd realize where the pattern frays—edges nudging against each other. Each footfall is a hollow thud, bouncing off the warped walls and ricocheting back. Above her, a chandelier hangs as if on a threadbare rope. The crystals dangle, some of them missing altogether. The light it casts isn't steady; it flickers in manic bursts, throwing erratic shapes that dart around. A massive staircase snakes upwards at the back, splitting in two directions, the wood creaking in protest.

Around her, voices drift from the connecting rooms, each conversation more surreal than the last.

"So, I told him the feather boa was cursed, and the idiot actually prayed over it. Like, hands clasped, eyes closed—full-on 'Dear Lord' while it's still tangled in my bra strap!"

A burgundy sofa sprawls against the middle banister of the staircase. Cracks and wear mark the leather; some parts peel, revealing stuffing that pokes out in the role of little bones. The couch is littered with strange objects: a doll's head with a single eye painted shut, a deck of tarot cards missing the Death card, and a feather boa tangled in what looks to be worn fishing wire. The cushions bear tiny cigarette burns, each resembling a puncture wound and smelling faintly of perfume or something sharper, stranger.

"I wouldn't kiss him unless he could name all four members of the Highwaymen. Man damn near fainted trying to remember Johnny Cash."

"So... did he get it right?"

"No, but I took pity when he started singing *The Gambler*. Close enough, I guess."

Taxidermy animals crowd the walls—deer, moose, mountain lions—all draped in Mardi Gras beads. A crow sits perched above the entrance, its feathers oddly glossy, almost wet, as though it's about to ruffle and fly off. A rabbit, fur matted and missing an ear, hangs barely above her head, positioned as if it's leaping from wall to wall.

Trish's voice cuts through the noise, dripping with pride. "Listen, Dolly is the reason this whole damn country hasn't fallen apart yet."

An exhausted groan rises from someone in a room that appears to be the kitchen. "Trish, for the love of God, please shut the fuck up about Dolly fucking Parton."

The animal's glass eyes tell Lace they've seen more than any girl here. Girls drift through the space, slipping in and out of rooms, each a strange and vivid figure that Lace can't keep her eye on for more than half a second before they disappear.

Lace's heart races, overwhelmed by the pulsing energy surrounding her, when Madam Lottie reappears behind her. "I know you aren't one of mine. Girl. Where did you come from?" Madam Lottie's voice drips with curiosity, her thin brows furrowing as she studies Lace.

"Wyoming," Lace replies, her tone steady despite the woman's intense gaze. Lace feels the need to clarify when the older woman doesn't respond immediately. "—Ma'am. I came from Wyoming. Big Piney, to be exact."

Brandi, Trish, and a growing crowd of unfamiliar girls hush their conversations. "Brandi and Trish found me and asked if I wanted to tag along." Lace gestures around the building. "Not sure what y'all got going on over here. But... I'm here."

Madam Lottie's gaze flickers over Lace, a leisurely, scrutinizing scan making Lace exposed yet resolute. "Can you do the wild thang?" Madam Lottie asks, her eyes narrowing with intrigue.

Lace's brows knit together in confusion. "Not sure what you're asking, Ma'am." If Madam Lottie believes Lace to be naïve, she certainly doesn't show it.

The older woman leans in closer, her voice dropping to a conspiratorial whisper. "Fuck. Fucking. You ever touched a man..." Lace inhales sharply. "—or woman. However, we don't get any of those around here, except for that one time back in '79. Women don't pay for pleasure.

Usually." Madam Lottie's question hangs heavy. The eyes of the other girls bore into her, waiting for her answer.

"No. Ma'am. I have not," she finally admits, her voice steady despite the butterflies flitting in her stomach.

Madam Lottie's expression shifts, surprise morphing her lips into an "o" as she processes Lace's admission. "Aha," she muses, beginning to circle Lace. A vulture sizing up its prey. Lace stands her ground, refusing to flinch. Returning to her original position, Madam Lottie declares, "Well. We all gotta learn someday." She turns, addressing the gathering of girls who have assembled behind Lace. "Ain't that right, girls?"

They chorus in unison, "Yes, Madam Lottie!"

Madam Lottie's gaze shifts back to Lace, a gleam of approval in her eyes. "Brandi! Since you and Trish brought this betty here, you gonna show her our ways. You're responsible for—"

"Lace. Name's Lace," Lace interjects, her voice cutting through the anticipation in the room. Madam Lottie dips her head in acknowledgment, her demeanor shifting as she considers the newcomer.

"I'll take mighty fine care of her, don't you worry, Madam," Brandi replies as a soldier reporting for duty.

Madam Lottie dips her head in acknowledgment, adding, "All the girls go by an alias here. Gotta keep some secrets, after all." She gestures around the room. "This here is Peach. She goes by Pegleg Annie." Her warm, tawny skin is covered in freckles, scattered close to a dusting of cinnamon on a freshly baked Snickerdoodle. There's something soft about her. She's never been roughed up by the world. Not yet, anyway. Her hair is cut in a blunt orange shag, and bangs too long, falling right into her eyes. Zuni cluster rings, necklaces, and bracelets clack together with every breath.

"Mint Julep!" Madam Lottie says with a flourish. She's got a knowing grin as if she's introducing her favorite hand-picked gem. "Mallory, but she goes by Mint Julep—got a touch of sweetness, but I'd warn you not to underestimate her." Mallory steps forward, her chestnut hair tied in an oversized bow, giving her a doll-like appearance, almost too perfect, too staged—a porcelain figurine brought to life. She flashes a sweet smile with the faintest curl at the edges, suggesting there's more than sugar behind that bow.

"Gold Rush," Madam Lottie calls out next, her voice smooth, a practiced tone knowing precisely how to sell the spectacle. The girl steps into view, her two long dark braids grazing the floor, each heavy and thick, functioning as ropes that tie her down. She stands barefoot, wearing a simple white dress, almost hospital-like in its plainness, starkly contrasting with her name. She speaks in a soft but clear voice, her lips barely moving. "My name is Gemma." There's something unassuming about how she says it; there is no drama or exaggeration, nothing but a fact laid bare.

"Now, Miss Beverly is Buckaroo Bliss," Madam Lottie says with a playful roll of her eyes. "Or, as I call her, trouble in pigtails." A girl with honey-blonde hair tied into loose pigtails smiles at Lace. Her wide eyes, rimmed in smoky grey kohl, dart around the room. A perfect reflection of a Western-styled Brigitte Bardot.

"Sloppy Gertie, also known as Sable," Madam Lottie says with a crooked smile. She gestures to Sable, who steps forward, a striking figure against the pink backdrop. High atop her head, Sable piles her coiled hair adorned with ghost and cactus flowers whose pale blossoms contrast her jet-black locks. They look almost out of place—rooted there on their own, part of her wildness.

There's nothing sloppy about her.

"Moxie. Sometimes called Milk and Honey," Madam Lottie says, "Our sweetest of all." Moxie steps up, her skin almost glowing under the low lights. Her albinism gives her an ethereal quality. Stark white hair is long and loose, and her blue eyes, pale as winter, carry a sharp contrast to the great beyond background. She looks delicate, almost unreal. Something sculpted out of moonlight.

Madam Lottie gestures again. "Pistol and Pillow," she says. Radiant red curls come into view, bouncing as she speaks, her Southern accent smooth and unmistakable. "I'm Petal," she says, a playful edge in her voice. A slit in her right eyebrow peeks through the wild curls.

She nears the end of the line, where Trish and Brandi stand hand in hand, beaming, suggesting they got away with robbing the nearest bank. Madam Lottie lets out a long, weary exhale, the kind that implies she's been dealing with these two far too long. "You know Trish—Three-tit Tillie. And Brandi—Bilious Bessie."

Trish flicks her hair over her shoulder, her smile sharp. "Got the name from my mama."

Madam Lottie mutters under her breath, "Lord help me." She turns to Lace, raising an eyebrow. "Alright, honey, you gotta pick a name."

Before Lace can think, the girls jump in, voices tumbling over each other in excitement.

"Lusty Lil' Lass!"

"Lickety Split!"

"Long-Legged Lulu!"

"Little Miss Leather!"

The chatter rises until Trish cuts through it all, her voice shrilling enthusiastically as an excited little girl. "I got it! Lone Star Lover!"

All the girls shut up at once, staring at Lace to see if she approves.

These girls are absolutely nuts... but God, there's something about it.

Lace's heart races, a mix of fear and exhilaration flooding her veins as she stands amidst the lively chaos of the Desert Delights Ranch. A meager smile playing on her lips.

Trish throws her hands up, grinning wide. "Fuck, am I good!"

6

Pucker-Free Policy

randi intertwines her pinky finger with Lace's, guiding her through the narrow, dimly lit hallway of the ranch. The air is thick with the scent of aged wood, dust, and something sweet—remnants of a perfume once worn by the house's former residents. Lace's footsteps echo off the creaky floorboards. Every sound is a reminder of the rich history held within these walls.

"The ranch? They built it about a hundred years ago, maybe more," Brandi says casually, her voice soft.

"It used to be a bed-and-breakfast, back when folks still passed through these parts for that kinda thing. Then, in 1971, when the government decided it no longer had a hankering for arresting men that was paying women to sleep with them, Madam Lottie saw an opportunity."

Lace follows, her eyes drifting over the strange assortment of objects littering the hallway. Mismatched frames hold black-and-white photos of women who look both glamorous and haunted, their eyes staring down as if continuously watching. Brandi's tone shifts, a note of reverence sneaking into her words. "Madam Lottie took all the money she got from her late husband's insurance and turned this place into something else."

They turn a corner and enter the kitchen. The room is a chaotic blend of old-world charm and bizarre eccentricity. Dark wooden cabinets line the walls in front of wallpaper patterned with faded roses, some petals seemingly half-torn off. Hanging from the ceiling are pots and pans in every imaginable size and color.

At the center of the kitchen stands a sizeable blue island, its chipped surface bearing scars from decades of use. In the middle of the island sits a ceramic bowl shaped like a woman's torso, but where one would expect fruit or cookies, it cradles only packs of cigarettes. Beside it, a lamp with a lampshade made entirely of stained glass flickers. Brandi leans in toward Lace, her voice lowering to a conspiratorial whisper. "If you ask me, Madam Lottie didn't have nothin' to do with that law passin', but the timing's too perfect to ignore."

Lace barely hears her, distracted by the strange decor. In the corner stands a life-sized mannequin dressed in an ancient as the hills gown, its head replaced by a mosaic of shattered mirrors. Every so often, it grabs the light and sparkles. The atmosphere is unsettling but oddly homey, as though each piece has its place, no matter how strange.

Brandi clears her throat, breaking Lace's trance. "This here is the kitchen. All the basics—flour, sugar, perishables—are covered. But if you're picky and want somethin' fancy, you'll have to get that yourself. Madam Lottie takes a fifty percent cut from all our earnings. She says it's for the roof over our heads, the water, the whiskey, and everything else we use."

Lace recognizes a woman at the counter, her back turned, standing calmly and unhurriedly.

Gemma?

The woman spreads peanut butter over toast, her absurdly long hair trailing as a hazard. Lace nearly trips over it as she steps to the pantry to return the jar. Brandi's voice grows louder as she addresses the woman. "Gemma came from Washington—the state, not the capital. Ain't that right, Gemma?"

Gemma turns, her eyes locking onto Lace with a calm, almost unsettling intensity. She grips her butter knife in one hand, and in the other, she has her slice of toast. "Yeah," Gemma says, taking a deliberate bite, persistently holding Lace's gaze. "It's been about two years now. Madam Lottie took me in when I had nowhere else to go."

Her eyes travel over Lace, sizing her up without saying much. Her expression softens momentarily. "Seems like she just about did the same for you," she adds with a slight smirk.

Gemma winks, slinging her braid-handles over her wrists as she exits the kitchen. As she walks past Lace, the faint scent of jasmine and tobacco clings to the air, a strange but not unpleasant combination. With a last glance over her shoulder, Gemma's voice is a soft murmur as she passes. "*Lone Star Lover.*"

Lace blinks, absorbing the encounter as Gemma leaves the room. Brandi chuckles softly. "She's a sweetheart," Brandi assures, giving Lace a pat on the shoulder. "They all are. It's just gonna take a minute for you to see that." Lace breathes it all in, realizing the ranch, with its peculiar charm and eccentricities, has more than simply history within its walls.

It holds people—each as odd and fascinating as the things they surround themselves with.

The grand staircase creaks beneath their feet as Lace follows Brandi up to the second floor of the ranch. A runner, once vibrant red but now faded, with patches of threadbare fabric showing through, adorns the stairs. Brandi reaches the top and flings open the double doors of the first room on the right. The sight and sounds of a space immediately assault Lace, buzzing with color and chaos. The walls are an unforgiving shade of bright pink, though most of the paint is barely visible beneath a mosaic of photos, magazine clippings, and scribbled notes.

Lace's eyes dart from one image to the next—unfamiliar girls with broad smiles and sultry poses, shirtless men with too-perfect abs, and scraps of words written in messy cursive, creating a jarring collage of lives she doesn't yet know.

In one way or another, the room's clutter is methodical. Half a dozen clothing racks, for all intents and purposes Lace can—or can't—imagine, press against the walls. School girl costumes, glittering sequined dresses, fishnet stockings, and an array of lingerie hang from hangers in an almost artistic disarray. The floor is no different, with pieces of fabric spilling out onto the worn hardwood beneath their feet as though the room is breathing with the life of the women who dress here.

Lace hesitates as she steps inside, her eyes darting around, taking it all in. The room's cluttered mess extends to the vanities lining the far wall in a crescent shape, a half-moon of mirrors. There are ten of them, each a reflection of the girl who uses it. Makeup tubes, brushes, jewelry, and strange trinkets cover any available surface, save for one—an empty vanity stands waiting for its new occupant.

Above each mirror is a photo, taped to the glass, of a different girl who resides at the ranch. Lace recognizes Brandi's picture at the vanity beside the empty one. Brandi leaves Lace at the entryway, strolling over to her vanity and leaning casually against the chair, tossing her hair over her shoulder. "This here's our closet-slash-dressing-room," Brandi says, gesturing broadly to the chaos surrounding them. "You can pretty much wear whatever you want. We share just 'bout everything. But, uh…" she wrinkles her nose playfully, "I'd recommend washin' it before you do."

Brandi's gaze shifts toward the empty vanity next to hers. "This one'll be yours. Right next to mine," she says with a grin.

Lace smiles back, but it's a nervous smile. Her hands unconsciously wipe the sweat off her palms onto her shorts.

"Brandi… can I ask you somethin'?"

"Sure, hun,"

Lace swallows, her throat tight. She glances at the room's disarray, at the fragments of lives lived in this strange place. "Why do y'all do this?" Lace finally asks, her voice soft but steady. "Isn't it—isn't it deemed wrong under the eyes of God?"

"Didn't take you for the religious type," she teases.

She pushes off the chair and moves toward Lace, her eyes never leaving hers. There's something in the way Brandi carries herself—confidence mingled with defiance. She stops in front of Lace, her gaze softening as she gently cups Lace's face, brushing a stray lock of hair away.

"Listen, Lace," her voice a whisper now. "Being born a girl—I. It's like a life sentence destined for humiliation and degradation. But this here ranch? It's our chance to take that sentence and throw it right back at the man."

Lace's lips part as if to respond, but no words come. Before she can find her voice, Brandi continues. "Change? It's scary. But you know what's scarier? Stayin' still. Never livin'. Never takin' that leap."

Brandi's hands fall from Lace's face, as she steps back, the warmth of her touch fading but her words remaining. "Oh! But hey, we've got some rules we stick to—might make you feel better, huh?"

She leans back against a vanity, crossing her arms with an almost sisterly smirk. "First thing's first," she says, "we let them pay after—it keeps them sweet like they're still trying to earn something. But if he so much as hints at not paying, you don't let him out that door without your money. No one walks out of here owing you a damn thing. And condoms?"

"Non-negotiable. I don't care if he claims he's the cleanest guy west of the Rockies. No rubber, no fun. Oh, and don't let him give you lip into some *oops* moment—it's not your job to manage his impulses."

Her fingers tap against the counter as if ticking through a mental checklist. "And you check him every time. Down there. If something looks weird—bumps, redness, whatever—you send him packin'. It's your body, not a damn science experiment."

Brandi leans in. "Never let him kiss you on the mouth. That's personal and intimate. It blurs lines you don't want blurring. And don't buy into any of his sweet talk, either. If he says you're the best he's ever had or promises to come back for you, he's lying. Always lying."

She straightens up, brushing a stray strand of hair out of her face. "Oh, and no freebies. No discounts. No, I'll pay you later. This isn't charity work. And if he tries to sneak in something extra—anal, rough stuff, whatever—you charge double or show him the door. You make the rules, not him." A pause following a dry laugh. "And always pee after he's gone. Trust me on that one."

Brandi takes a deep breath, her gaze drifting somewhere far away, and exhales. "Except James Dean," she murmurs, a faint smile tugging at her lips, "That man was a masterpiece. I'd let him do whatever he wanted to me. If he walked in here right now, I'd toss every single house rule out the window—hell, I'd set the whole rulebook on fire. God rest his perfect, rebel soul."

Finally, Brandi taps Lace lightly on the chin. "But the most important rule? You don't do anything you don't want to do. Period. Madam Lottie won't make you, and neither will anyone else. If something feels wrong, you walk out. No shame in that." She steps back with a slight shrug. "That's the code around here. It's not perfect, but it keeps us safe. Mostly."

She walks to the door, her presence filling the room even as she prepares to leave. Lace stands there for a beat, frozen, her mind swirling with thoughts she hadn't expected. Her whole body as though it's teetering on the edge of something unknown, something she isn't sure she's ready for.

Brandi reaches the door and turns, her expression softening into a smile. "Just give it a chance, babe," she says gently. "If you hate it, you can always leave. You ain't no one's prisoner here." She winks at Lace before pushing open the door. "Now, c'mon," she adds, "tour ain't over yet."

Brandi and Lace interlock pinkies once more as they round the corner into a long hallway. Lace's feet sink into the shag carpet beneath her, its garish orange both inexplicably welcoming and out of place. It's soft, nearly luxurious, though its color screams of a past which has long since faded. Ten doors line the hallway, all painted with depictions that make Lace blink twice. Each door shows a different sexual position, illustrated in vivid detail as though inviting the curious to step inside. Lace's pace stalls, her feet dragging as Brandi moves ahead, seemingly unaffected by the strange art. Old mannequin parts—arms, legs, and torsos hang from the ceiling by thin ropes, swaying gently. Some mannequins wear masks, while others have neon-colored scarves wrapped around them.

Lace stops, allowing Brandi to continue trailing down the hallway as she recites more of the ranch's history—stories Lace tunes out, too focused on the doors. Lace hesitantly follows, glancing left and right at each passing door. Muffled moaning drifts from one of the unidentified rooms, piquing her curiosity.

Missionary, doggy style, golden arch, reverse cowgirl, sixty-nine, standing, lotus position, cowgirl, and scissors.

A muffled moan slips through sixty-nine, making Lace pause for a moment before continuing. Brandi stops at the second-to-last door, her hand gleaming in the dim hallway light as she closes in on the handle.

Lace surveys the door before them. It's slightly ajar, revealing only a sliver of the room beyond.

"This one's yours—Bondage," Brandi says, her voice gleeful.

"Last girl left about two weeks ago for a ranch up north. Funny timing, innit." Lace looks up at the painting on the door. The image is arresting—an ethereal woman on her back, her arms tightly bound beneath her, while an enormous tattooed hand travels from above, covering her mouth. Despite the compromising position, the woman's eyes are wide and inviting, as if daring someone to join her in her vulnerability.

Brandi pushes the door open fully, and the painting vanishes from Lace's sight, replaced by the room beyond. The same strange orange shag carpet as the hallway spills into the room, but other than that, it's oddly bare. Wood-paneled walls give the room a dated, almost cabin-like feel, except for the centerpiece—a white, lace-canopied bed in the middle of the space. A handmade felt horse dangles from the canopy, a whimsical touch in the otherwise stark room. A sizable heart-shaped window adorns the far wall. Lace moves across the room to peer out as Brandi throws open a cramped closet directly in front of the bed.

Peering out the window, Lace gathers she is facing the front of the ranch; her view encompasses the parking lot and the vast, empty open range stretching endlessly. The sound of Brandi rummaging through items draws Lace's attention back to the room. She notices a large bell nailed to the wall above the front door, a long red string trailing down into the adjacent wall. The floral wallpaper inside the closet contains little except a dozen metal hangers acting as a perch for a small Colt single-action army revolver, its brown handle intricately engraved. Brandi stretches up to the top shelf, pulling down a dinky box.

Lace keeps her eyes on the gun, feeling a mix of fascination and unease. "This girl could've at least cleaned out the room before she bolted," Brandi scoffs, stepping back to stand shoulder-to-shoulder with Lace.

She sighs, smiling, but her expression falters as she takes in how captivated Lace is by the weapon. Brandi waves her free hand around dismissively.

"Oh... don't be startled, hun. That's for your protection. All the girls got one." She grabs the gun off the hangers, supporting it delicately. "Never seen a lady having to reach for one, but hey, better to be packin' than prayin'," Brandi says, placing the gun in Lace's hands. Lace doesn't move except for her eyes fixated on the weapon. Despite the desert heat, the metal is cool to the touch.

"You do know how to use it, don't you?"

Lace shifts the gun in her hands, a slight tremor betraying her uncertainty. "No. My mama never had one, and my daddy was never around to teach me."

Brandi's expression softens as she takes the gun back from Lace, a flicker of understanding in her eyes. "Oh! Well, it's easy here—"

Brandi raises the gun, pointing the barrel merely inches from Lace's forehead. Lace freezes, crossing her eyes to glare down the barrel.

"First, you cock the hammer," Brandi instructs, using her thumb to pull back the silver hammer, the motion smooth and practiced. "Pick your target." She steps back from Lace, straightening her arm, the gun motionlessly aimed at her. "And bang, you're dead," Brandi whispers, her voice low and theatrical.

She pulls the trigger.

Lace flinches, scrunching her eyes shut. After a moment, she hesitantly peeks one eye open, watching Brandi return the gun to the hangers. "Real simple. Just make sure to load it if you need to bust 'em up."

Lace, her eyes now wide open, takes in a shaky breath. "You're fuckin' crazy, aren't you?" Brandi twirls on the balls of her feet, heading for the door. She peeks her head back into the room to look at Lace.

"Go on and settle in... I'll bring your bag up."

She disappears from the doorway, but Lace hears her call from the hallway, "You're a true American whore now!"

7

Chin High, Tits Higher

ace lies on her back. Her gaze fixated on the felt horse swaying from the delicate lace canopy above her bed. It is a strange artifact, vibrant and whimsical against the dull, oppressive atmosphere of the wood-paneled room. With each passing second, memories claw their way to the surface—Jean's pure and untainted laughter ringing in her ears as they run wild through plains, their imaginations turning the ordinary into magic. Those carefree days impossibly fabricated, fading into a cacophony threatening to consume her. The sharp image of Darlene shouting, venom lacing her voice, slices through the warmth of those memories, dragging Lace back into the harsh reality that keeps trailing her like a bloodhound on her scent.

Right as the suffocating silence closes in, the ring of the bell above the door shatters. It resonates similar to a warning, each chime reverberating in her chest, sending a jolt of anxiety through her.

She blinks, disoriented, as she strains to listen to the laughter and shouts from the hallway—a cruel reminder of her isolation.

Before she can gather her scattered thoughts, the door bursts open, and Trish appears. She stands framed by the doorway.

"Well, don't just lay there! C'mon, we got a lineup!"

She glances at Trish, confusion knitting her brow. "Lineup?" she echoes. Trish doesn't pause to explain; her excitement too infectious. She darts out of the room, her laughter trailing behind her. As Trish calls out to another girl, the hallway beckons Lace, tempting her to step out of her comfort zone.

Gathering her resolve, Lace crosses the threshold into the hallway, joining the throng of girls.

Lace pauses at the top of the grand staircase, her gaze sweeping over the foyer below. The low light of the chandelier reflects off the scarlet drapes, which hang in heavy waves from the ceiling, casting a warm, intimate glow across the room. From her vantage point, she can see a smaller man lounging on the crimson sofa, his back turned to her, but his presence unavoidable.

He sits with his legs spread wide, his arms resting on the back of the sofa, claiming the space. Nearby, Madam Lottie stands to the side, watching the room in imitation of a hawk, her eyes clicking back and forth like she's a conductor preparing to cue the orchestra. She clasps her hands before her, her fingers tapping lightly against her knuckles.

In front of the man, nine girls form a perfect crescent. Their postures are sharp and deliberate, each adjusting their stance enough to seize the man's attention—arching backs, letting their hips sway ever so slightly.

Lace hesitates at the top of the stairs, unsure of her next move. Her hand rests lightly on the banister as she looks down. With a deep breath, she makes her descent. As she closes in on the bottom, her uncertainty only grows stronger. She scans the room, unsure where she's supposed to stand and where she fits in this arrangement. Brandi snatches her eye from the line of girls and gives her a slight nod, significant enough to direct Lace's attention to the empty space beside her.

Lace hurries across the floor without hesitation, slotting herself into the line. She inhales sharply, forcing herself to hold steady as her gaze locks onto the man. He appears to be in his early thirties, though his tan skin makes him look older. His clothes are rough—dark blue jeans and an ill-fitting black T-shirt. Dirt streaks his face, haphazardly smeared across his brow and chin. A cigarette hangs loosely from his lips, and his eyes move ever so slowly over the line of girls. His gaze is unhurried, like he has all the time in the world to inspect each of them.

When his eyes land on Lace, they stay, scanning her from head to toe, lingering in a way reminiscent of Billy Rae. He gives her a deliberate wink when their eyes meet. Lace's throat constricts, a prickly knot blooming in her gut, spreading a discomfort pinning her in place.

Before Lace can react, Madam Lottie steps forward, instantly commanding the room's attention. Her presence is a force, a power which can't be ignored. Her eyes scan down the line of girls, lingering briefly on Lace at the far end, the furthest from her watchful gaze.

"Alright, girls. You know the drill." Her voice is firm, as if she's spoken the same command hundreds of times before. It isn't a suggestion; it's an expectation. With a quick gesture from Madam Lottie, the first girl, Moxie, steps forward. She moves with delicate precision, offering a tiny curtsy.

"I'm Milk and Honey," says Moxie.

A faint snort breaks the quiet, drawing attention to Peach, who stands beside Brandi. She tries to cover her mouth to stifle the laughter.

Peach whispers, "Did she just fucking curtsy?"

Moxie's face flushes with frustration as she steps back in line.

Madam Lottie's gaze snaps to the culprit, her voice slicing. "Girls! Not another word." With a nod to the man, who's oblivious to the brief exchange, Madam Lottie signals the next girl forward.

One by one, each girl steps forward, offering her *name*.

"I'm Mint Julep," says Mallory.

"I'm Gold Rush," says Gemma.

"I'm Three-tit Tillie," says Trish.

"I'm Buckaroo's Bliss," says Beverly.

"I'm Pistol and Pillow," says Petal.

"I'm Sloppy Gertie," says Sable.

"I'm Pegleg Annie," says Peach.

"I'm Bilious Bessie," says Brandi.

Brandi nudges Lace softly, breaking her out of her trance. Lace blinks, realizing all eyes are on her now. The man's gaze burns into her, waiting.

"Lac—Lone Star Lover."

The man shifts, leaning forward. His forearms rest on his knees, and his cigarette now forgotten on the floor. Eyes stay locked on Lace. His attention is unnerving, lingering far longer than anyone else. The room is silent, heavy with expectation. Finally, the man stands up, the sound of his boot crushing the cigarette against the tile echoing in the space. He runs his eyes down the line of girls once more before turning back to Lace.

"Her—Lone Star Lover."

Lace's eyes widen. The other girl's shift, whispering complaints. Madam Lottie clears her throat, stepping toward the man. "Well, now, Lone Star is a newbie. Just touched her feet on this here soil. The other girls are far more experienced."

The man shrugs off her words with a dismissive flick. "Then why's she standing in front of me?"

Madam Lottie opens her mouth to respond, but no words come. Lace, cheeks burning with heat, steps forward, her breath shaking. "It's alright. I'm a big girl."

The man chuckles softly, his voice low. "Yes, you are."

Brandi gently touches the back of Lace's arm as she steps back in line, a quiet gesture of solidarity. Madam Lottie throws up her hands, exasperated. "Well, I'll be damned."

Lace perches at the bed's edge, her body a game board of *Operation*, limbs and curves waiting for a careful hand, each breath trembling, on the brink of lighting up the board. This isn't fear—not exactly—but something close. It's the unease of what's just around the bend, pressing against her chest.

She's agreed to this. Told herself she's ready.

However, it does little to stop the nerves from crawling up her spine. Her foot taps against the carpet, the steady *tap, tap, tap* barely breaking the thick silence. Each sound anchors her. Keeps her present. She focuses on the motion, the sensation of her toes meeting the floor because everything else carries itself as too ample.

Too overwhelming.

She's aware of the man crowding her space, a stranger whose name she doesn't know and whose face she hopes to forget. The deal has been made. The decision hers—this isn't being forced. But it's... strange, almost like she's on the edge of a cliff, unsure of how far the fall will be. Her hands fidget in her lap, thumbs picking at each other as her eyes level with his belt buckle. His towering presence doesn't go unnoticed. A bead of sweat rolls down his forehead, dropping onto her cheek. Lace flinches, disturbed by the cold wetness, but she doesn't wipe it away. It's a minor, almost insignificant thing.

She steals a glance up at him and sees his face—dirty, lined, eyes half-lidded with expectation. He's not old, but life has worn him down. His hands move for his belt, and the metal buckle clinking echoes too loudly. Lace swallows hard, her throat tight, but she keeps her eyes down, watching the leather slide free, watching his hands fumble with the zipper of his jeans.

She has imagined this moment so many times, but now that it's here, it's nothing like she had expected. There is no romance, no excitement, only flesh trading places. The fragile part of her adsorbs the disappointment.

His dirty hands, scarred and rough, reach out to touch her. Lace stiffens. The touch isn't violent, but it is cold and impersonal. The hard press of his wedding band against her cheek, a strange reminder this man has a life outside of this room, outside of this moment. But there is no softness in him, no comfort. He is only here for what he came for.

"Touch it."

Carefully, she raises her hand, hesitating for a second.

Two.

Three.

Four.

Her palm rests against the bitty bulge in his boxers. He exhales sharply, a shudder passing through his body as her hand makes contact. His reaction is immediate, and something in her tightens, a strange mix of power and disdain. She knew it wouldn't be perfect—how could it be? With a stranger? But this... this is different. She thought it would be over quickly, would be something to get through, a moment to endure. But now, as her hand lingers on him, she realizes how much power she has over this grown man.

Is this it? The thing that makes Trish and Brandi walk through the world as if it can't touch them? The power is heady, sharp as a blade, carving through her doubts and leaving something dangerous in its place. But the man's patience runs thin.

"Enough of this."

His hands are on her, pushing her back onto the bed. Lace's body tenses as her back hits the mattress, her breath quickening. His movements are clumsy, almost desperate, as he pulls at her shorts, yanking them down with little grace. Her eyes dart to the ceiling, focusing on the cracks in the plaster, on anything but him. Her hands curl into fists beside her, gripping the sheets as he moves on top of her. She could stop it, but she won't. Doesn't wish to. Not entirely.

I have to see it through.

His breath is muggy against her neck, his body pressing into hers as he fumbles with himself. With her. Lace squeezes her eyes shut, trying to block out the sensations, trying to keep herself detached. But it happens. The sharp, unfamiliar pain as he thrust inside of her, the invasion claiming her breath and making her body tense in ways she hasn't expected.

The sharp trill of the bell on top of the door lingers in the air, breaking the quiet like a lone rider's shadow stretching across the desert.

Echoing through the house.

Bouncing off the walls of the ranch.

Lace lies stationary, her body cooling as the sweat on her skin dries. The room is quieter now, the heat of the moment replaced by a strange emptiness. She turns to watch him pull on his clothes, his movements quicker now.

Oh. Now he's in a hurry.

He doesn't say much. Just mutters something Lace doesn't care to catch under his breath. As he adjusts his belt, he walks toward the window and slaps a hundred-dollar bill onto the sill with a careless flick. The sound is soft but final, a pitiful punctuation to what happened.

Lace stares at it, her eyes narrowing as the crumpled bills settle. A flutter of emotions hits her all at once—disgust, shame, and something cloudier. She sits up; the sheets sliding off her bare legs, a hollowness crawling in her chest—pitching a tent—setting up camp for the winter. But as she stares at the money, something shifts inside her.

One hundred dollars.

She clutches the bills between her fingers, rubbing the worn edges of Franklin with her thumb. The rough texture. Real. Lace looks down at the money again, and a thought blooms in her mind—an idea filling the emptiness with a slow-burning fire.

This could be more.

Her hand clutches around the bills, and a strange sense of power washes over her for the first time. Someone paid her for something she never imagined giving away under these circumstances, but now... now she contemplates how much more she could get. Not just a hundred, but two hundred, a thousand! Men wearing the same face are willing to pay for something that Lace now realizes she can control. Her reflection stares back at her, hollow-eyed but determined. Lace knows this could be dangerous, but the hunger inside her is louder than the warnings in her head.

It's not about the sex. It's about the power that comes with the exchange. The money means something now.

It's not about survival anymore—it's about ambition, about control.

She turns away from the window, clutching the bills in her hand. Her lips curl into a quiet smile. More to be made out there, more men who'll come knocking. And next time, she won't be only seeing Benjamin.

8

Price Of Lace

The days blur together as Lace explores her newfound power, the thrill of control, and the allure of money driving her forward. Headfirst, she dives into the work, her appetite growing with each encounter; the brothel becomes a place where she tests boundaries and turns desires into transactions.

Lace becomes insatiable—her curiosity pushing her into the farthest reaches of the ranch, her body a canvas for boundless exploration. Lace becomes fascinated by the different men who venture through those bubblegum pink doors—the businessmen in their suits, smelling of aftershave and whiskey; the ranch hands with rough skin and sunburned necks; the young ones, barely further down the road than her, nervous and eager. They all hunger for something different, and Lace learns to give it to them. She understands their fantasies and their needs. She pushes herself to fulfill each one, no matter how strange or demanding.

She finds herself in twisted positions, bodies tangling together on the bed, her legs over a man's shoulders while he grips her thighs, his eyes wide and desperate. Lace lets herself get lost in it—the thrill of giving in, of being exactly what they need. There are nights when she takes on more than one man at once, her body awash in sensation—hands gripping, pulling, mouths tracing her skin, her breath breaking into shallow gasps. She craves its chaos—the magnetic pull of being at the heart of it all. The way they look at her, touch her, something they can't resist. She plays into it. Her moans echoing off the walls, her body moving between them, her mind sharp, calculating the money she will make from each encounter.

She starts experimenting, pushing the boundaries of what the clients desire. She books couples—a man and his wife, the wife's eyes wide with a mixture of curiosity and nervousness. Lace moves between them, her fingers trailing over the wife's skin, her lips brushing against her neck, while the husband watches, his breath heavy. Lace kisses the wife gently, her eyes open, tracking the husband's reaction. Guiding the couple, her hands on their bodies, positioning them, showing them how to touch each other, how to touch her.

She tries positions once spoken of in hushed tones, her body bending, stretching, and muscles aching in ways that leave her breathless. Straddling one man, her hands on his chest, while another stands behind her, his hands on her waist, the three of them moving together in absolute rhythm. Twisting, arching, and head thrown back as Lace lets herself get lost in the pleasure, the heat of the moment, utterly consumed by it all.

Some clients want more than sex. They want control. They bring ropes, scarves, and things to tie her up, and Lace lets them.

She lies back, her wrists bound above her head, her body open and vulnerable, as they take what they came for. Feeling the burn of the rope against her skin, the way it digs into her wrists, the way her body responds to being entirely at their mercy. And she loves it.

She loves how they look at her, how they need her, and how they can't get enough. Each angle tells a different story, all of them hers. Encountering men who have a thirst for being dominated, who plead with her to take control, to push them down, to make them beg. She stands over them, her foot on their chest, her eyes cold, her voice commanding as she tells them what to do—watching as they obey. As they look up at her with a mix of fear and adoration, the power surges through her, filling her up.

Lace pushes herself further and tries things she never thought she would—positions that leave her sore for days, men who leave her covered in bruises, and couples who make her feel as though she's part of something larger than herself. She throws herself into it all, her body a vessel for every fantasy, every whim, every strange, obscure desire coming her way.

In the quiet moments, Lace sits alone. The money spread out in front of her, the worn bills a tangible reminder of what she's done, of what she's capable of. She runs her fingers over them, her mind swimming with possibilities. Envisioning the future, about what she could do with more—more money, more power, more control. It's a constant, gnawing need driving her forward. It makes her smile when she dwells on what comes next.

I could go see Vegas with this money. I could go to fuckin' Antartica with this money.

The brothel is her world now, a place where she can be whoever she wants to be, where she can take what she aches without apology.

Lace moves through it with confidence, her eyes always on the next target, her mind always on the next move. She knows there's more out there for her, more to take, more to conquer, and she's ready.

The hunger inside her isn't going away—it's only growing.

9
To Cum Or To Not Cum

ace sits cross-legged on the cool wooden floor, her back against the deflated red leather couch. The rest of the ranch girls lay scattered along the sofa. A deck of tarot cards splatters in front of Mallory. "Let's see where fate says you'll end up, shall we?" she purrs, flipping over a card with flair. "Ooh, the Queen of Pentacles. Looks like luxury and status are in your future, Miss Peach. I see you in pearls, sipping martinis by a pool owned by a hedge fund manager named Gerald."

Peach arches a brow, unimpressed but curious. "Gerald? That's the most tragic prediction I've ever heard. I was hoping for something with a bit more mystique."

Mallory grins, undeterred. "Mystique, huh? Fine." She pulls another card, hoisting it up dramatically, "The Fool! Oh, it's all clear now. Gerald's your cover story. Really, you're off to join an underground speakeasy circuit in Paris. Velvet gloves, secret doors, piano jazz... the whole shebang."

Peach sighs with faux exasperation, reaching for the deck. "All right, if we're playing mystic, let's see what your future holds." She shuffles, pulls a card, and smirks. "The Knight of Wands. Bold and impulsive. I'd say you're one road trip away from starting a painted rock stand in the middle of the desert."

Mallory gasps, clutching her heart. "Painted rocks? In the desert?"

Mallory flips another card, all mock seriousness now. "And you—The Devil. Oh, honey, I'm sorry to break it to you, but it looks like you're gonna marry Gerald after all. And it'll be so deliciously boring."

"Ya'll aren't even doing that right." Gemma chimes.

"*Lace*... LACE!" Beverly's voice cuts through the chatter, pulling Lace from her reverie.

Beverly commands attention at the front of the room, her presence magnetic. She wears a black mesh button-down shirt, leaving little to the imagination, and a plaid miniskirt, which flirts with the line of decency. A paddle in her hand, emblazoned with the words "GUILTY! BEND OVER." Seemingly both a weapon and a trophy.

Behind her, a giant rolling chalkboard stands as the backdrop, covered in crude drawings and humorous diagrams of sexual positions, the words of dirty talk scribbled in wild, enthusiastic strokes.

Lace, dressed in a playful schoolgirl outfit, blinks, snapping her attention to Beverly's expectant gaze. A ripple of laughter goes through the room as she registers the playful challenge in Beverly's expression.

"I'm here! Sorry!" Lace responds, a grin spreading across her face.

"She ain't even fuckin' paying attention!" Beverly throws her hands up in frustration. "What did I just say?"

Lace's eyes flick back and forth, trying to recall Beverly's last lecture. "Something about cock and ball torture?"

Beverly puts her hands on her hips. "Wrong. That was ten minutes ago. I see where your mind is at. Nasty." Turning abruptly, Beverly grabs a piece of chalk from the ledge of the board. "We're diving into the art of moaning!"

Peach gasps as she flips another card, "The Empress!"

Beverly writes in bold, exaggerated letters: "MOANING!" Trish pops a bubble of gum.

"Now, ladies, listen up!" Beverly declares, her tone serious. "We all know men can be selfish in bed—like it's all about their pleasure. But here's the deal. We have to make them believe they're doing an amazing job."

"Or at least pretend they are," Trish chimes in.

Beverly bobs her head, feeding into the energy. "Exactly! We can make them feel like kings, total sex gods—think Tom Selleck in Magnum P.I.!"

"Impossible." Moxie chokes.

"Unfortunately for us ladies... that just sadly isn't the fucking case. But what we can do is pretend. Fucking act our perfect asses off." A murmur of collective agreement ripples through the room. "Using our voices is a great tool. Men are ignorant. Selfish. Only care about themselves—"

Sable whispers, "That's the same thing."

Beverly continues, "They don't notice OR know what the body of a woman who is enjoying herself looks like!" She gestures to the girls with her paddle. "So, how do we do it?" Beverly leans in closer, her voice dropping conspiratorially.

"FAKE IT!" the girls shout in unison.

Beverly drops to her knees, the paddle raised as a scepter. "Alright, ladies, here's how it goes," she declares. "Imagine you're in the heat of passion."

She wriggles, her eyes squeezing shut as she mimics a wild encounter, bouncing her hips up and down and waving the paddle in a spanking motion. "*Ahh! O.. Oh!... Aghh! AAAH!*" The exaggerated sounds spill from her lips, and the room erupts into laughter.

"*Mmm-ahh. A-aahh... Ahn... Mngh-ph! Uhmn. AH!*"

Brandi tilts her head, biting her fingernail, confusion painted on her face. "I don't even know what fuckin' position that's supposed to be," trying to suppress her giggles.

Beverly rolls onto her back, legs in the air, embodying pure theatricality. Peach, unable to resist the moment, jumps up and kneels beside Beverly. She grabs Beverly's legs, mimicking a vigorous hump.

"*Uh-uhh. Haahhh. Mmmm-mmh. Nnmm...*" Beverly cries out, her voice grasping a new level of hilarity. The room is alive with joyous noise, each girl laughing and shouting in encouragement.

Madam Lottie appears in the doorway, her apron adorned with frills. Her hands land on her hips. The laughter momentarily fades as everyone turns to her. "Honey, that's not how you do it right," Madam Lottie remarks, before disappearing into the kitchen. The girls burst into laughter again, their voices filling the foyer.

Lace leans back against the couch. As the laughter settles, Beverly pushes herself up and wipes a faux tear from her eye. "Alright, alright! Let's get back to business," she announces. "Who's next?"

Trish struts to the center of the room, taking her place in the spotlight. Beverly waves the paddle. "And... *action!*"

Trish takes a deep breath, her hands flying to her sides as she moves with the imaginary rhythm of passion, *"Ooooh, yeah... Ahhh."*

With each exaggerated sound and movement, Trish transforms into a wild vixen, embodying the spirit of uninhibited joy. *"Mmmm... don't stop, don't stop! Ahhhh! Yes!"* Her voice echoes off the walls.

As the girls cheer her on, a sense of empowerment washes over Lace. They've become each other's safe space, a sisterhood bound by laughter and shared experiences. Eventually, Trish flops onto the floor, breathless and giggling.

Beverly picks up the chalk and adds, "TRISH CUM - YES."

"Oh! I've got one more mantra I live by that I want to pass on to you girls," Beverly exclaims. She closes her eyes, takes a deep breath, and hums deeply from her gut, the sound resonating as if channeling some ancient wisdom. After a few moments, she holds her arms out wide, pointer finger touching the tip of her thumb. With a proud smile, she declares, "She won't do kissing, but she will do anal!"

The other girls exchange glances of shock, mouths hanging open, while Trish nods along, a sly smile creeping onto her lips.

"Okay! Who's next?"

10

A Cowboy Walks Into A Bar With Ten Sex Workers

escending the grand staircase, Lace moves with seasoned grace. Her hair, styled into two soft plaits cascading down her shoulders, sways gently with each step. She wears a poorly cropped white tank top clinging to her curves, revealing the delicate lace of her baby pink bra beneath, while lace-trimmed boy shorts ride up her thighs.

Knowing this is the game she plays, a role she has come to embody.

The dim light of the chandelier casts warm amber silhouettes on the worn-out pink walls, illuminating the rustic beauty of the ranch. Lace glides down the staircase with the other girls, their steps a silent rhythm, a slow unraveling. They spill into a loose crescent, poised yet distant, each adrift in the quiet tides of her own thoughts.

Lace knows the routine well.

This is precisely another night at the ranch, another performance. A dark figure lounges lazily on the couch, but she barely acknowledges him. She's seen too many men come and go to be anything but indifferent.

Taking her place next to Brandi, Lace's gaze drops to her dirty nail beds. She has been so caught up in the chaos of her life that her self-care has taken a backseat. The routine begins.

"I'm Milk and Honey," says Moxie.

"I'm Mint Julep," says Mallory.

"I'm Gold Rush," says Gemma.

"I'm Three-tit Tillie," says Trish.

"I'm Buckaroo's Bliss," says Beverly.

"I'm Pistol and Pillow," says Petal.

"I'm Sloppy Gertie," says Sable.

"I'm Pegleg Annie," says Peach.

"I'm Bilious Bessie," says Brandi.

Lace hesitates before stepping forward. The eyes of the man across the room find her before she can look up, deep and probing, pulling her gaze upward as if magnetized. It's strange how one glance can ensnare so much power. She locks eyes with him for the first time.

Fuck.

He's the most handsome man Lace has ever seen.

Late forties. Stands out in the abyss. His tall, weathered frame tells a story etched by the sun, the tattoos winding down his arms, revealing a life lived boldly. His chestnut hair, thick and tousled, curls at the edges, showing the first signs of gray creeping in near his temples. It suits him, those flecks of silver—a mark of age curiously sharpening his appeal rather than dulling it.

A neatly kept beard, rugged but deliberate, frames his face; it hints at both neglect and intention, as if he could go days without caring, but also knows exactly when to trim it. The lines around his eyes are deep. Carved out from years spent squinting against a harsh sun, or maybe just from seeing more than he ever asked for.

He wears a black T-shirt that fits snugly against his chest and a scorpion belt holding his deep blue jeans. A collection of gemstone bracelets clinks softly on his left tattooed wrist, contrasting his rugged exterior. Next to him rests a brown cattleman cowboy hat, an unassuming prop carrying the entirety of his identity. And there are his eyes—dark, almost brooding, but with a spark buried deep within, akin to embers glowing faintly under a layer of ash. They're tired, sure, but sharp, scanning the room with a kind of calm wariness suggesting he's always a little on guard, particularly when pretending not to be. There's an undeniable charm in his half-smile, the type to disarm you if you let it. His eyes, surprisingly soft and kind, lock onto hers.

A jolt of electricity fires through her.

He gives her a crooked smile, sending her heart blooming. The man rises from the couch, grabbing his hat without breaking eye contact. As he crosses the room, the heat rises in her cheeks, an unfamiliar mix of excitement and anxiety flooding her senses. She's frozen, caught in a moment that's suspended in time. He stops inches from her, his presence looming similar to a gentle giant.

Lace forces herself to meet his gaze.

His voice is deep but soft. "Howdy, rosebud."

Lace's heart stutters. His hand, rough and calloused, gently grasps hers. He lifts it to his face and, with the softest of touches, presses his lips to the back of her hand. His eyes remain locked on hers, unwavering, and the world around them fades away. Lace twitches, her body tense with nervous energy. She forces a slight, trembling smile as she glances back up at him, her face flushing.

She hears a not-so-discreet whisper from the lineup but can't make out who spoke, nor does she care to pay any mind.

"Is this fucking allowed?"

Lace tries to steady herself, her eyes meeting him once more. A spark passes between them, igniting something deep within her, a flicker of hope in a hopeless life. She smiles again, this time with a touch more confidence.

Lace sits on the edge of her bed as she watches the strange man move through her room. His hat rests casually behind his back, held in one hand, while his eyes lazily sweep over the room, absorbing every detail. The thought of him exploring her personal space thrills her; she's amused by how he seems to uncover hidden secrets in the mundane. He pauses at the window, peering out into the dimming sky, where the sun dips low, casting the landscape in hues of gold and red.

"You know. Dusk is my favorite time of day. For most folk, it signifies the end of their day." He glances back at her, his eyes soft yet curious. He whispers, "Onto the next."

His boots make no sound as he walks toward her, and she watches, heart pounding in her chest. She tries to hide her nerves, to appear composed.

"But for me. It's just the start of my day." He stands directly in front of her now, his broad frame towering over her, which is oddly comforting rather than intimidating. His voice levels out, and he barely makes out a whisper. "It's where I come alive." He gently cups her chin with his thumb and forefinger, guiding her face toward his.

She melts under his touch. He grins at the sight. "You're as pretty as a picture." She marks what his tattoos depict: "Lucky" - top of the hand, Skull - forearm, "Never Again" - knuckles, and a Baby Lamb covered in spikes on his other forearm.

Lace forces herself to meet his gaze, the heat in her face here to stay. "Thank you."

His smile widens, revealing perfect white teeth. Lace lowers her gaze, her eyes drawn to his belt buckle, polished with age and stories untold. She reaches forward, fingers brushing against the cool leather, fascinated by the world he represents. He chuckles softly, catching her wrist and nuzzling her hand away.

Lace stammers, "Oh, sorry..." She shifts back on the bed, sliding her shirt off with one smooth motion, both daring and vulnerable. Her legs part a few inches as she rests her hand between them. An invitation. Lace makes sure to put on a more sultry tone in her voice, "You can just fuck me, then."

His eyes trail down her body, lingering but making no move to close the distance. Instead, he picks up her discarded shirt from the floor, inspecting it with an amused expression, as if it supports the secrets of her soul. Lace spots tally marks scratched inside the brim of his hat as he places it upside down on the edge of her bed. The significance of those marks intrigues her, igniting her curiosity about his life. His weight sinks into the mattress beside her as he hands the shirt back.

"How old are you, sweetheart?"

Lace hesitates, her fingers clenching the shirt as she pulls it back on, the fabric evoking an invisible shield.

"Twenty."

He leans back, a chuckle escaping his throat. She endures a mixture of pride and embarrassment.

"You're just a baby. What you doin' in a place like this?" Lace looks away, cheeks flushing as doubt creeps in. Does he see her as a child?

"Wanted something bigger for myself... see what that so-called American dream is all about."

He nods serenely, as if he understands her words. "—I don't get it. You don't want to have sex?" She gives him a fleeting wink, her voice dipping low. "Don't wanna knock boots with me?"

He shakes his head. "Not tonight. I want to talk."

"Why? You're paying me to fuck you."

"You seem like an amiable lady." The man speaks reassuringly and truthfully, as if he wholeheartedly believes the truth he claims. Lace's heart races at the compliment, but her mind spins with uncertainty.

This must be a game or some kind of fetish Lace isn't familiar with yet.

"Okay... well, what's your name?"

"Bo."

"Bo..." She relishes in how it sounds coming out of her mouth. "Well, I'm Lone Star Lover. You didn't give me a chance to say it earlier."

He frowns. "No. Your real name."

Lace hesitates, her lips parting, but the words catch somewhere in her throat. Bo waits, eyes locked on hers, and flashes another Hollywood smile, inevitably prying the truth out of her.

"Lace."

"*Lace.* It suits you."

Her eyes drift to his hat, still on the edge of her bed. "You a cowboy or somethin'?"

Bo chuckles, crinkling his eyes with a grin, "The meanest motherfucker in the valley."

Lace giggles, brushing her fingers through her braids, simply lighter in his presence. "Is that so?"

Bo raises an eyebrow, and she can't help but smile back at him.

"Well, I don't believe you... see, you already broke the cowboy hat rule."

"Really? And what does this cowboy hat rule state?"

Lace sits up on her knees, stretching for the hat. The hat is heavier than she expects, imbued with the stories of its owner. "Never set it on the bed. It's just bad luck. All your luck is in this here hat."

She flips the hat around in her hands, glancing inside to count the nine tally marks etched on the brim. Each mark intrigues her, inviting her to ask questions she's unsure she ought to know the answers to.

She whispers, "don't sit it upside down."

Gently, she places the hat atop his head. A playful smile brings up her lips as he chuckles, the sound resonating with warmth.

"You sound like a cowboy yourself."

"Maybe I am."

She settles back on her feet, a comfortable silence enveloping them. Bo watches her with arms crossed, his expression thoughtful, as if he's piecing together a puzzle, which is her. "What's Miss Lace's version of the American dream?"

Lace sighs, a smile breaking through as she allows herself to dream out loud. "A big city. With lights and people from everywhere—where anything's possible. Vegas. Las Vegas."

Bo tilts his head, amusement sparking in his eyes. "Vegas? That's your American dream?" Lace's confidence wavers, the words tasting bittersweet on her tongue.

"Yes."

The mattress groans again as Bo stands up.

"Well, I guess I have to take you, then." Lace says nothing as his words hang, a tempting proposition. "Las Vegas. It's your dream, right? And as an American cowboy, it seems like my God-given duty to help you reach it." Lace laughs, shaking her head, yet a smile plays at the corners of her lips.

"Yeah, right."

But the idea lingers, brightening her spirits and filling the room with an electric potential. Her heart races at the concept of adventure. Bo walks to the door, pausing before he leaves. He turns to look at her, a smirk tugging at his lips as if he already knows she's someone worth holding onto.

"Care for a little drive?" He waits, hand on the knob, his body halfway out, ready to disappear but would stay if she claimed the word.

"Right now?" She asks.

"Why not?" Bo replies, his voice low and easy, as if the idea of a nighttime drive with a stranger is as casual as lighting a cigarette.

He steps out, leaving the door ajar.

Lace feels the pull.

She quickly hops off the bed.

11

Jesus Take The Wheel

The air outside is nippier than she expects when she follows him.
Bo's a good ten yards in front of Lace as they walk toward his
topless blue 1978 Ford Bronco truck parked under the faint pink glow of
a flickering Desert Delights Ranch sign. He doesn't look back at Lace.
Not once as she trails behind him as if he is nothing, but sure, Lace will
follow.

Stopping at the passenger door, he swivels around, giving Lace the
brightest boyish smile she's ever seen. His right hand clasps the rusty
handle, opening it gently with a soft click. He gestures his free hand for
Lace to hop inside, tilting his hat in acknowledgment as she crawls in.

"You didn't put any shoes on," he says, leaning his arms against the top
of the frame, peeking his body inside the car.

Lace shakes her head, teasing, "You wouldn't get it."

The truck's engine growls as they pull out onto the dusty trail. The ranch falls away quickly, swallowed by the pitch black, leaving only the headlights cutting through the night. Lace rests her head against the window, the engine vibrating through her body. The endless stars above, cluttered so closely it almost makes up for the absent sun.

Bo drives with one hand on the wheel, the other draped casually over the open window. He's quiet, letting the night speak for itself, the wind whipping through their ears.

"Where we going?" she asks after a long stretch of silence.

"Nowhere in particular," he replies, eyes fixed on the road ahead. "Just wanted to show you the quiet."

There's a sense in which they don't need to fill the space with meaningless words. The isolation is nothing but palpable out here.

Only two people left in the West.

The truck speeds up, and the stars blur in her vision. "What do you do?" Lace shouts.

Bo lightly shouts back as they make a sharp right turn, the wind picking up, "Ranchin'."

"Ranchin'?" Lace repeats, leaning a little closer, curious now. "What's that like?"

Bo shrugs. "It's hard," he admits, "sunup to sundown, you either fixing fences, wrangling cattle, or trying to keep the land alive. Most days, it feels like you're fighting against something bigger than yourself."

Lace studies him, intrigued. "But you love it?"

Bo chuckles, the sound deep and gravelly. "Sometimes. Ranchin' is in my blood. My great-granddaddy built that place from nothing, and my old man kept it running until he couldn't anymore. Then it fell to me."

He pauses, and there's a flicker of something in his voice—pride. "It's not the kind of life you choose. It's the kind that chooses you."

There's something heavy about Bo running deeper than his peaceful smiles and charm. She imagines him out there, under the blistering sun, dust kicking up around his boots, sweat on his brow, working his generational land. There's a quiet strength in that kind of life, but also loneliness.

"Ever think about leavin'?" she asks, the question slipping out before she can stop herself.

"All the time."

Lace turns her head, surprised by the honesty of his answer. Bo keeps his gaze fixed ahead, but she can see the tension in his shoulders and how his hands tighten on the wheel. "But I never do," he continues, shaking his head as if he could brush off the thought. "That land's in my bones. Even if I wanted to, I'm not sure I could walk away."

There's a sadness in his words, tugging at something inside Lace. She has that similar vein of feeling trapped, to have a part of you tied to a place you can't entirely escape from, no matter how desperate you may be. She leans back in her seat, watching him, questioning if maybe that's why he's here now, with her, in the middle of nowhere.

Maybe he's running, too, even if he won't admit it.

Lace's eyes flutter shut, letting the sensation wash over her—the rumble of the truck, the rush of wind, of Bo's presence next to her. Something dangerous but thrilling, waiting to be unleashed.

After a long stretch of silence, Bo speaks again. His voice is rough, mimicking the scrape of boots on a dusty porch. "I'd give it all up, though. If I met the right lady."

Bo doesn't elaborate. Nothing else left to say. He only presses his foot harder on the gas, and the truck surges forward under the guise of outrunning the past if they just drive quick enough. The speed makes Lace's pulse quicken, making her crave to do something reckless.

Without a word, she stands up, pushing herself through the open roof of the truck. The cold and exhilarating wind hits her, whipping her braids behind her. She stretches her arms out wide, the stars spinning in a dizzying blur overhead.

For a moment, she's weightless and untouchable. She closes her eyes, letting the night swallow her whole.

I can be anything or nothing at all.

Bo lets out a low chuckle from below, and Lace grins, the sound sending a thrill through her. She arches her back, leaning into the wind, her fingers drifting down her body. Exploring the curves of her skin as if it's the first time she genuinely felt herself.

She sucks in a breath of cold air as she touches the bare skin beneath her shirt, her fingers moving in deliberate circles over the soft fabric of her shirt. She reaches her left arm up, aspiring to touch the stars if she solely extends high enough.

Below, Bo glances up at her through the rearview mirror, his eyes brushing back and forth between the road and her silhouette against the sky. He can see the way she moves.

The unrushed motion of her hands as they explore her body. She slides her hands lower, her back touching the hood, teasing herself as the world rushes past, her heartbeat matching the wild rhythm of the engine. The stars blur, the sky spins, and Lace lets out a soft, breathless laugh, which the wind snatches back.

Bo's hand gravitates to her left ankle, softly grasping it as if he can stop her from flying off. Her right hand slips down the front of her shorts, connecting with the soft fabric of her underwear. She doesn't stop herself from slipping her hands under until she meets bare skin.

Touching herself with a boldness she hasn't understood until now. She let out a soft gasp, barely audible over the rush of the wind, her body swaying with the truck's movement. Her hand moves at a snail's pace, teasing herself, each touch sending sparks up her spine.

Bo's eyes dart to the mirror again as she leans back against the roof's edge, lost in her world.

He doesn't look away. Something magnetic about the way she moves, the confidence in her posture.

Lace—a wild spirit, untamed, burning bright in the night.

12

Little Harlots On The Prairie

Sweat clings to Lace's back as she steps off the porch into the dry backyard, the boards creaking under her weight. The air smells of dust and summer heat, mingled with the sweet tang of crushed wildflowers. A few chickens scratch at the edges of the fence, where men mill about, boots propped on overturned crates or the backs of wheelbarrows. Murmurs turning to wolfish whistles and loud laughter competing with the buzz of bees rising from their combs.

Moxie props against the rickety clothesline pole, an ankle kicked over the other, smirking as she adjusts the strap of her lace camisole.

She pretends not to register the man beside her. When he finally speaks, fumbling for words, she cuts him off with a sly grin. "Go on, spit it out. Or you scared of a girl who bites?"

He laughs nervously, scratching the back of his neck. "Depends on how hard."

Gemma has taken over the porch swing, rocking steady. A glass of sweet tea sweats in her hand as she sizes up a man leaning against the post. "Careful, sugar. Stare too long, and your eyes might stick."

"Can't help it," he drawls, tipping his hat. "You sittin' there like you put a rubber stamp on sin."

Gemma chuckles, low and throaty. "Sin's free, sweetheart."

Mallory is near the cornrows, flipping an ear of corn back and forth as if it were a baseball. Her skirt flutters in the breeze as she eyes a man with a grease-stained hat. "You ever seen a woman husk corn this fast?" she asks.

The man grins, arms folded. "No, ma'am. But I bet I can do it faster."

Mallory tosses the corn at his chest. "Bet you can't. And I don't take kindly to losing."

Trish has claimed the water trough, leaning against the edge as if it's a bar counter. A cowboy inches closer, his grin wide as he looks her up and down. She dips her fingers into the hot water spreading it across her chest. "Hot out here, huh?" she says, her voice low and teasing.

"Hotter with you around," he fires back, stepping closer until there's barely an inch between them.

She hooks a finger into his belt loop and gives it a playful tug. "Careful, cowboy. You keep flapping your gums sweet like that, and I might think you're serious."

His grin doesn't falter. "What if I am?"

Trish tilts her head, brushing a speck of dirt off his collar. "Then you better start proving it." Her hand lingers only a second too long, and when she turns to walk away, she glances back over her shoulder, her smile daring him to follow. He does, stumbling a little, completely forgetting how his legs work.

Beverly lingers near the wildflowers, plucking petals from a daisy as a man follows her every move. She doesn't say much, humming to herself, but she turns with a honeyed smile when he steps closer. "You here to talk, or you just gonna hover there like a cloud?"

The man blushes. "Uh, talk. Yeah. What's your name?"

"Buckaroo's Bliss," she says, pulling another petal loose. "But you can call me whatever you hanker for—just don't get in my light."

Petal glides barefoot through the grass, her sundress clinging to her as she passes a group of men. She tosses an apple to one of them, watching with amusement as he barely catches it. "You look hungry," she says, her voice as sweet as the fruit. "Careful, though. It's sour."

Brandi perches on the edge of the picnic table. A vision ripped out of a Marlboro ad, her cutoff shorts leaving little to the imagination. Her shirt knotted at the waist, sweat-seeping at the collar, while a cigarette dangles from her lips as she smirks at a man struggling with his lighter. When he finally manages to strike a flame, she exhales a plume of smoke and teases, "Took you long enough. What are you, a virgin?"

The man grins, leaning closer. "Maybe I just wanted to savor the moment."

"Keep savoring, cowboy," she purrs, blowing smoke into his face.

Peach is front and center near the barn, perched on a stack of hay bales with a man standing between her knees. She trails a finger down his chest, stopping an inch above his belt buckle. "You ever had a woman make you blush like this?" she asks, her voice dripping with mock innocence, though the grin on her lips says otherwise.

The man shifts his weight, his hands brushing against his thighs like he doesn't know where to put them. "Blush? I don't blush," he stammers, his grin faltering.

Peach leans forward, close enough that her breath fans his neck, her hands resting lightly on his shoulders. "Sure you do. You're just bad at hiding it." Her nails trace circles on the fabric of his shirt, and he sucks in a breath so sharp it earns a round of laughter from the other men nearby.

"Careful, sweetheart," one man shouts. "He might pass out."

Sable is by the fence, one boot propped on the bottom rung as a cowboy slides up next to her, trying not to trip over his feet. She gives him a once-over; her smile sharp enough to cut. "What's the matter, handsome? You lost a bet?"

The man blinks. "Uh, no. Why?"

She smirks, leaning close enough to make him squirm. "'Cause you're standing here like you don't know what to do with your hands."

He shoves them awkwardly into his pockets, trying to recover. "I know what to do."

"Oh, do you?" she says, arching an eyebrow. She grabs his hand and places it on her hips.

Across the yard, Madam Lottie sits near the bed of roses, her sharp eyes scanning the scene—a hawk perched over her territory. She doesn't interfere much; she only watches, her hands folded over her lap, her wide-brimmed hat shading her face. Lace glances toward her, comforted by knowing she's always there.

The men don't seem so sharp. Edges of their grins suggest they're not so dangerous.

She even finds herself laughing when one of them slips in the mud by the water trough, his buddies hooting as they haul him back to his feet.

A hand on her shoulder pulls her out of it. Lace stiffens, her muscles tensing before her mind can catch up. She recognizes him immediately—Nate.

His hat, battered by years of sun and dust, sits low on his brow, its brim curling as if it were the edge of a dry riverbank. His face is a map of hard living, creased and rugged. He'd spoken to her on her second day here, leaning against her door frame with his hands shoved into his pockets. Right after, he instructed her to strip and place her hands on the wall. Telling her she reminds him of his daughter back in Idaho, the same quiet way she carries herself.

He'd smiled when he spoke about it.

"Sweet ole Lone Star Lover," Nate practically drools. "You're a tough cookie to catch. Been meanin' to speak to you."

Lace forces a smile. "Guess I've been busy," she says, glancing toward Brandi and the others, but they're too caught up in their own noise to notice.

Nate chuckles, stepping closer. "Too busy to say hi? That don't sound polite."

His words don't hit wrong, but the way he says them does. She straightens, gripping the fence tighter as he moves in close enough for her to smell the beer on his breath. "You remind me so much of my girl," he murmurs, his voice dropping. "Got that same quiet sweetness to you."

Lace shifts her weight, the knot in her stomach tightening. "That's nice," she says lightly, trying to step back, but his hand is already on her arm, locking her in place.

"Don't be shy now," Nate says, his grip tightening. "Ain't nothing wrong with gettin' comfortable."

Before she can pull away, he pulls her into his lap, his arms snaking around her waist as he sits on a nearby overturned crate. Lace freezes, the noise around her fading to a low hum as his hands slide down her thighs. His grip is firm but too familiar, making her skin crawl.

"Let me go," she says sharply, her voice cutting through the air. She pushes against his chest, but Nate only laughs.

"Relax, darlin'," he murmurs. "You're too stiff. Ain't nobody here gonna hurt you."

Her pulse pounds in her ears as she struggles, glancing around for someone—anyone to intervene. She jerks her head toward Madam Lottie, but for once, she doesn't pick up on it, too busy plucking roses and dropping them into a woven basket. Lace twists against Nate's grip, panic rising in her throat. She finally catches someone's eye.

He's across the yard, sitting in the shade of a time-tested chinquapin oak tree with one knee bent up, his hat pulled low over his face. Bo.

She doesn't know how long he's been watching or how long he's been here, but his body tenses as their eyes meet. He flicks the cigarette from his hand and rises, his broad frame cutting through the haze of sunlight.

The yard stills as Bo strides forward, his boots crunching against the dirt in a deliberate, steady rhythm. When Bo reaches them, he stops, his shadow stretching long over Nate and Lace. His jaw tight, his hands loose at his sides, but there's a weight to him, making the air thick.

"Let her go," Bo says. The words come out heavy as a memorial stone.

Nate freezes for half a beat before he chuckles, his grip loosening momentarily, but not enough.

"C'mon, we're just messin' around."

Bo tilts his head, his gaze narrowing. "I said, let her go."

Nate hesitates and finally lifts his hands in surrender. Lace stumbles to her feet, her heart skipping a beat as she backs away from Nate, but Bo doesn't move. His eyes stay locked on Nate, the air around them crackling as if it were dry lightning.

"Don't know why you're gettin' so worked up," Nate mutters, brushing the dirt off his jeans as he stands. "She's fine."

Bo steps forward. "That's what you think?"

His presence alone is a warning, but the words never come. Bo's fist crashes into his jaw. The sound sharp and heavy echoing across the yard as Nate staggers back into the dirt. Blood drips from his lip as he groans, but Bo doesn't stop. He grabs Nate by the shirt and hauls him upright, slamming him against the fence hard enough to rattle it. The wood groans under the weight, trembling as though it might give way, but Bo's grip is unyielding—unyielding just as the look in his eyes.

Madam Lottic's voice slices through the air, sharp and commanding. She's on her feet now, her hat pushed back, her eyes blazing.

"Enough!"

Bo doesn't move for a moment, his fist clenched as he stares down Nate. He steps back, letting Nate collapse into the dirt with a pitiful groan. Bo turns to Lace, his expression softening, but his voice is firm when speaking. "You alright?"

Lace nods, but her voice traps in her throat. The yard hums with the murmurs of the other men, their unease palpable.

She hears Trish speak up. "That was kind of sexy," she turns to face Gemma. "You know, I've always loved a big, muscular man who could pick me up and throw me around." She drawls, twirling a strand of hair around her finger. "Especially a man in a uniform. Though there was this soldier I was with once. Spent the whole night crying in my arms about—"

But Lace can't focus on them. Her gaze stays on Bo, on the tension in his shoulders as he turns and walks away, disappearing out of the yard and into the parking lot without another word.

Madam Lottie watches him go, then turns to Lace, her gaze steady but unreadable. "Get inside," she says, her voice quieter now but no less firm. Lace's legs shake as she heads toward the house. She glances back once at Nate, crumpled in the dirt, his blood mixing with the dry soil.

It's way too fuckin' early for this.

13

Hey Robert Plant, I Have Your Next Vacation Spot!

A s the sun makes its gradual, dramatic exit, painting God's country in the kind of orange belonging to a cheap postcard. Lace and the girls tumble out of Trish's Pontiac and Gemma's pristine white Audi Quattro into the rodeo dirt lot. Trish, ever impatient, decides doors are purely aesthetic and vaults herself over her car, landing in a colossal heap of horse manure. The shriek she lets out is high enough to scare a grizzly.

She lifts her pastel pink cowgirl boot, now accessorized with a generous smear of barnyard luck. "Jesus H. Christ! We're going home! I am NOT walking around with shit on my boots!"

Lace chokes back a laugh, but it slips out. Trish whips around, her eyes wild, mirroring Anna from *Possession*.

"This ain't funny, Lace! How the hell am I supposed to snag some dreamboat wrangler when I smell like livestock?" Her voice cracks with the tragedy of it all, on the verge of tears.

Lace shrugs, quietly laughing, "Maybe they'll like you better now?"

Trish tiptoes out of the mess, hands in the air, surrendering to the manure gods. Her gaze lands on Lace's clean black leather boots. She throws herself down in front of Lace, clutching at her left boot, acting as if it's a life preserver. Lace stumbles back, landing squarely on her butt.

"Oh, c'mon, Lace, please! You never wear shoes anyway!" Trish wails, clawing at the boot in a way only a rabies-infected raccoon could relate to. Lace flips onto her stomach, scrambling away from Trish's desperate grip, digging her fingers into the dirt to escape.

A family of four strolls by, the parents quickly shielding their children's eyes from the rodeo's real wild show.

"You drove here! Go back and get another pair!" Lace shouts. "And these aren't even my boots—they're Brandi's!"

Trish manages to yank Lace's boot halfway down her calf. "I am *not* driving back alone! It's nearly dark!" She widens her eyes for effect. "Some psycho's gonna snatch me up and eat me alive. You *have* to come with me!"

Moxie and Brandi bicker about Robert Plant.

"There's just *no* way Robert Plant pays for sex. No way," Brandi says, rolling her eyes as if she's argued this a thousand times before. Her voice has that finality, trying to close the book on the conversation. Moxie takes a deep drag of a joint, but her comeback gets strangled by the smoke.

She coughs, eyes watering, but finally squeezes out, "I—know a girl—who fucked him—for a hundred bucks—and a pack of Runts."

Brandi looks at her like she's sprouted a second head. "You're lying. Robert Plant could stick his dick in anyone for free. You want to know why? Because he's *fucking* Robert Plant!" She taps her forehead for emphasis.

Moxie's continuously wheezing tries to gather her dignity. "Well, don't come crying to me when Robert strolls up to the fucking Desert's Delight and picks *my* room," she huffs, handing the joint off to the Sable. Brandi's eyes widen as she bursts out laughing, nearly doubling over. "*If Robert Plant shows up here, I'll fuck you myself!*"

Moxie narrows her eyes. "Forget it," she says, side-eyeing Brandi. "I think he's gay, anyway."

Brandi grins wide, the joint back in her hand now. "Gay, straight, whatever," she says with a shrug, blowing a smoke ring. "You're still full of shit about the Runts."

Beverly, Peach, and Mallory stand around Lace and Trish, watching as the two wrestle in the dirt. Lace shrieks as Trish climbs on top of her, pinning her arms behind her head. "Ah! I feel it! You smeared your shit on my thigh. I'm gonna yack!"

Two ropers in their early thirties slow their pace as they pass by, one giving a low whistle. "Well, fuck me. Those buckle bunnies get crazier every year."

Lace and Trish freeze, breathless, staring after the men as they stroll through the gates. Trish pushes herself off Lace and plops back into the dirt, crossing her arms with a dramatic huff. "Buckle bunny? Who do they think they are?" Trish juts out her chin indignantly. "I am not no damn buckle bunny."

Flat on her back, Lace gazes up at the open sky, swiping a hand across her forehead to clear away the dust—only to smear it further, painting herself in a fresh layer of grime. Shit and dirt now wholly cover her short denim overalls, American flag bikini top, and wide-brimmed cowgirl hat. A patriotic mud pie.

Peach clears her throat, eyeing the dirt-smeared pair. "Y'all done?"

Trish and Lace scramble to their feet, brushing themselves off with little success. Trish lets out an exaggerated sigh. "Yes."

As they weave their way through the maze of cars and trailers toward the rodeo gates, Trish mutters to herself. "Buckle bunny... Ha! In their fucking dreams."

She huffs, tossing a glare over her shoulder.

They shuffle into the bleachers, surrounded by the din of the rodeo. Sharp tang of sweat and leather hangs thick, laced with the smoky whisper of grilled meat and the buttery lure of popcorn. Somewhere close, the sour bite of cheap beer sloshes from a plastic cup, mingling with the lingering musk of horses and cattle—earthy, raw, alive. Several people wrinkle their noses as Trish and Lace pass by. The chatter dips as the spotlight swings to the middle of the arena, casting its glow on a lone figure.

There stands a stunning woman not much older than the girls, topless but calm as a preacher on Sunday, her guitar slung across her chest no less than some kind of musical armor, barely hiding what God gave her. Her white cowgirl hat perches jauntily on her head. She gives the crowd a pageant grin.

Her voice is one that could melt fat in a hot pan, a honey-sweet drawl. She belts the national anthem, each note rising and falling as though weaving a story rather than singing a song. There's no sense of rushing—each note is savored. Each pluck of the guitar's strings deliberate.

The anthem sounds... different in her hands. The girls turn to one another to ensure they see the same thing.

Brandi asks, "Now, why isn't she one of ours?"

"If she doesn't watch it, some cowboy's gonna rope her right out of that arena," Gemma remarks loud enough, causing a couple of men in the row ahead to grin, tipping their hats in agreement.

As the last note fades, the woman tips her hat to the crowd, tossing her head back with a lingering laugh. She struts out of the arena, men breaking their necks to catch a last glimpse. The announcer's voice crackles through the speakers, pulling the crowd back. "Alright, folks, hope you enjoyed that little slice of American pride!" He laughs, and the bleachers rumble with applause.

Lace slouches back, elbows hooked over the splintered bench behind her, as the announcer's voice comes back on, "Time for our first saddle bronc rider. Let's give it up for Jim Hold-On-For-Dear-Life Hankins from Snakebite Ranch! Last time he rode, he managed to stay on all of... three seconds. Let's see if he can beat his record!"

The first rider barrels out of the chute, clinging to a bucking horse, looking mean enough to chew nails. The cowboy lasts maybe two seconds before he's tossed like nothing more than a rag doll, landing in the dirt with a thud, making the crowd wince and cheer in equal measure. He scrambles up, waving to the crowd with a grin as the pickup men dart in, distracting the horse and ushering it back to the pen.

Trish bolts up from her seat, hands cupped around her mouth. "That's alright, Jim!" She hollers, her voice carrying over the crowd, loud and proud.

A few heads turn, chuckles ripple through the bleachers, and Jim glances up, tipping his hat toward the unexpected support. The announcer picks up on it, adding to the laughter. "Well, looks like Jim's got himself a fan club up there in the stands! Maybe he'll give you his autograph on a busted boot, miss."

Trish grins, plopping back down nudging Lace. "Gotta show some support, right?"

Lace shakes her head, laughing. "Sure, Trish, but maybe try pickin' one who actually stays on next time."

"Oh, please," Trish scoffs, "I'm all about the underdog!"

A woman in her late 40s sitting in front of them, her teased hair sprayed into an immovable dome, turns around with a sour twist to her lipstick-smeared mouth. Her voice cuts sharp over the applause. "Underdog? Is that what they're calling sluts these days?" She says, her tone dripping with disgust.

Trish freezes momentarily, her grin faltering before snapping back into place, broader and sharper. She leans forward, resting her elbows on her knees, her voice sweet and dangerous. "What's that, hon? You drop somethin', or you just runnin' your mouth for the fun of it?"

The woman doesn't flinch. She crosses her arms, her nose wrinkling as if she smells something foul. "Just calling it how I see it. Screamin' for a man who couldn't even last five seconds—sounds about right."

Sable tugs at Trish's sleeve, a nervous laugh slipping out. "Let it go, Trish. She's not worth it."

But Trish isn't about to let it slide. She tilts her head; her cross earrings catching the light as she sizes the woman. "Listen, sweetheart, if you wanna jabber on about lasting five seconds, maybe look to your own backyard. Or your front porch. Hell, wherever it is, you lost your fuckin' manners."

The woman's lips curl into a smirk as she turns halfway back toward the girl's, her voice loud enough for the surrounding crowd to hear. "I know you," she sneers. "You're those whores from the ranch, aren't you? Thought you'd go unnoticed, huh? Must be nice, takin' a break from spreading your legs."

The words land as a slap, and Brandi leaps out of her seat before anyone can blink, her face twisted with rage. "You wanna say that again, you dried-up hag?" she snarls, clawed fingers aimed right at the woman's bouffant hairdo.

"Brandi!" Lace grabs her from behind, wrapping her arms around her waist, pulling her back down with all her strength.

Brandi kicks her legs, trying to lunge forward. "Let me go, Lace!"

The woman jumps out of her seat at the sight of Brandi's fury, but recovers quickly. "What's the matter? Can't take a little honesty? It's the truth—you lot are nothing but a walking petri dish. Go on, roll around in the mud with the cowboys all you want, but don't think you're fooling anyone."

Her husband, a wiry man who looks all too familiar, grabs her arm. "Betty, just leave it. Come on, let's go."

But she shrugs him off, clutching her purse tight against her side like it's shielding her from contamination. "I'm not sittin' here another second with the likes of them. Who knows what diseases they're carrying?" She spits the words out loud enough for the nearby rows to turn their heads.

"That's fine, sweetheart. Go ahead and find another seat—preferably one far enough away so we don't catch your bitterness. Pretty sure that's contagious." Trish fires back, her grin is razor sharp, arms crossed.

The crowd murmurs as the woman scurries off, her husband trailing behind with his head down, muttering about how she "never knows when to shut up." Brandi settles back into her seat, still fuming, while Lace loosens her grip, heart pounding.

Trish plops back down with a satisfied huff, glancing at Brandi. "Next time, at least wait until after the bull riding. No sense getting thrown out before the real fun starts."

Lace shakes her head, half-exasperated, half-amused. "You're all crazy."

Brandi crosses her arms, glaring down at the empty seats where the woman had been. "Damn right we are. Crazy enough to not let anyone run their mouth to us like that and walk away."

Trish winks at Lace. "Underdogs. Remember?"

A wiry guy who doesn't look a day over eighteen walks out. The announcer's back at it: "And there's Young Willy... holdin' onto that rope like he just found out his girlfriend's daddy's the sheriff!"

Beverly cocks her head. "Look at him—hat's bigger than his head. Think he knows how to use that rope, or is it just for show?"

Moxie shakes her head, smirking. "Please, he probably stole it from his sister's My Little Pony set." The girls hoot and holler, watching as Young Willy flies across the arena, hitting the dirt with a spectacular roll, leaving him looking dazed and balled up.

Brandi doubles over laughing. "Oh yeah, a real outlaw right there. Someone get him a juice box."

Lace calls out. "Better luck next time, cowboy!"

The loudspeaker crackles, "And now, bareback ridin' out of Blackthorn Ranch, give it up for Bo, stickin' to that horse like the bank's about to close, and he's got a loan to pay!"

Lace perks up, her eyes snapping at the gate as the crowd lets out a collective cheer. All eyes fall on Bo, who's sitting in the right delivery of the chute. Nothing but all the time in the world, as his one hand grips the leather rigging. The sleek black horse beneath him shifts, all muscle and nervous energy, as it paws at the dirt, but Bo looks calm, waiting for the right moment.

The gate swings open, and the horse bolts out. Bo's body moves with every wild buck, every twist, riding each brutal jolt. Nothing but instinct. The crowd's on their feet, yelling and stomping, but Lace can only watch.

He looks untouchable. Painfully handsome.

But, as the horse kicks their legs up unnaturally high, boiling over with a sudden jerk, Bo's body leans too far, his hand slipping. For a split second, he tries to recover, but the animal bucks again, quick as a rattlesnake, and Bo flings sideways, hitting the dirt with a hard, sickening thud.

The crowd gasps, voices rising in shock and groans, some whistling in sympathy, others cheering. Lace's stomach drops as he lies there, hat off, dust clinging to his deep red snap-button shirt.

The masses wait to see if he'll move. After a beat, Bo plants a hand in the dirt, pushing himself up, shaking his head with a half-smile tugging at his mouth. He picks up his hat, giving it a good slap, setting it back on his head as he glances up at the crowd, tipping his hat to them with a grin.

Pure Bo—easy and unbothered, acting like he didn't eat dirt seconds ago.

Bo takes a step back toward the gate. Just before he turns away, his gaze sweeps up to the stands, landing on Lace. For a moment, he pauses, his eyes locking with hers.

With that same half-smile, he gives her a quick, knowing wink so subtle she almost questions if she imagined it.

But the flicker in his eyes say he knew she watched all along. The heat in her cheeks spreads as he finally turns and strides out of the arena.

Brandi nudges Lace.

"You know, I think I kind of like it better when they do fall."

14

This Little Piggy Went To The Rodeo

bout twenty minutes have passed since Bo hit the rodeo dirt, and Lace can focus on nothing more, even as she watches Mallory chase after a piglet. After the last go-round, the announcer clicked on the loudspeaker, calling for children and any enthusiastic adults to come down to the muddy pig pen, "Alrighty, folks! Come on down! It's time for the 7th Annual Greased Pig Round-Up! We've got our pigs—all slicker than a fresh wax job on a Cadillac!"

Mallory's leg bounces impatiently as she watches below. The mud pit is alive with squealing pigs and flailing contestants, and each failed attempt to grab a pig has the crowd in stitches. A cowboy in a sweat-stained hat dives for a piglet and misses, landing face-first in the mud. The stands erupt in laughter, but Mallory doesn't join in. Her lips twitch with something closer to ambition.

"I could catch that pig," she mutters.

Peach, next to her, smirks. "What was that, Mal?"

"I said I could catch that pig. Probably faster than anyone down there." Mallory sits up straighter, scanning for the best route to the gate.

Peach raises an eyebrow. "You serious?"

Mallory stands, brushing off the back of her denim shorts. "Dead serious. That scrappy little guy in the corner? He's mine."

Before Peach can reply, Mallory's already on the move, weaving her way down the bleachers. The rest of the girls trail their gaze on Mallory. Brandi leans forward, craning her neck to get a better look. "Now, where she going?"

The announcer's voice booms over the speakers as Mallory hops the rail near the gate. "And it looks like we've got another brave contender! Give it up for—what's your name, ma'am?"

"Mallory," she calls back, tying her hair into a quick knot at the base of her neck.

"Well, folks, Mallory here thinks she's got what it takes to wrangle one of our greased-up speed demons. Let's see if she can prove it!"

Mallory grins and steps into the pen, the mud squelching under her boots. She keeps her eyes on the pigs as the farmhand slathers another layer of grease onto the one she's been eyeing. It snorts and darts nervously in the corner, as if it knows its freedom hangs by a thread.

The crowd counts down. "Three... two... one!" Pigs scatter in sporadic directions, but Mallory doesn't hesitate. She darts forward, boots slipping, her focus locked on the scrappy pig bolting toward the far fence.

The arena erupts in cheers as Mallory takes a spectacular nose dive into a patch of mud. Her laughter rings out as she scrambles to grab hold of the slippery pig. Mallory lunges, arms wide, just as some poor young soul flies in from her right, both of them gunning for the same pig. Without thinking, she slams into him full force, sending them both crashing into the mud.

But for Lace, the noise blurs into a distant breath.

Her focus shifts, and her gaze pulls to the right.

Bo stands near a sleek, jet-black trailer with the name of his ranch emblazoned in bold gold letters on the side, *Blackthorn*. The horse he'd ridden stands tied off to a post, shifting its weight lazily. Bo moves unhurriedly, his hands steady as he adjusts a lead rope, his broad shoulders tearing against the fabric.

Lace takes a breath, steadying herself as she steps away from the bleachers. She passes a booth framed in blinking string lights, its banner proudly declaring: "The Higher the Hair, the Closer to the Crown!"

Four women stand on podiums, their hair teased to outrageous heights, each a masterpiece of aqua net and ambition. One sports a rhinestone-studded beehive, another a wild lion's mane of curls. A redhead waves dramatically, her towering hair swaying in the breeze, while the fourth contestant flaunts a feathered mohawk, defying all laws of physics.

The judge, a lanky man with a bolo tie, circles the contestants, nodding thoughtfully as he speaks. "Height's not enough, folks! Volume, structure, and wind resistance decide this crown!"

A gust from a giant fan sends a ripple through the hairdos, and the crowd gasps. The women clutch their heads, similar to queens protecting their crowns. Lace keeps moving, nearing Bo's trailer.

He doesn't acknowledge her at first, his hat tipped low enough to shadow his face, but when she gets close enough for her boots to crunch against the gravel, he glances up. A smile tugs at the corner of his mouth, casual, as though he'd known she'd come to find him all along.

"Well, hey there," he drawls, brushing his hands off his leather chaps. Bo's grin comes easy, lazy, as his eyes drift over Lace, taking in the streaks of dirt across her arms and legs. "You look like you've been through it. What happened to you?"

Lace shrugs, her lips twitching into a sly smile. "Had a little wrestle with my friend Trish in the parking lot."

Bo lets out a low whistle, his grin spreading wider. "Now, that's somethin' I wouldn't mind seein'." He leans on the fence post, "sounds 'bout right for Trish, though. She's always been a spitfire."

Lace freezes for a moment, narrowing her eyes at him. "How do you know Trish?"

Bo pauses, scratching the back of his neck, his voice dropping into something smoother, more casual. "Name and face stuck with me from this mornin' in the garden. Pretty sure she was around then, wasn't she?"

But Trish would've introduced herself as Three-tit Tillie.

Lace's brow furrows, her mind racing. She doesn't remember Bo meeting Trish, not like that. But his voice carries a simple confidence, and his grin is disarming.

"Yeah," she says, watching him close. "Guess she was." Bo shrugs, pushing off the fence and shoving his hands into his pockets.

She shifts her weight, the question already burning in her chest. Finally, she glances at him, her voice cutting through the crowd's roar. "Why'd you punch that man earlier? In the garden."

Bo doesn't look at her right away. His jaw tightens, the muscles working under his tan skin, but his expression doesn't change. After a long pause, he shrugs, "seemed like he deserved it."

"Seemed like," Lace repeats, narrowing her eyes at him. "You just go around knockin' out men who seem like they deserve it?"

Bo tilts his head. "I ain't in the habit of it if that's what you're askin'."

Lace doesn't smile. She's watching him too closely, the way his shoulders stay loose, but his eyes flick toward her, sharp and measuring. "He didn't hurt me, you know," she says, quieter now. "Not really."

Bo finally turns to her, leaning one elbow against the rail, his dark eyes locking on hers. "That what you think? 'Cause from where I was sittin', he looked about a step away from doin' somethin' you couldn't brush off so easy."

Lace stiffens, her grip tightening on the fence. "I'm startin' to get used to it. Men always grabbin' at me. I could've handled it."

"Maybe," Bo says, his tone soft but firm. "Maybe you shouldn't have to. A man who's lost his way ain't got nothin' worth offerin' to a good woman like you."

Lace folds her arms across her chest. "I saw you fall," she says softly, skipping past topics she would preferably not discuss. "It looked bad."

"Wasn't my best ride," he admits, reaching up to adjust his hat. "But you take the hits as they come. No use fussin' over it."

"You could've gotten hurt," she presses, her brow furrowing.

He chuckles, a low, warm sound rolling over her. "Lace, it's a rodeo. If I let every fall get to me, I'd never get back on. You just dust yourself off and move on. Simple as that."

"You make it sound so easy," she murmurs.

The announcer's voice roars in the background, Mallory's triumphant laughter ringing through the arena as she finally catches the piglet. Lace whips her head around in time to see Mallory, drenched in mud, clinging to the squealing creature high above her head in victory.

Her grime-smeared grin widens as a rodeo clown drapes a sash over her, declaring her the new "Piggy's Princess 1986."

The horse shifts its weight, releasing a sudden snort, startling Lace and bringing her attention back to Bo. Its muscles ripple under its sweat-darkened coat as Bo adjusts the lead rope. Lace hesitates at the edge of the scene, unsure if stepping closer is the right move. But Bo looks up, catching her in his steady gaze, and the faintest smile tugs at his lips.

"You ever been this close to a horse before?"

She shakes her head, her hands fidgeting with the frayed edges of her overalls. "Not this close."

Bo tilts his head, his smile softening as he pats the mare's neck. "She's gentle," he says, stepping to the side. "C'mere. You wanna try?"

Lace blinks, glancing at the horse and back at Bo. "I don't... I mean, I wouldn't know what to do."

He chuckles softly, his hand resting lightly on the horse's flank. "Ain't much to it," he says, his tone coaxing, almost teasing. "Come on. She won't bite. Names Licorice."

Lace takes a hesitant step forward, the earthy smell of the horse and the faint warmth of Bo's presence pulling her closer. He extends for her hand, his touch firm but gentle as he guides it toward Licorice's neck.

"Here," he murmurs, positioning her fingers against the sleek, damp coat. "Start slow, right here."

Her breath stops as her hand makes contact. She strokes hesitantly, her movements stiff at first, but Bo's hand doesn't leave hers. He stays close, his thumb brushing lightly against her knuckles as he guides her.

"See?" he says, his voice low and tender. "Nothin' to it."

Licorice huffs softly, its ears twitching, and she lets her hand move confidently. But it's not only the horse harnessing her attention—it's Bo. The way he stands so close, his touch firm but unhurried.

"You're a natural," he says, his voice carrying the trace of a smile. "Might have to take you ridin' one day."

She laughs softly, the sound nervous but genuine. "I'd just embarrass myself."

"Doubt that," he replies, his voice dipping lower, the words meant only for her. "Fortune favors the bold."

The moment stretches, her hand stroking the horse, his guiding hers, though she's sure she doesn't need the help anymore. She glances up at him, catching the faint line of sweat at his temple, the way his lashes cast shadows against his cheeks.

"You didn't wanna win?"

Bo's lips curve into a smile. He pulls his hand away, letting hers linger against the horse's neck. "There'll be others," he says, his tone soft but sure.

A promise.

All she can do is stand there, caught between the noise of the rodeo and his gaze. Before she can consider what else to say, Bo tips his hat subtly, guiding Licorice back to her trailer, the conversation slipping away as quickly as it began.

15

Hot To The Touch

The moon hangs so low as if it vigorously awaits to join them, slipping into their circle. Merely another restless girl. Lace watches it and supposes, for sure, *the moon is female*. Only a woman could hang in such a manner, luminous and quiet, longing to be part of something but keeping her distance. The night air carries the lingering echoes of the rodeo—shouts, laughter, the pounding rhythm of boots against hard-packed earth.

The girls have been riding that energy for hours, as if they could keep galloping across nature's bounty, untamed and unbroken, forever. They sit in a circle behind the ranch, a stolen bottle of whiskey being passed around, its amber glint catching in the flickering firelight of the modest bonfire.

Lace picks at a loose thread on her overalls, her teeth chewing her bottom lip.

She takes a deep breath and blurts out, "Trish, you know a man named Bo?"

Trish pauses mid-swig, the bottle hovering before her lips. Her eyes narrow as she considers the question. She takes her gulp anyway, swallowing hard before handing the bottle off to Brandi. "Bo?" Trish says, smacking her lips like she was tasting the name. "Hell, I don't know. Sounds familiar, but I meet a lot of men, Lace. What's he look like?"

"Older," Lace says quickly. "Tall. Dark hair. Wears a hat most of the time. Talks like he owns the damn sky."

Trish snickers, leaning forward to warm her hands against the fire. "Sugar, that could be half the cowboys in Nevada. Did he say he knew me?"

"Basically," Lace says a little defensively. She glances at the moon, still slung low.

"Well," Trish says, brushing ash off her knee, "like I said, I see a lot of men. Some stick, some don't. But if he's got a mouth like that, I probably wouldn't forget him." She grins, wicked and sharp. "You sweet on him or somethin'?"

"No!" Lace snaps, her voice sharper than she intends. The others glance at her, curious, but she waves them off. "I'm just... trying to figure him out. That's all."

Trish shrugs, already losing interest. "Men like him? They're not puzzles, Lace. They're storms. Best you can do is wait 'em out."

The fire crackles louder as Lace turns back to the moon, watching as if it understands. The flames in front of her snap and hiss, a living thing refusing to be ignored, but her eyes stay fixed on the sky, searching for answers in its cold, distant face.

"We should do something," Brandi says, her voice husky from the dust and drinks.

Trish laughs. "Like what? Tip a cow? How old are you?"

"No," Brandi smirks, pulling out a miniature branding iron behind her. The iron has two hearts conjoined, crude but unmistakable.

"Oh. So you do see me as a cow? Were you gonna push me over too?" Trish asks, raising an eyebrow. "What you do? Steal that from some wretched rancher?"

"Found it in the junk heap," Brandi says with a grin, twirling it above her head as a lasso. Moxie, sitting beside her, quickly ducks down. "It's cute. Got two hearts on it."

The girls immediately chime in with their remarks.

"We can see that," Peach says, a laugh bubbling up, half nervous, half amused.

"Absolutely not," Sable deadpans, shaking her head.

"Bitchin'," Mallory says, her grin stretching wide. Proudly wearing her Piggy's Princess sash.

"You're serious, aren't you?" Petal says, eyes widening, a half-cocked smile on her lips.

"Damn right, I am," Brandi replies, her wicked grin spreading.

"I think we done lost out marbles," Beverly says, shaking her head, but there's a gleam in her eyes.

"I'm in," Gemma says, her voice steady.

"If we're gonna do it, we all have to," Mallory adds, shrugging with a sly smile.

"No way," Peach adds, a nervous laugh escaping her. "You're bat shit."

"Yeah, I kind of like my skin not melting off. So I'll pass," Moxie says, her blue eyes widening.

Trish remarks, "you've got the Miami Vice logo tattooed on your left ass cheek. Pretty sure the ship for caring about body art has sailed, babe."

"I didn't know you were from Miami," Gemma cocks her head toward Moxie.

"She's from Boca Raton," Trish quickly replies.

Moxie throws up her arms. Her translucent skin practically absorbs the fire's light, resembling her to a written fable passed down from generation to generation. "I like Miami Vice, okay? The pastel suits, the cars, Don fuckin' Johnson! Boca Raton. Miami. Whatever, same fuckin' thing! Why you always gotta bring that up?"

Trish snaps her head to meet Moxie. "No, it ain't! My California ass even knows that. Boca's the kind of place Miami folks go when they need a nap."

"This is a stupid fuckin' argument," Beverly says to no one in particular.

Before Moxie can open her mouth to respond, Trish jumps up, almost landing in the flames. She grabs a nearby tall stick, using it as a makeshift cane, and rolls her back, mimicking a cat hacking up a hairball.

"Oh dear, let's not go to the club, Moxie; we might miss bingo night and all the excitement of Harold's endless stories about his gallbladder surgery." Trish stammers, clearly mimicking an elderly voice.

All the girls double over in laughter, copying Trish's elderly impression. The only one who isn't laughing is Moxie, who throws herself across the bonfire, tackling Trish.

Lace can't help but have tunnel vision on the iron. It's reckless, it's insane, but the thrill of it. She brings her attention back to the girls. Akin to a gathering of Salem witches conjuring their sacred rites under the veil of twilight.

Witches. Burned for being women.

Oh. Why the hell not?

Lace moves past the flickering light of the bonfire. The laughter around the fire swells, punctuated by the shrieks and jeers of the girls egging Trish and Moxie on. Trish's voice rises above the others, snappy and sharp, "You wouldn't last two minutes in Miami. You'd melt like butter in a skillet!"

Moxie's comeback is half laughter, half growl, her arm twisting around Trish's neck as they roll over, "Oh please, you'd fit right in with those housewives. All you'd need is a little facelift and a bigger credit limit!"

"Jokes on you! I don't even have a credit card!" Trish howls.

The girls roar, leaning in, pushing and pulling the tangled mess of limbs, their shadows jerking against the firelight. Lace barely glances their way, her eyes fixed ahead on something glinting in the dirt beyond the fire—the branding iron. Two hearts intertwined, rusted, and cruel. She picks it up, its weight solid and unyielding in her hand.

She steps closer to the fire, and the heat rushes up, licking her skin. She plunges the branding iron into the heart of the flames, watching as the metal glows red, bright, and angry. Her fingers tighten around the handle, knuckles going white.

The noise behind her blurs. Voices fuse into a distant hum. Time stretches, warped by the pounding in her ears. She pulls the iron from the fire, the two hearts blazing at the tip. Lace turns her head, her gaze sweeping over the bonfire crowd—Brandi's eyes catch hers for a second, her laughter freezing mid-syllable. But Lace doesn't stop. She moves swiftly, unbuttoning her overalls only enough to expose her left hipbone, skin pale and unmarked in the firelight.

She presses the brand to her skin.

The sizzle is immediate. A searing pain shoots up her side and rips a gasp from her throat. Her knees almost buckle, her vision blurring at the edges as the metallic scent of burned flesh fills her nostrils. But she latches on, her teeth clenched, her heart pounding in her ears louder than the girl's voices.

All eyes turn toward her, the laughter fading into stunned silence. Two hearts. Forever seared into her skin. The pain is almost unbearable. Lace drops the branding iron, letting it clatter to the ground. Her breaths coming in ragged, shallow gasps. The girls stare wide-eyed, a mix of shock, awe, and a little fear etched across their faces.

Lace straightens. Curling her lips into a faint smile.

The silence lingers before Peach steps forward, embers crackling behind her, casting a fiery glow around her silhouette. If someone were to capture her aura, it would blaze with an intense orange light, almost blinding in its brilliance.

Her lips pull into a half-smile. "You're the fuckin' crazy one."

16

Vultures Ahead

ace drifts through sleep, her breathing steady, and her face softened in the glow of moonlight spilling through the heart-shaped window. Her blankets are heavy and warm, cocooning her in safety. She's deep in a dream, the kind that feels too real, as if she could reach out and touch the scenes unfolding in her mind. In the dream, she's running.

The horizon stretches beyond her—vast and sinking low in the sky, painting the world in hues of orange and pink. Bo is at her side, his hand wrapped firmly around hers, pulling her forward. They're both laughing, breathless with excitement, the wind sweeping through their hair. Their footsteps kicking up dust behind them.

Bo's brown hat sits low on his head, contouring his face, but he locks his soft, full eyes on hers. He grins, a crooked, perfect grin, his voice echoing through the dream. "We're almost there, rosebud."

The world around them blurs as if they're outrunning responsibility, expectations, and life itself. She imagines this is what life would be like if she left it all behind. If she could just keep running with *him*.

No ranch, no judgmental eyes, no past to weigh her down.

Just Bo and the open road ahead.

As they run, the sky shifts to dusk, that magic hour Bo loves. The stars piercing the fading light, and in the distance, the glittering lights of Las Vegas shimmer as a mirage, dangerously within grasp. So close she could touch it. But only as the lights grow closer. Her grip on Bo's hand slips, and the world tilts. Her breath falters as the landscape crumbles. She tries to scream his name, but the words die in her throat as the dusky veil swallows the world.

A sudden crash from the other room steals her thoughts, making time freeze for a heartbeat.

The dream shatters. Lace jerks awake, the laughter and warmth from her dream fading instantly as cold fear grips her chest. Her heart still whirling, but it's not from joy or exhilaration this time. It's the sound which ripped her from her dream.

She barely has time to process the crash before a scream—a blood-curdling, bone-chilling scream—rips through the quiet. Lace bolts upright, kicking off her sheets and running to her door. The sound of more crashing follows, and another scream, remarkably louder than the first.

Her heart pounds so hard she hears it in her temples, the remnants of her dream slipping away entirely as dread floods her body. Her hand hovers over the door handle, trembling. She listens, her breath shaky, but there's only silence now, a tense, suffocating quiet that may be worse than the screams.

Glancing toward the closet, where the gun barrel peeks from the shadows, the metal gleaming faintly. She considers grabbing it, her fingers twitching, but something inside her freezes.

Her mind spins with the possibilities—who's hurt, what's happening, why is this happening? She forces herself to move, her hand trembling as she cautiously cracks open the bedroom door.

The hallway is dim, lit only by slivers of moonlight creeping in from various windows. Half of the girl's doors hang limply open like gaping wounds. Lace tiptoes forward, her feet soundless on the carpet, each step calculated, her breath shallow. As she moves down the hallway, the distant sobs and shouts grow louder. Figures flicker and stalk on the walls, cast by the movement in the room ahead.

Then, a deafening gunshot.

Lace freezes, her body going rigid. Her ears ring from the sound, but she nonetheless hears the heavy thud of footsteps—a rush of boots hitting the floor.

Two older men—disheveled, their faces cruel—burst out of the door painted in missionary. They're rugged, dressed in basic tees and unzipped jeans, and their faces contorted in smug satisfaction.

Lace presses herself flat against the wall, holding her breath as they sprint past, their heavy boots slamming against the floor in quick succession.

They don't bother to look at her. They don't care.

The men disappear down the stairs, their footsteps fading into the distance. Cold and numb as she watches them vanish, but her mind screams at her to move. She takes a shaky step forward, her breath catching in her throat. When Lace steps into the room, the scene before her is completely surreal. Something straight out of a nightmare.

Scattered across the floor lay an overturned nightstand, shattered lamp, and jagged pieces of glass. A large cracked mirror lies in the corner. Its splintering pieces reflect the room in fragments, distorted and broken.

Gemma sits on the bed, knees pulled tight to her chest. Her bunched-up nightgown rides high on her thighs, and she trembles violently, her raw sobs shaking her whole body. She's trying to fold in on herself as if making herself condensed might make the pain disappear. The shell-shocked girls, eyes wide with disbelief and tears streaming down their faces, scatter around the room.

Madam Lottie runs in breathlessly, wearing her sheer pink nightgown, carrying a similar model to Lace's gun. Without a word, she crosses to where Gemma sits, her movements slow and measured.

She lowers herself beside Gemma, the gun resting loosely in her lap as her hand extends toward the girl. But she hesitates, her fingers hovering in the space between them. Gemma flinches at the faintest shift, her body too rattled to accept comfort. Madam Lottie's gaze doesn't waver, fixed on Gemma as if she's willing her strength into the girl.

She stands back up. "I'll see to it that all the doors are locked."

The tension is suffocating, their silence deafening in the wake of chaos as Madam Lottie exits the room. Brandi is the first to step forward, her movements almost afraid Gemma might shatter if touched. She climbs into the bed, her breath shaky as she sits before Gemma.

Brandi doesn't say anything. She rests her cheek gently against Gemma's knees, offering her presence, her warmth.

Gemma's sobs hitch, but she doesn't pull away.

One by one, the other girls move toward the bed, hesitant but driven by an understanding. They need to be close, to embrace each other through the horror of what's happened.

Carefully, they climb onto the waiting quilt, tangling themselves together in a mass of limbs, bodies overlapping as they curl around Gemma in a protective shield.

After Lace's stunt of branding herself, the rest of the girls followed one by one. Moxie became the last to give in, picking her spot next to her Miami Vice tattoo. What merely hours ago felt as though a powerful, shared act now hangs heavy. A death sentence. Lace becomes highly aware of each branding on the girls while they huddle around Gemma, trying to offer her some comfort they know they can't give.

Am I next? Did I just seal my fate?

Lace watches from the doorway, her throat tight and her heart heavy. The warmth of the girl's intertwined bodies draws her in. She climbs onto the bed wrapping her arms around Sable, sinking into the collective embrace.

They stay as such, huddled together in silence, as Gemma's soft, muffled sobs fill the room.

A lone sound in the unsettling hush.

The girls scatter throughout the softly lit foyer of morning light. Their bodies bent low as they clean in near silence. Each one on their hands and knees, scrubbing at the filth left behind, their movements heavy with exhaustion.

The night's violence clings to their clothes, the walls, their minds. Once bustling with life, the ranch now hollow, a place emptied of its soul. Lace moves mechanically, reaching down to pick up a tiny shard of glass that glints. Her fingers tremble as she turns it over in her hand, hypnotized.

The room blurs around her, and all she can focus on is the tiny sliver of light in her hand, the sharp edge biting into her skin.

When it draws blood, she barely reacts. A single drop of crimson wells up and falls, splattering against the cold tile floor, leaving a puny mark that feels rightly insignificant compared to the surrounding wreckage.

Her mind is a tangled mess, spiraling as the past few hours bear down on her. The screams, the gunshot, Gemma's sobs—it all plays on a loop in her mind. She can't not see the fear etched on Gemma's face, her trembling body as they held her.

A loud clatter jars Lace back to the present. She looks up sharply to see Gemma standing in the middle of the room, her broom abandoned at her feet. Her hands shake, her eyes wide and vacant, lost in her inner turmoil.

"Don't y'all see..." Her voice cracks, as she swallows hard, forcing the words out. "We thought joining this ranch was us reclaiming our power..." Tears well in Gemma's eyes, glistening in the dim light. Her face is pale, the bruises on her skin stark against the backdrop of her vulnerability. Lace can see the fear persistently gripping her, lingering in every word she speaks.

"But it's exactly what they wanted from us... a false sense of security." Gemma's words falter, her voice barely maintaining control. "All this... it's just four walls chaining women. They got us exactly where they want us."

Her words blanket over the room as a heavy fog, suffocating the already fragile sense of peace. The other girls stop, exchanging nervous glances, but no one speaks. They all know the truth of what Gemma's saying, but acknowledging it is too dangerous, too real.

The girls return to their cleaning, the sound of brooms and mops filling the space, but the eerie silence remains. It's as if Gemma's words have shifted something inside them all, something they can't quite face yet. Lace, though, can't move. Her gaze stays locked on Gemma, who stands in the center of the room, staring blankly at the floor, her body trembling.

Another drop of blood falls from Lace's finger, unnoticed, mingling with the grime on the floor.

It all presses down on her—the violence, the fear, the sense of being trapped in this place, pretending they have control when, in reality, it's slipping through their fingers.

The girls and Madam Lottie stand outside the ranch, their bodies stiff, weighed down by the moment. The dry wind tugs at their clothes. Trish leans heavily on Brandi's shoulder, both weary from everything they've endured. They watch in silence as Gemma hoists two suitcases into the trunk of her Audi, the thud of the cases against the metal breaking the quiet stillness.

Gemma turns to face them, her cheeks stained with dried tears, her eyes red and swollen. Her lips tremble as she forces herself to smile, the gesture shaky and sorrowful. She takes a deep breath, moving down the line, wrapping her arms around each girl, one by one. The hugs are tight and desperate, like she's trying to anchor herself to something slipping away, her arms pleading for the moment to outlast time itself.

When she approaches Madam Lottie, her movements lag, the embrace lingering. Madam Lottie's hand cradles the back of Gemma's head, their foreheads pressing together in a moment of understanding.

Neither speaks, but the exchange is palpable. Madam Lottie, usually so steady, now on the verge of breaking, but she holds Gemma a tad longer, knowing it's likely to be the last.

Gemma pulls away, her eyes shimmering with fresh tears. She steps back, her breath ragged, and looks at the whole bunch as though she's just pressed their faces into a pin art toy, aching to capture their essence—an imprint she could clutch when the warmth of their presence slips through her grasp. She forces another smile, but it falters, painful in its effort.

Turning back toward her Audi, she climbs inside; the door shutting with a final, hollow thud. She offers a soft, tentative wave through the passenger window, her hand barely lifting as if her decision to leave is too much to bear. The girls, standing together, quietly return her wave, their arms limp at their sides.

There's no sound but the wind and the faint shuffle of feet as they shift uneasily.

Inside the car, Gemma wipes her eyes with the back of her hand and exhales. She reaches up and pulls down the sun visor.

A CD falls into her lap, a reminder of simpler times. She slides the CD into the player. "Dream a Little Dream of Me" by The Mamas and the Papas fills the car. Gemma's face softens, though the tears continue to flow freely.

She grips the steering wheel with both hands and pulls out of the lot. The vast expanse of the desert stretches out before her, an empty, endless path. Behind her, the girls watch the car shrink until it says hello to the earth and sky, their quiet sobs filling the void Gemma has left behind.

Trish buries her face deeper into Brandi's shoulder while Brandi's trembling hand strokes Trish's hair. Lace stands near the end of the line. Her arms crossed tightly against her chest as if trying to lock herself together. Her throat is tight, her vision blurry with unshed tears.

Madam Lottie's eyes remain on the dust cloud in the distance long after the car has disappeared. "I pray you find what you're looking for, baby girl," she whispers.

Lace wipes a tear from her cheek, feeling the loss.

Now, I just pray to survive long enough to save myself.

Lace sits atop the kitchen counter, her legs swinging gently beneath her, a rhythm echoing the unease. The girls scatter throughout the room, each absorbed in her own world. With her long, painted nails, Trish reaches into the busty bowl on the counter, retrieving a pack of cigarettes. She lights one with a flick of her lighter, the flame momentarily illuminating her face, revealing a flicker of vulnerability before she inhales deeply.

Despite being in the heart of the home, no one eats or drinks.

Lace clears her throat. She whispers, "you think she's right?" The other girls perk up at the question, their eyes shifting toward Lace, curiosity piquing amidst the melancholy.

Petal, her voice tinged with a bittersweet sadness, speaks up. "Wh—when I close my eyes... it feels like the chance of a man truly loving me slips further away with each passing day." Her confession lingers thick with resignation. The room falls silent.

Lost in thought, Brandi stares out the window at the landscape stretching wide and unbroken, her eyes tracing the rusty barbed wire twisting along the fence posts, the wind kicking up little whirlwinds of dirt, sending them tumbling. "I feel like a ghost," she murmurs, "haunting the spaces where I'm wanted but never loved."

Mallory scoffs softly, her expression a mixture of defiance and hurt. "They always say you're pretty... like that makes a damn bit of difference."

Sable leans against the counter. Her brow furrowed in contemplation. "Every night's got its own kind of rush," she says, her voice steady yet reflective, "but I can't help wonderin' if this is really what I want. Feels like I'm chasin' something, only to end up empty after it's all said and done."

Beverly's eyes glisten with tears as she adds, "I'm homesick for a love that I've never known. Afraid I'll never know."

Moxie, with a distant look, speaks of her fractured past. "I don't talk to my mama no more... she never could understand why I came out here. Truth is, some days I don't rightly know either."

Peach, her voice trembling, poses a question that echoes the confusion in their hearts. "Why do I feel strong one day, then turn 'round and convince myself I ain't worth no love the next?"

Trish, the cigarette now a thin ember between her fingers, chimes in with a bitter laugh. "Ain't met a man yet that ain't called me a whore."

Lace's heart aches as she reflects on her past. "I used to dream about sex," she admits, her tone laced with regret, "rough and messy like there wasn't a lick of love in it. I reckon I just wanted to feel like somebody needed me that bad, like they couldn't catch a breath 'til they had me. But now. I don't dream about it anymore."

A heavy silence blankets the room as the girls absorb each confession, their shared pain creating an invisible bond binding them together. Footsteps shuffle around the corner before Madam Lottie appears in the entryway, her presence commanding yet comforting. She takes in the heartache etched on the girl's faces and exhales a deep sigh.

"Girls. I think it's time we put on another show. Tonight."

Brandi furrows her brow, uncertainty flickering in her eyes. "Madam Lottie," she questions softly, "do you really think that'll help?"

Madam Lottie responds with fierce determination. "We need to cleanse the negative spirit in this here ranch."

Sable, skepticism evident, "Shouldn't we oughta hold off for a spell?"

Madam Lottie's gaze hardens, a motherly authority emanating from her. "It's this, or I'm sendin' for the priest again... and we sure as hell remember how that went last time."

Trish rolls her eyes. "That was one time."

Madam Lottie waves her hand dismissively. "Go on now, spread the word." She turns to leave the room, her confidence filling the space. She calls out, "I want that theater packed tighter than a cattle drive at sundown."

Moxie looks puzzled. "The fuck is a cattle drive?"

Trish snorts. "Fuckin' Florida people."

Lace chuckles softly. "We got a fuckin' theater?"

17

God Bless The Troops, And God Bless Dolly

"I look like a fuckin' calico queen." Beverly declares, tilting her head to the right as she examines herself in the mirror.

Sable, watching her reflection, lets out a snicker. "You literally are one."

Beverly swivels around to face her. "That's like calling a stripper a stripper. The correct term is *exotic dancer*. Adds a touch of class, don't you think?"

"Who gives a rip? It's 1986, babe," Sable replies with a shrug. "Didn't you get the memo? We're all about being sex-positive now."

The energy is contagious, a complete electric chaos vibrating similar to the anticipation before a sandstorm. That blue funk of what's to come. Warm candlelight mingles with the soft glow of old-school Christmas lights, casting a cozy yet frenetic ambiance throughout the dressing room. A Fisher-Price record player crackles to life, spinning Dolly's "9 to 5."

In front of their vanities, a few girls sit fully nude, faces focused in the glow of the lights as they paint themselves slightly paler. Some tease their hair, transforming it into exaggerated styles, ensuring it's the right height to fit the lampshades they're about to wear.

In another corner, Moxie and Trish lean over Trish's vanity, their faces intent and determined. They dip their heads down, snorting a thin line of cocaine without missing a beat, the movement fluid, and practiced, an artist preparing for the next brushstroke.

The rest of the girls slip into sheer dresses of varying colors, each a delicate wisp of fabric remaining tantalizingly transparent, barely held up by a single strap. The material flows loosely, demanding the girls to gather the excess fabric in their hands, careful not to trip over the billowing hem as they move.

Brandi stands over Lace, who is wholly exposed and lacking undergarments, wearing a black version of the sheer dress. Her body adorned with sparkling Playboy nipple piercings glinting in the light, and a meticulously trimmed landing strip adds a hint of allure. Brandi's right hip bone bears the mark—a patch of raw, puckered skin still healing from the branding.

The edges are raised and angry, an unnatural red fading to shades of deep purple. Thin scabs crisscross along the lines of a spider's web while the surrounding skin swells, flushed with a heat which hasn't cooled.

In contrast, Lace dons a pastel pink dress in the same style. With a lipstick brush in hand, Brandi carefully outlines a vivid red heart at the center of Lace's lips, the color striking against Lace's plastered pale complexion.

Soft pink eyeshadow dusts her eyelids, while clumpy eyelashes give her a fragile, doll-like appearance. Brandi steps back, a satisfied smile spreading across her face as she admires her handiwork.

"Aaaand done!" she exclaims, her voice bright with triumph as she gestures toward the mirror. Lace turns to examine her reflection, her fingers grazing the ends of her hair styled in soft, inward-curving waves with a middle part framing her face.

"I think my mother would drop dead if she saw me right now," Lace laughs, a lightness in her tone that belies the heaviness lurking beneath.

Brandi wraps her arms around Lace from behind, their eyes meeting in the mirror. The laughter fades as Lace's expression shifts, reality creeping back in. "—Are we just supposed to forget about what happened?" Lace whispers, her voice barely above a breath.

"No. No, we ain't," Brandi replies softly. "But we gotta make peace with the cards we got, right?"

"But we chose this... what if these aren't our cards?" Lace questions, the uncertainty reflected in her eyes.

"Got anywhere else better to be?"

"... You never told me how you ended up here. Or literally anything about you."

Brandi steps away as she squares her shoulders, the confidence she carries as armor. She drags her vanity chair across the floor, planting it directly in front of Lace.

Her hands grip Lace's armrests. "I had a sister, Lace. *Anna*. She was seven years younger, sweet as sugar, always carrying around this stuffed rabbit with one ear missing. Mama used to say we were like salt and pepper—opposites—but we worked together."

A faint smile flickers on her lips, but it vanishes just as quickly.

"Daddy wasn't in the picture, and Mama... well, Mama wasn't much better. She was a waitress at some bar off the highway and had a knack for pickin' men who only stuck around long enough to ruin things. One of 'em moved in when I was eighteen, and right away, he started looking at Anna like she was dessert." Brandi's voice falters, but she pushes through. "I told Mama. Screamed it at her. But she called me jealous—said I didn't want her to be happy. So I kept my mouth shut after that."

Lace's heart strains, but she doesn't dare interrupt.

"One night, I woke up to Anna shaking me, tears all down her face. He'd been in her room. That was it for me. I grabbed her, grabbed the little cash Mama kept hidden in a coffee can, and we took off. We were just kids, Lace. Eighteen and eleven, running down the highway like a couple of idiots."

Brandi's grip on the armrest hardens. "We hitchhiked. Got picked up by this woman, real nice, said she was headin' to Texas. I thought we were lucky. She bought us food and even let us sleep in her car at a rest stop. But when we got to Houston..." Brandi's voice trails off, her jaw clenching. "Turns out, she wasn't some good samaritan. She worked for this guy. Said we could earn our keep if we stayed with them. I didn't know what that meant at first—thought maybe we'd just be doing dishes or somethin'. But the minute I saw Anna's face, I knew it wasn't that simple."

Lace's eyes widen, horror washing over her. "No."

Brandi nods, her voice trembling but steady. "I fought back. Told them they weren't layin' a hand on her. Took every hit, every scar, to make sure she stayed untouched. I made myself useful, started running errands, doing whatever I had to keep her safe. But one night, Anna got sick—real sick. Fever, coughing blood, the whole nine yards. I begged them to take her to a doctor, but they wouldn't. Said it wasn't worth the trouble."

She pauses, her voice cracking. "She died three days later. In my arms. Just me and that damn rabbit." Her words hang in the air, sharp and raw, before she continues. "After that, I just ran. Took buses, hitched rides, didn't even know where I was goin'. Ended up in this little diner in the middle of nowhere, starvin' and half-dead."

Brandi's gaze barely softens. "That's when I met her. This girl named Ruby. She was sittin' at the counter, all dolled up and smokin' like she didn't have a care in the world. She could tell I was in trouble, didn't even hesitate. Bought me a plate of eggs, gave me a cigarette, and muttered, *Honey, you don't have to fight so hard anymore.*"

Lace watches Brandi's face, the faintest trace of warmth breaking through her armor. "Ruby brought me here. Told me I could make good money and that no one would ever lay a hand on me again unless I wanted it. I didn't believe her at first, but..." She shrugs, glancing back at the mirror. "Been here ever since. Not everyone's like me, though. Not every girl in this room came from a life full of abuse and trauma that they had to claw their way out of. Hell, most of them didn't. You'd be surprised. A lot of these girls? They came from good families. Parents who loved them. Took care of them. Some of 'em even went to college."

Her voice softens, but the words hit just as hard. "They wanted this. They chose it. They love the money, the sex, the way it all feels. Not everyone's carrying a bag of bricks around like I am. And that's okay too."

Brandi squares her shoulders, her armor sliding back into place. "So yeah, Lace, maybe I didn't choose this life. But I choose it now. And it's a hell of a lot better than where I came from."

Silence fills the room, thick with the weight of Brandi's story. Lace doesn't know what to say, but her heart aches with an understanding she didn't have before. Brandi looks at her, her eyes steady.

"We don't always get to pick our cards. But we do get to decide how we play 'em."

Brandi stands, her movements smooth but resolute, and turns to leave. Instinctively, Lace leans out, her hand catching Brandi's for the briefest moment. Her fingertips brush against Brandi's palm, a quiet, unspoken *I'm sorry*. But Brandi keeps walking, her hand slipping away as she moves across the room. She makes her way to Beverly's vanity, her reflection in the mirror already composed, untouchable. Picking up a tube of mascara, she twists it open and applies it with practiced precision, her focus unyielding.

Left at her vanity, Lace stares at her reflection, her thoughts drifting deeper into the depths of her mind.

"Oh, ain't you a sight!" Trish squeals, her excitement infectious as she rushes over. She runs her fingers through Lace's hair, fluffing the waves as she admires her. "You excited?"

Lace forces a smile, though Brandi's voice lingers. "I guess... not really sure what we're doin'."

Trish laughs, reaching for a can of aqua net from Lace's vanity. She douses Lace's hair in a heavy mist, causing her to cough and wave a hand in front of her face, the chemical scent sharp and overwhelming.

"You'll be fine! It's fun, really—getting to be someone else for a night. Every little girl's dream, innit?" Trish replies, her grin wide as she sets the hairspray can back down. "Speaking of that, I gotta go do one last thing!" Trish exclaims, scurrying back to her vanity six spots away.

A loud ring echoes through the room as the bell on top of the door goes off, signaling something—or someone—exciting. The girls erupt into chatter, scrambling to finish their preparations. Oversized, fringed lampshades are grabbed from a nearby table, a flurry of movement. Lace stands, moving toward the table to claim her own.

Across the room, Trish kneels at her vanity, eyes closed, hands pressed together in prayer. A partially lit candle bearing a magazine cutout of Dolly Parton's image flickers in front of her, a makeshift shrine.

Brandi walks over, disbelief etched on her face. "Are you prayin' to a fuckin' Dolly Parton candle right now?" Trish doesn't open her eyes, her concentration unwavering. "You're not even from the south! Or religious!" Brandi continues, incredulous.

Trish cracks one eye open, peering at Brandi. "Don't be a Jolene! And who said you gotta be southern to appreciate Dolly!" she retorts, a hint of sass lacing her words. Brandi huffs in response, crossing her arms as Trish fully opens her eyes and blows out her candle, the flickering flame snuffed out instantly.

She turns to face Brandi, eyes wide with mock horror. "You bitch! I told you I wanted to wear the black one!"

Before Brandi can respond, Madam Lottie throws open the dressing room door, her presence commanding attention. "Girls! I rang the bell! No more time to wax your pucker! Get those lampshades on, and let's go!" she barks, her voice carrying authority.

The room bursts yet again into a whirlwind of motion as the girls rush to put the lampshades on their heads, the fringes swaying wildly as they hurry out the door. Lace grabs hers, placing it atop her head. The lampshade is so large that the fringe almost obscures her face, a whimsical yet absurd look. Noticing some lampshades are lit, Brandi slides up beside Lace.

"Flip the switch inside," she instructs.

Lace tries to tilt her eyes up to see inside the lampshade, but the angle is awkward. Instead, she extends her arm in, fumbling until her fingers find a microscopic switch nestled within.

With a quick flick, she turns it to the other side, and her face lights up in a soft glow, illuminating her features with a warm radiance.

The backyard door swings open dramatically, revealing Madam Lottie standing tall in the entryway. Her silhouette backlit by the shimmering glow of the moon. As each girl steps outside, Madam Lottie takes a moment to light a three-pillar altar candle, her movements fluid and intentional. She hands each candle to the girls. The intricate carvings on the bases depict a busty woman, her details radiating a silent, spiritual strength.

A palpable shift is not only recognized but welcomed—something electric, something sacred. All the girls carry their heads slightly higher. Their movements imbued with a deliberate grace as if they shedded their old selves and adopted different personas—more confident, more assured. Lace steps forward, reaching for her candle.

A drop of hot wax spills over the edge, splattering onto her skin. She flinches at the sting but doesn't pull away; instead, she watches with a strange fascination as the wax cools, hardening quickly, forming a white trail on her hand.

The girl's hands cradle the only flickering lights, licking across the dust-choked yard as they glide in a steady line toward a sprawling building. Simple and boxy, standing one story high but emanating an odd sense of height. Its white paint chips and peels at each and every corner, leaning scarcely to the right, giving the impression a strong wind can send it crashing down at any moment. Lace had always assumed the building was either abandoned or used for storage. It never occurred to her to ask about it—she'd never seen anyone go inside.

At the forefront of the line, Brandi grips the well-worn handle, her hand steady and resolute. Behind the group, Madam Lottie follows. Lace glances back at her before turning her gaze forward once more.

With a haunting creak, the door swings open, revealing a flickering beam of red light spilling out from the inside. It douses over the girls as liquid rubies. A low, thrumming bass rolls out, harmonizing with the flickering glow—a hypnotic pull beckoning them into the obscured.

They enter a cramped corridor, barely wide enough for two people to brush shoulders. The girls move forward, their hips swaying in time with the music, their shadows stretching and morphing against the walls.

Her fingertips brush against the wall as Lace walks, surprised by the soft velvet meeting her skin, inviting yet strangely unsettling. At the end of the hallway stands a massive curtain, its dark, heavy fabric almost alive in its presence.

The red flood light washes over the fabric, leaving Lace unable to discern its correct color. Brandi reaches the curtain first, halting shy of its significant folds. She turns, extending a look back at her friend. Their eyes meet, and she gives Lace a soft smile, accompanied by a wink.

Peeking through the curtain, Brandi frames her figure in the warm candlelight, and the faint thrum of music beyond bleeds through as the curtain parts. Above the entrance, a rusted marquee flickers weakly, its bulbs struggling to illuminate the golden letters spelling "THE BIJOU."

"Bang Bang (My Baby Shot Me Down)" by Nancy Sinatra shrouds them. As Lace steps through the heavy curtains, she quickly drowns in the theater's lavish embrace. The walls, draped in rich purple velvet, whisper secrets of the past while swirling gold filigree traces every inch of the room, from the ornate archways to the lofty ceiling. The oval dome above looks almost too grand for such a place, its opulence mingling with an air of melancholy.

At the heart of the room hangs an enormous crystal chandelier swaying gently, its weight seeming almost too much for the aging chains holding it aloft. The stage—subtle but imposing—framed by layers of deep red brocade curtains, heavy and decadent, tied back with thick gold cords. Above the stage, a massive mural spans the entire backdrop.

It depicts a fantasy version of some far-off, forgotten cabaret—ornate arches, velvet-draped balconies, and glittering chandeliers, a mirror image of the theater itself but more ethereal. Figures shimmy across the mural in swirling silks and feathers, their movements frozen in time, faces half-hidden behind jeweled masks.

Rows of velvet armchairs, deep reds and purples faded from years of use, lines the room in a haphazard arrangement. Some are oversized, their cushions sagging invitingly, while others are plush settees with gold tassels brushing against the floor. There are no rigid aisles; instead, clusters of seating form cozy enclaves, encouraging intimate whispers and private disclosures. In the far corners of the room, plush velvet booths hug the walls, obscured by sheer curtains of black lace, inviting clandestine conversations.

Dozens of men occupy the scattered seats, their faces obscure by swirling cigar smoke and tilted brims. Their attention drifts toward the girls, who appear from behind the curtain, standing in their famous half-crescent formation. Lace takes her place at the tail end of the group, positioning herself on the left side of the crescent, next to Beverly.

She makes a conscious effort to straighten her spine and keep her chin up despite the flutter of nerves in her stomach.

A low whistle threads its way through the room. The velvet walls swallowing the tune whole. Madam Lottie steps forward from behind the girls, planting herself a couple of feet in front of them.

"Welcome, gentlemen, to The Bijou!" she announces. She pauses, anticipating any sort of applause. A cough from the back breaks the silence, nothing more. "Well, we have a mighty fine night planned for you... gorgeous performances from our lovely girls that you all know oh so well. So sit back and enjoy the show." With a sweeping gesture of her arm, she signals toward the girls. "Our girls will now come around with some drinks."

Lace's eyes lock steadily on the bar, where Brandi is already exchanging her altar candle for a tray of crystal glasses. Next to the bar, a larger-than-life head of a woman sticking out her tongue sits on display. The woman's nose is now replaced by a nozzle, and Brandi yanks it upward, causing brown liquor to pour out. She dips each glass beneath the stream, filling them before walking over to a group of men lounging on plush, velvet armchairs.

After all the girls go, Lace sets down her candle and picks up a tray topped with four glasses. She pours the drinks, her eyes sweeping over the room. The front and middle of the room are filled with men and women swapping glances and whispers, all indulging in the lavish scene.

In one corner, Lace spots Trish sitting on the knee of an older man, giggling as he whispers something in her ear, his fingers digging possessively into her waist. Her gaze falls upon an unoccupied man sitting at the back.

She makes her way over to him. When she approaches, he looks to be in his late eighties, his light gray suit hanging loosely on his thin frame. His white hair stands spiked in all directions as if frozen in time. The pasture-worn man grunts excitedly as she nears him, pushing himself up from the armchair with trembling hands. Even barefoot, Lace stands taller than him by a couple of inches.

She takes a step back, startled by his sudden closeness.

God. Why are they always so fuckin' old?

"Polite for a man to stand in the presence of a young lady," he rasps, stepping forward until he's an inch away from her. His gummy smile widens as he reaches out to grasp her waist before Lace can react. Her tray clatters as it presses between them, acting as a barrier. The man's grip tightens, and Lace forces out an uneasy laugh as one glass sloshes, spilling its contents. "Bet none of these young-ins would do that for you," he lips, breathing swampy and reeking of whiskey.

Before Lace can formulate a response, a firm hand clamps down on the man's shoulder. Relief floods her as she instantly recognizes the tattoos.

Bo.

Towering over the man as old as a dry riverbed, Bo's presence immediately causes him to recoil, mumbling incoherently. Bo gives the man a crooked grin. "Looks like the lady's spilled a drink," Bo says, his voice low and smooth.

His black button-down shirt opened enough to reveal the dark hair on his chest, suddenly making it the most captivating thing in the room to Lace.

The man opens his mouth to speak but falls short as his dentures tumble out.

Bo's hand stays firmly on the man's shoulder as he gives Lace a quick wink. "Sir, why don't you sit back down, and I'll have another girl bring you a fresh one?"

He raises an arm motioning across the room, signaling for a girl. Lace looks over her shoulder and sees no one coming—better yet no one looking. A giggle slips out before she can stop herself. The old man grunts but obeys, settling back into his chair with a huff.

Lace makes out a muttered curse under his breath—"son of a bitch"—as he painfully slowly picks up his teeth, wiping the excess onto his shirt.

Bo has already turned his attention fully to her. His grin widens as he gently takes the tray from her hands. "Vegas girl..." He gestures with his head toward a secluded booth in the corner where his cowboy hat sits. "Come sit with me."

Lace hesitates, her eyes peeled to the booth, its black curtains offering the promise of privacy. "Oh, I don't know if I'm allowed..." she begins, her voice wavering. "I think I have to hand these drinks out."

Bo picks up two of the glasses and downs them quickly, leaving just one for him and one for her, making it clear she won't be handing any more drinks out. He places the other lightly on the small of her back. The warmth of his touch sends a shiver up her spine. He gently turns her around to face the front of the room. Lace can visualize nothing more but his solid chest pressing against her back, the heat of him seeping through the fabric of her dress.

Bo leans down, his mouth brushing her ear, his voice a seductive whisper. "Truth be told darlin'... I don't think anyone will notice." Lace's eyes scan the room. All around her, the girls are engaged in confidential exchanges.

The men lost in their selfish gratifications. Madam Lottie deep in conversation with a man at the front of the room.

No one is watching. No one cares either.

This is technically my job.

Gently, she turns to face Bo, their bodies only an inch apart.

"I think you might be right."

Bo's hand lingers on her back, his thumb tracing minor circles that make Lace lose all sense of self. She finds herself leaning into him, her body drawn to his hard-ridden grace.

"You gonna sit with me or keep playing bartender?"

18

What Would Nancy Do?

ace sits in the middle of the booth, her legs tightly tucked under her, the cool velvet of the seat pressing against her bare skin. The soft black lace curtain flaps up, though the theater is sticky with blaze. Bo sits beside her, close enough for her to absorb the heat of his body, but far enough to keep her guessing. His arm resting casually along the back of the booth, fingers occasionally brushing her shoulder, sending tiny sparks down her spine with each accidental touch.

The distance between them is almost intentional. He waits for her to close it. Each move he makes is deliberate, but he carries an effortless charm.

He's in control, but in no rush.

Bo reaches for one of the two remaining glasses on the tray before them, lifting it to his lips. Lace watches his throat bob as he downs the liquor in one swift motion. He sets the glass back down with an unapologetic clink, his eyes finding hers. His gaze lingers like he peels her open one layer at a time.

A smile ruffles her mouth as she decides to match his pace. She grabs the last glass and throws her head back; the liquor burns its way down her throat, but she doesn't flinch. A streak of brown trickles down her chin. She wipes it away with the back of her hand, inviting the warmth to spread throughout her chest.

Bo releases a laugh, making him look ten years younger.

"You drink like a man."

Lace lifts an eyebrow, her smirk deepening. "You don't know jack about me." Her words daring him to challenge her.

Bo leans in a little, the gap between them shrinking but remaining painfully open. "I know more than you think, baby."

Lace's heart picks up, but she keeps her expression calm. "Oh, yeah?" she asks, cocking her head. "Like what?"

Bo leans back, his gaze drifting over her, settling on the oversized lampshade perched upon her head. "Well, I know you're into giant lampshades, and you've got a thing for drawing hearts on your lips," he replies, clearly mused.

Lace rolls her eyes but can't stop the grin tugging at her lips. "You're a real Sherlock, you know that?"

Bo slides in a little closer, enough for his thigh to brush against hers. "I know you've got brains," he breathes, his voice intensifying.

Another inch.

"Guts."

Closer.

"And you're secretly a romantic."

His thigh fully presses against hers now, making her heart palpitate. His hand, resting casually behind her, moves lower, his fingertips gently grazing her neck. The touch is light, barely there, but it sets her whole body alight.

"Am I right?" His voice is low, almost a whisper, vibrating through her.

She tries to maintain control. She doesn't need him to know how much he affects her, but it's getting harder to pretend. "You don't know me like that," she whispers, her voice wavering.

Bo chuckles softly, his breath warm against her ear as he leans closer. "No? I think I've got you figured out, sweetheart." His lips brush the nape of her neck, feather-light. Lace has to bite down on her bottom lip to keep from gasping. "You're sexy as hell," he murmurs.

Lace's breath heaves, her skin tingling under his touch. His hand slides lower. Thumb tracing a lazy line along her spine. Her entire being screams at her to lean into his touch—to close the gap, but something holds her back. Her heart thunders in her chest.

"You don't know that," she reiterates.

Bo's lips barely graze her skin, his breath shivering through her. "I know what I see," he says, his voice deep and sultry. "And I want more."

Lace closes her eyes for a second, letting herself get lost in the moment. His hand secures on her waist, pulling her a tad closer, his chest pressing against her back. "What's that branding on your hip?"

She glances down, the faint outline of the double heart branding peeking out from the sheer fabric of her dress. Her fingers twitch, remembering she is utterly exposed under the dress, leaving nothing to the imagination.

He presses his lips onto her collarbone, his voice softer now, carrying a low, unshakable timbre, "You don't mark yourself like that unless it means somethin'. What's the story?"

She swallows hard. Her eyes land on Brandi, who's tucked into the far corner, her head thrown back in laughter at some man's joke, which couldn't possibly be that funny.

This means something. That's what Brandi said after we all lined up like fools and lit the iron.

A family. A union.

Branded together for the rest of our lives. But now, every time I feel it sting, I think about Gemma. How she was hurt worse than any of us that night. And what are we doing now? Sitting here, laughing with men who don't care about us, putting on this act like it's all fine. Like, the mark on my hip is anything more than a scar of that night.

We lost someone who was our sister. She's gone, and all this—the naked bodies, the winks, the theatrics—it's just a distraction. A bad one. Feels wrong.

Feels like a lie.

I can't even say it out loud. It was supposed to mean something. Now, it just hurts.

"It's not a story worth telling," she says finally, but her voice tremors give her away, yet again.

Bo sighs, his breath brushing her hair. "You're allowed to carry what you carry," he says, his tone gentler than she expects. "But you ain't gotta carry it alone."

She stiffens, her walls snapping back into place. "I'm not some sob story, Bo. I'm fine."

He shifts. His hand skims higher to rest between her shoulder blades. His thumb brushes against the ink etched there, tracing the lines of her tattoos. "And these?" he asks. "Stay Away." He pauses, letting the words hang, "—and this cowboy getting bucked. They sure as hell don't scream fine."

Her breath shortens again, her shoulders tightening. "They're just tattoos," she replies, sharply turning to meet his gaze. But his eyes, steady and patient, anchor her in place.

"You don't gotta act so tough all the time," he mumbles. His thumb lingers over the cowboy, tracing each curve of the bucking horse. "You're allowed to be soft, Lace. Allowed to be a little feminine. Ain't no shame in it."

She wants to laugh, to scoff at his words, but the heat rises to her cheeks yet again.

Blushin' like a fuckin' school girl.

His gaze stays locked on hers, unshakable. "Bein' soft, don't make you weak. It just makes you real," Bo whispers against her skin, his lips brushing the sensitive spot below her ear. "I'll come see you in the morning. You and me."

Before she can answer, the room bursts into applause. The lights dim, and the stage lights up in a blinding flash. Lace has no clue who's even in charge of these theatrics.

Sable stands front and center, wearing skintight black leather pants with gold detailing. Her jacket unzipped only enough to show a tantalizing hint of skin.

She owns the stage, her back to the crowd, head dipped low. Waiting for the perfect moment to strike. Nancy Sinatra's "These Boots Are

Made for Walkin'" blasts through the speakers, and Sable snaps her fingers to the beat, her hips swaying sensually as she spins to face the crowd, lip-syncing with all her might.

She struts across the stage, her boots stomping in perfect rhythm. Lace can't tear her eyes away from Sable, mesmerized by how she commands a room's attention. It's like every woman in her life, Madam Lottie included, has the effortless ability to command a room's attention without giving it a second thought.

Lace ponders if they ever believe the same to be true about her. Bo, noticing Lace's distraction, gently turns her face back to him, his fingers brushing her jawline.

Their noses almost touch.

"Do you want me to?" Bo murmurs, his voice thick with intensity.

"Yes," she whispers.

Nancy's voice echoes in the background as Sable dances across the stage, kicking her boots onto a table.

"Kiss me," Bo coos.

He drank too much.

Bo lets out a moan, pleading again, "Kiss me."

The other people in the room are fading away.

The only ones left are you and me.

Bo's lips press against hers, firm and deliberate, and Lace's body responds instantly. His kiss is sure, not asking for permission but clarifying his intentions. A rush of heat blooms in her chest as her fingers curl into his shirt, pulling him closer. The way his stubble grazes her skin sends a shiver down her spine, and she leans into the kiss, meeting his intensity with her own.

His hand skims her waist, but he doesn't rush. Lace's breath chokes as his touch lingers on her bare skin, enough to leave her wanting more. Her heart pounds, but she keeps her composure, the steady rhythm of her breathing betraying only a fraction of what she's feeling.

Bo's lips trail down her neck, each kiss purposeful, as if he's memorizing the contours of her skin. Lace tilts her head to a slight degree, giving him a little more room, her fingers tightening their grip on his neck.

"Lace," Bo breathes against her skin, his voice a low rumble, making her stomach flip.

That fuckin' voice will be the death of me.

His lips return to hers, more urgent now, and Lace matches his intensity, losing herself in how their bodies fit together, how each touch ignites her.

She's wanted this longer than she'd care to admit, but now that it's happening, it feels more than desire.

19

Stupid Fuckin' Hat

ripping her dress tighter, the fabric bunching in Lace's fist as she ascends the foyer's grand staircase. The hour is early—just shy of the morning, though the show ended long ago. Cleaning up, taking down props, and Sable drilling them with a new dance to "Sixteen Tons" has stretched the night thin.

Yet, despite the exhaustion, Lace's mind keeps drifting back to Bo.

He had left not long after the show, saying he'd be waiting for her in the foyer as soon as the sun slipped above the mountains. Bo isn't the other men who drift in and out of the ranch. Eyes glazed with liquor and lust.

He sees her. *Truly* sees her in a way that seems like she's more than purely another girl spinning through the motions of survival. The life he paints for her—a life beyond these walls—feels real.

She can almost touch it.

She smiles softly, imagining what Darlene would say if she knew.

But Lace isn't the same girl who left that dusty trailer park. She's more intelligent now, less credulous. Learning to stand in her skin, heavy with scars and stories no one else will understand.

Every heartbeat's a defiance, a quiet 'I'm still here.'

As she reaches the hallway to the girl's bedrooms, hushed whispers seize her ears. The dressing room had been full of girls when she left, scrubbing paint from their faces, swearing under their breath as they yanked off lampshades tangled within their hair.

Who had slipped into their room undetected? Lace decelerates her steps, careful to walk on the balls of her feet as she nears Petal's room, the door slightly ajar. Lace's gaze falls on the inky figure inside.

A man, shirt fully undone, struggling with his belt buckle.

She freezes. Her stomach drops when her eyes land on the cowboy hat resting casually on the edge of Petal's bed.

Bo's cowboy hat.

Her feet move before her mind can protest, carrying her forward and urging her to look away. But she can't. The image immediately sears into her vision, her chest tightening as the realization claws at her insides. As she's about to disappear down the hall, Petal steps into view. She doesn't catch sight of Lace as she softly pushes the door closed, her back toward Lace.

But Bo does.

Their eyes met, locking for a fleeting moment. It's quick—so brief that if Lace had blinked, she would've missed it. His face carries no explanation, no apology. He doesn't try to stop her, doesn't call out. He simply let the door close behind Petal. The hallway grows darker and colder. Lace freezes in place, staring at the closed door.

Her mind races, tangling in knots she can't unravel quick enough. There is no way that was Bo. She'd never even seen him speak to Petal before! So why was he in Petal's room now, and not hers?

Her heart pounds in her chest, a nauseating rhythm making her head spin. It doesn't make sense. She stares at the painting on Petal's door. *Standing*. Turning in a circle to look at all the paintings as if they're mocking her with their certainty, their intimacy.

Lace wants to scream. To cry.

But all she can do is stand there, her hands trembling, as Bo's betrayal settles.

A stone in her gut.

Has she been so stupid to believe him? Or has she just wanted to believe?

The Bullet That Could've Been

orning cracks over the far ridge, washing the ranch in a hard, pale light. Lace's eyes rim with exhaustion, her face ashen from a night spent sleepless and spiraling into endless thoughts.

Bo. His name echoes through her mind as a ceremonial drumbeat, driving her completely erratic.

Bo.

Bo.

Bo.

It's maddening how one person can occupy so much space in one's mind. She had spent all morning trying to convince herself that it wasn't Bo in Petal's room. Plenty of men were in the theater; anyone could've been there.

But deep down, Lace knows.

There's no mistaking him. Bo has carved himself into her, slicing her open with precision.

Burying himself deep beneath her skin, leaving a part of him lodged there, only to sew her back together with thread pulled tight—binding her to the pain and the permanence of his presence.

No matter how hard she tries, she can't forget his boyish smile or how his eyes go through her. She doesn't know if he has left or spent the remaining hours of dark in Petal's bed. All she knows is Bo declared he'd come to see her in the morning, and with the sun creeping through her window. Lace can't help but curse herself for letting her imagination run wild, crafting fantasies for a man she has spoken to only a handful of times.

Stupid.

The shrill ring of the bell above her door splits the quiet fault line.

He's here.

She doesn't need a mirror to know that she looks like hell. Lace can feel all the leftover hairspray and crusty mascara dragging her features down. She considers staying in bed until they'd have to come with a shovel to peel her body off the mattress. But would it change anything?

She has two choices: face him or crumble.

She stands up, takes a deep breath, and heads toward the foyer.

Bo is there, hands casually in his pockets, looking as if he doesn't have a care in the world.

Typical.

He wears fresh clothes, but the same cocky grin remains, and, of course, he clutches his stupid cowboy hat to his chest as if it were a second skin. He stretches out to take her hand, lifting it gently to his lips. His eyes muddle as he kisses the back of her hand with deliberate care.

Lace holds nothing but irritation. "Do you ever wear that fucking thing?" she asks, motioning to the hat.

Bo's lips part, clearly caught off guard by her tone. The smooth charm he always wears falters, only for a blink of an eye.

But he quickly recovers, his face shifting back to an easy smile.

"Why don't we go upstairs to your room?" he says, his voice thick with suggestion.

Lace crosses her arms, fixing him with a cold stare. "You know where the bedrooms are," she says, her tone sharp and unwavering. "Lead the way, cowboy."

He looks at her, measuring her, dissecting her next move before she knows it herself. With a short tip of his head, he turns and heads up the stairs, the sound of his boots thudding against the wood.

Lace follows, her insides twisting.

It's a shot-for-shot scene from when they first met. Lace perched on her bed, Bo shifting around her room, relishing in his complete jurisdiction. She taps her bare foot against the carpet, leaving no sound except the mattress bouncing underneath her shaky leg. Bo moves silently to her closet, his face wearing a permanent smirk. Lace watches as he grasps the doorknob and creaks open the doors. There's nothing in there except a few T-shirts, two bras, and a handful of panties.

The gun is laid flat on top of the hangers, unmoving since Brandi touched it.

Bo releases a soft "ah" as his eyes lock on the revolver. He takes the gun off the hangers, flipping it lazily, examining it. Clicking open the chamber, he sees there are no bullets. Kissing his teeth, he looks up and sees a couple of loose bullets laid astray on the top shelf, right next to her box, filled with all the cash she has earned.

Lace holds her breath as she watches him closely. Taking one bullet, he slides it oh so carefully into its rightful place. Lace, previously carefree from the lack of sleep, is now on high alert. He spins the cylinder, slamming it shut, bullet inside, and looks at Lace.

He sees the fear in her eyes; it's evident. How could he not? This appears to amuse him as he lets a deep chuckle. "Did you have a good time last night?" he asks, his tone teasing.

Lace doesn't take her eyes off him as he crosses the room to stand a couple of feet directly in front of her. He smells of tobacco and dirt.

She forces her chin up, attempting to mask the concern slapped across her face.

Her voice barely cracks, "Yes."

Bo tilts his head approvingly, murmuring, "Good... good." He paces back and forth. "You just seem off compared to last night."

"No. No, I'm just really tired. Didn't get much sleep."

Bo chuckles again, this time softer, but his eyes never leave her. The gun continues to twirl in his hand, flipping over his fingers. Complete second nature. Lace's heart pounds in her chest, a sick knot forming in her stomach. "Tired, huh?" Bo muses, stopping his pacing to stand directly in front of her. "Tired of what? Life on the ranch? Tired of the work? Tired of me?" He bends down, bringing his face close to hers.

Lace swallows hard, "I'm just tired, Bo. That's all."

Bo grins. "See, I don't think that's it, sweetheart." He crouches down so they are at eye level. "I think you've been thinking too much. I think you've been letting your pretty little thoughts get you in trouble." He taps the side of his head with the barrel of the gun.

Lace flinches. "What are you talking about?" she asks, her voice wavering enough for him to detect.

He leans closer, his lips inches from her ear. "You saw something last night, didn't you?" he whispers, his breath slick against her skin. "You saw me. With Petal." Lace's heart stops. Her stomach drops.

I can't breathe. Don't let him notice.

"I didn't see anything," she lies, but before the words even leave her mouth, she knows he doesn't believe her.

Bo pulls back and smiles. "Oh, you didn't?" He brings the gun up to his lips, kissing the cold steel. "Funny, because I could've sworn I locked eyes with you, Lace."

Lace's skin prickles as she sits frozen, unable to strategize what to say. His smile is too sharp, his eyes too focused.

He stands up, towering over her now, looking down on her with a mix of amusement and something a tad grimmer, something coiling between them. A silent threat. "You know what I think, Lace?" he says, his voice dropping low. He brings the gun to his eye line as he waves the weapon around the room. He points to the front door, the window, her felt horse, and finally at her. "I think you don't know what you want."

Lace's breath pulls back, her eyes widening as the cold barrel of the gun aims directly at her. Her heart pounds in her ears, so loud she's certain Bo can hear it.

For the love of God. Why do people keep pointing guns at me?

"Thing about steel, Lace," he says, voice smooth and almost conversational, "is it's simple. Don't ask questions or wait around to see if it's loved or feared." He gives a half-smile, eyes never leaving hers. He lifts the gun high enough to gesture around the room. "And I get the feeling you're still figuring out which one you are—lover or fighter."

He chuckles softly as if the whole thing's simply a joke between them, something light, almost intimate. But his gaze sharpens, a spark of warning beneath the charm. His voice hits low enough to draw her in. "You just need someone to hand it to you, nice and clear."

The gun returns to his side, relaxed, but the message hangs heavy.

Bo continues, his voice almost tender, as if telling her a secret, "I know exactly what you need. You need to get out of here. Away from this place. Away from the other girls. With me."

He leans closer. "Run away with me, Lace. Forget about the ranch. Forget about everyone else. I'll take care of you."

Lace's mind races. Is this the same man who, only hours ago, made her believe in something better? The same man who made her believe that maybe, just maybe, she's capable of being loved?

"You don't know what you're saying, Bo," she whispers, heart pounding.

Bo's expression turns serious. "I'm not lyin'. I want this just as much as you do. Look, I came here because I see something in you—a fire you can't snuff out, not in a place like this." He studies her face, his tone softening, almost tender. "And you know it, too. Otherwise, you wouldn't be sitting here, holding your breath like I'm the only one who's ever really looked at you."

Bo lowers the gun, resting it on his knee with an easy grip as though it were a third person active in the conversation. "All I'm saying is, if you come with me, you won't have to stay stuck here, selling pieces of yourself. You can be something so much more." He gives her a knowing smile. "We're the same, Lace. People like us don't fit in cages."

Lace looks down at the gun, her heart fleeting. The allure tugging at her, the pull of his words weaving through her hesitation. "I—"

"Let's get out of here," he urges, his tone coaxing and soft. "You don't have to be alone anymore. Just say yes, and I'll take you to the lights of Vegas."

Her resolve crumbles.

Decays.

Erodes.

"Okay," she whispers.

Bo's smile widens, the relief washing over his features. He leans to plant a rough kiss on her cheek. Standing up, he plants another kiss on her forehead. "I'll be in the parking lot in an hour."

Bo rushes out of her room, gun and hat in hand, before she can swallow the words and bury them where they belong.

21

No Shoes, No Clue

There isn't much to pack. Lace didn't bring many belongings with her, but the task stretches, time unfurling just as the worn shag carpet. Each moment drags as she meanders through her room. *How did I get here?* But something, not at all deep, something right at the asthenosphere, already knows she's sliding down a slippery slope. So speedy that she doesn't know how to yell *stop!* But why wouldn't she trust Bo? He's been around the corral, seasoned by life's storms—surely he knows more than she does.

Life had to have taught him something she hadn't learned yet.

Why would he lie?

Her gaze fixates on a cigarette burn in the carpet, mind flashing to a few nights back. All the ranch girls gathered in Lace's room.

It was late evening. The kangaroo rats and jackrabbits were already running amuck through the open range. Trish had brought her boombox into the room, spinning her pride and joy, a mixtape full of Lee Hazlewood and Bronski Beat. Lace didn't recognize the track playing.

"Mama always said, Don't look back."

"A girl like you's gotta stay on track."

Petal's the first to spot the burn. "Lace, honey," she drawls, trying to stifle a laugh, "your floor's got its first battle scar."

Brandi snorts, stretching out on the bed, "First? With this carpet? Please. That orange has been through hell since it came outta the factory." She eyes the mark thoughtfully. "Think of it as character. Gives the room a real lived-in vibe."

Lace sighs, reaching down to pick at the remaining ashes. "Lived-in? It looks like a crime scene now."

Moxie exhales, "Little dramatic. No?"

Flicking through an issue of *Smash Hits* in the corner, Gemma doesn't look up. "Honey, we're all crime scenes at this point. Look at us—everyone has a burn, a bruise, or a tattoo of some guy we can't stand anymore."

Petal raises her hand like she was in elementary school. "Present!" she chirps, flashing a heart tattoo inside her wrist with a name so aggressively scratched it's impossible to translate.

"That's why we're the burned-out beauties club," Brandi jokes, taking a drag off her cigarette. "We just leave our marks wherever we go. Whether it's on men's hearts or Lace's carpet."

Lace groans, running her hand over the burnt spot again. "You know," she says, "it's kinda nice, us just being able to veg out. No clients, no pretending. Just... girls, being people, not anyone's idea of something."

Moxie inhales. "Even more dramatic."

Gemma nods, her voice quieter than usual. "Yeah. No show to put on, no one to impress." She looks around the room as if seeing it fresh. "Just us, as we are, mess and all."

Brandi chuckles. "Feels weird, right?"

Trish shrugs, rolling her eyes. "I don't know about y'all, but sitting around isn't exactly my idea of a hot Friday night."

Lace groans, tossing a pillow at her. Trish dodges the pillow, laughing. "Hey, I'm just saying, this whole being *people* thing doesn't exactly pay the bills."

Beverly snorts. "Technically, you have no bills to pay."

Gemma raises an eyebrow, grinning. "Baby, we could be sitting in church, and you'd be wondering if there's any way to make a buck off the choir."

Trish shrugs with a wicked grin. "Maybe I just think multitasking is a virtue. A little chat. A little cash—what's the harm?"

Brandi snorts, tapping ash onto the carpet. "Trish, one day they're gonna put that on your tombstone: she'd rather be having sex... for a fee."

Lace throws up her arms, gesturing from Brandi's flicked ash to the carpet burn. "Did you not just learn anything?"

Brandi quickly sucks back in the smoke she exhaled, "Okay, but I didn't do the last one. That wasn't my fault. I blame Trish."

"I'm literally not even smoking right now. Do you see a cigarette in my hand?" Trish exacerbates.

Petal raises an imaginary glass. "To Lace and her carpet—both survivors of lousy decisions and burn marks."

They all laugh, clinking imaginary glasses.

"Run away, turn away."

"Leave the ashes where they lay."

"Burned my bridges, scorched the floor."

"I can't stay here anymore."

A soft touch on her shoulder breaks the spell, jolting her back to the present. She spins around, heart galloping, to find Brandi's concerned face inches from hers. The worry in Brandi's eyes washes over her like a cold splash of water. Brandi's gaze drifts from Lace to the lopsided duffle bag sprawled on the bed, the sight of it pulling at the threads of reality.

"You leavin'?" Brandi's voice trembles.

Lace swallows, tears threatening to spill. Brandi exhales sharply, frustration lacing her voice as she sinks beside the duffle bag. "Why?"

Lace settles down beside her, "I—I found a new path. A better path."

Brandi's eyes widen in disbelief. "You have a better path. You're living it right fuckin' now." Lace shakes her head, embarrassment and anger swirling within her. "You're not fleeing with some fella, are you?" Brandi gasps, her voice a mixture of horror and concern.

Lace meets Brandi's gaze, the walls of her heart closing in. "It's what I want."

Brandi jumps back, hands flailing in exasperation. "Of course it is! But what the fuck do you know about what you want?" Lace narrows her eyes, defiance surging through her. She rises to meet Brandi at eye level. "You're so young, for God's sake," Brandi whispers, disbelief washing over her.

Lace's chest clutches with the sting of Brandi's words. "You're the same fuckin' age as me!" The realization rolls through her, paralleling a wave crashing against the shore, mixing anger with a sense of betrayal.

How can she not see?

This isn't a flight of fancy; it's a desperate bid for freedom.

I'm not asking for much. I just want to breathe.

"I don't want to be here anymore," she snaps, her voice rising as emotions claw their way to the surface. "I never wanted this!" She reflects back to a time when Brandi painted a pretty picture of their life together, *the glamor of the ranch*, the men they entertained.

An illusion, vanishing the moment she got too close. "You brought me here. You saw someone weak and naive, thinking, *oh*! She could make a pretty penny for the ranch."

A bitter laugh escapes her lips, a sound laced with pain. "You never even asked if I wanted to sell my body to men for money before you threw me in the back of your fuckin' car! It's all a goddamn joke. This place is a prison. Gemma was right. We aren't reclaiming our sexuality by having outrageous amounts of sex. That's the complete fuckin' opposite of what we should be doing. It was never ours to begin with!"

Lighter with each accusation, she hurls the truth, spilling out as a broken dam. Lace steps forward, closing the distance between them, her voice low and fierce. "I found a man who likes me for me. In this godforsaken place, that's like sticking your fuckin' shovel in the earth, thinking you'll hit solid *gold*."

What is so wrong about wanting that? She's tired of pretending. Tired of fitting into a mold as foreign as the cold metal of iron pressed against her skin.

Brandi's laugh comes soft yet bitter, a sound tinged with sadness. "News flash, honey, look around you. You're in a fuckin' brothel. Do you know how many men have whispered promises to whisk me away to the edge of the earth? Just about every fuckin' one of them, and trust me, there's been a lot. I may be almost the same age as you, but I've lived a life of despair far longer than you. This happily ever after bullshit isn't real. It's fiction, babe."

"In their eyes, a woman can only be sexy if she doesn't know it, doesn't own it, doesn't ask for it. The second she takes the reins, it's not sexy anymore—it's dirty, it's desperate. Remember that."

But what if he sees me?

More desperation creeps in.

What if he knows me for who I truly am?

She wants to shout, to plead her case, but the words tangle in her throat, heavy with doubt. She wants to believe Brandi. Wants to trust her experience, but the hope flickering inside her refuses to be snuffed out.

"You said I could leave if I wanted."

Brandi huffs. "Yeah. I did. Keyword *you*."

"It–it doesn't really matter."

Brandi steps back, "It actually fucking matters a lot," the hurt in her eyes is a direct shot to Lace's heart. "This isn't some Bonnie and Clyde bullshit. You used to be someone's baby. It's been time to go be your own baby now."

Before Lace knows it, Brandi is gone. Lace hears a soft clatter on the heart-shaped window behind her. She turns, wiping away false tears, and finds Bo standing at the hood of his Ford, his presence both a beacon and a tightening noose.

Brandi's words linger, seeping through her ears.

Crawling through her skull.

Yet, as she looks at Bo, a flicker of something ignites within her—a blend of thrill and trepidation.

She stands at a crossroads, ahead shrouded in mystery, yet the promise of the unknown calls to her.

Lace swears she hears a distant train whistle.

22

Not Looking Back, But I Peeked

on't look at them. Don't make eye contact.

She tells herself, moving with purpose down each step. The foyer fills with the ranch girls, laughter spilling as they gather around the floor, but the tension in Lace's chest weighs heavier than ever. She's leaving. There's no turning back. Her eyes flick briefly to the game they're playing—chess. But the pieces are tiny sculptures of naked women in yoga poses, frozen in time.

Lace feels a pang of pity for the little figures, their bodies twisted into eternal submission—spines arched, limbs bent, mouths silent.

Trapped in their elegance, they'll never move on their own, only at the mercy of the hands that play them.

Sable, with her usual reckless energy, smashes her bridge pose piece against Petal's downward dog, sending the insignificant figure skittering across the floor until its head pops clean off.

"Check motherfucking mate!" Sable shouts, leaping up in triumph.

"You airhead!" Petal huffs, gesturing to the broken piece. "Now look—she's broken. And you totally cheated."

Sable, hands on her hips, tilts her head, trying to make sense of the board. "Yeah. I don't know what I'm supposed to be lookin' at," she says, unbothered.

The room erupts into giggles, a sound which would've warmed Lace's heart only a few hours ago but now distant, muffled by the whirlwind inside her head. Her duffle bag slams against her side as she hits the bottom of the stairs, the noise drawing all eyes on her.

Don't look. Don't you dare look.

But there's Trish, her voice soft and hesitant, cutting through the noise. "Hun... where you goin'?"

The words slice through Lace's resolve, her grip clenching around the doorknob for a split second. *Open it*, she tells herself. She knows if she turns around. If she sees their faces. She'll crumble. These girls—her new sisters—they're more than just co-workers, more than the strangers they were when she first arrived. They're her family now, the only proper family she's ever known. Nevertheless, something inside her burns.

Telling her she has to leave. It's not about them, not about Petal. It's about survival. About getting out before this place swallows her whole.

She stands frozen by the door. Her heart thrashes in her chest, louder than the giggling and the noise in her head.

"Lace..."

The whisper of her name undoes her. Against her better judgment, she turns.

Slowly, painfully. She can't help it.

There they are—all of them, no more giggling or playful banter. Merely wide eyes and heavy silence.

They know. Trish stands now, her expression pleading.

Lace's throat tightens painfully as her watery eyes tell each girl more than she could ever express with words.

Trish.

Sable.

Petal.

Mallory.

Peach.

Beverly.

Moxie.

She pushes open the front door.

Stepping out into the daylight, a solid wall of stuffy heat slams into Lace. Bo leans against his topless blue Ford, arms crossed. His dark sunglasses hide his eyes, but the grin spreading across his face when he sees her is unmistakable.

"There she is," Bo says, his voice smooth and sure, dripping with confidence. He steps forward casually, grabbing her duffle bag. "I'll take that, darlin'," he says, lifting it quickly from her shoulder.

Before she can react, he leans in, his lips pressing softly against her cheek, leaving a warmth that lingers. Cologne and engine oil surround her, and for a fleeting moment, the anxious knot in her gut loosens. Her chest tightens again just as quickly, though, nerves battling with something else—something eerily similar to excitement.

"You ready?" Bo asks, eyes hidden but voice steady. Lace swallows hard and tilts her head in acknowledgment, unable to trust her voice. He tosses her bag onto the truck bed beside his worn brown leather bag and swings the passenger door open for her. She slides into the seat, the smell of the cracked leather filling her nostrils. The door slams shut with a finality, sending a jolt through her as Bo joins her on the driver's side.

Lace's eyes drift back to the ranch as the truck lurches forward. The girls stand clumped together outside. Madam Lottie now at the center. It's a scene all too familiar to Gemma's departure. But no tears this time, only somber faces and quiet murmurs.

Their stares say it all.

They know what's coming, and there's no sparing Lace the pain.

Lace glances up at her heart-shaped bedroom window. Brandi's figure stands there, barely visible in the harsh sunlight, watching as a distant sentinel. Brandi can't see her from this distance, but Lace can see her clear as day. Lace raises her hand, a barely there wave, not meant to be seen, a gesture she can't stop herself from making.

She snaps back to the present when Bo's rough hand slides onto her inner thigh, his fingers squeezing lightly. The contact grounds her back to reality. The truck picks up speed, leaving the ranch—and everything it meant—behind them.

23

For The Love Of God

"**Y**ou're not in any rush to get there, are you rosebud?" Bo asks.

He briefly takes his attention off the two-lane dirt road winding before them, the tires crunching against the dirt. It's only been an hour since they left, but to Lace, it resembles a lifetime spent staring blankly out the windshield, the landscape blurring into a canvas of dusty browns and sun-bleached yellows.

The cabin of Bo's truck is a cluttered sanctuary of Americana littered with cans of root beer, a worn issue of Time magazine from 1981 featuring Ronald Reagan's face splashed across the front cover, a flask tucked in between her seat and the door, and rusty tools such as wrenches and pliers.

An American flag air freshener dangles from the rearview mirror, swaying violently with the jolts of the trail. A tiny wooden cross hangs an inch further down, its presence grounding amidst the chaos of their journey. Lace shifts in her seat, the ripped-up leather tickling the back of her thighs.

There is no middle console to separate her from Bo, an invitation. She lays flat across the seat, her head gently finding a resting place in his lap, longing for the connection after the strenuous day behind her.

With her bare feet kicking out of the cranked-down window, she smiles up at him; the sunlight filtering through—creating a halo effect around him. "No. But aren't we only a couple of hours from Vegas?"

Bo glances down, his brown eyes sparkling, and a crooked smile spreads across his face. He lifts one hand from the steering wheel, his fingers brushing against her cheek. "Yes, ma'am, but I thought we could take our time. Maybe hit the sack in some dirty motel out in the middle of the boonies."

Lace giggles, the sound music to Bo's ears. "We're already out in the boonies." He chuckles, the sound rich. The sun shifts with the car, creating a shadow of the cross sticking to Bo's cheek.

He's beautiful, she muses. Her heart flutters as all her worries about the ranch, the gun, and Brandi dissipate, floating away into a strange dream. Lace can't shake that perhaps this all feels surreal—that Bo has magically swooped in and rescued her from her old life as if it had never existed.

"I wouldn't have taken you for the religious type." Lace teases, her hand reaching up to trace the outline of the cross against his stubble.

The words barely leave her mouth before she remembers—Brandi had once asked her the very same thing.

Leaning into her touch, Bo nips playfully at her palm, a grin spreading wider. "I ain't."

His straightforwardness intrigues her. She narrows her eyes, wanting to understand. "Then why you got a cross in your truck?"

He shrugs, a casual confidence enveloping him. "Maybe I just like its shape. I don't think God would mind." Bo lets the car drift to the middle of the road, bringing the cross over his right eye. "I don't believe in wasting this life hell-bent on believin' in somethin' no one can prove. We're all gonna end up in the same place, no matter if that's in the dirt, the pearly gates of heaven, or the pits of hell. Me believing what I choose ain't gonna change nothin'. Stupid of us to think we have any sway in this."

She drops her hand, resting it against her chest as she absorbs his philosophy. She's never encountered such a firm opinion about faith before—not belief, but the absence of it. Her mother, flawed as she is, has always instilled in her a belief in something greater, a sense of hope. Lace's lifeline.

Bo looks down at her. Brow furrows in curiosity as he studies her reaction. "You religious?"

She turns her gaze out the window, the desolate landscape stretching endlessly before them. "Yeah. I don't pretend to be the best Christian, but I do pray. I do believe in God."

The truck spins out, jolting Lace back to reality. Bo, whose attention has remained entirely focused on her and not the road, snaps his head up, seizing the wheel with both hands as the truck swerves dangerously. Lace's heart races as she instinctively covers her eyes with her arm, pulling her knees to her chest, trying to shrink herself as the truck groans beneath them. In a heartbeat, Bo regains control, steadying the vehicle as he lets out a shaky breath.

"Holy hell!" Lace gasps, her heart pounding in her ears.

Bo sinks his head onto the center of the wheel, triggering a blast of the horn. He sits there for what seems to be eternity.

Bo finally turns to her. Concern etched across his rugged features. "You okay, baby?"

Lace nods, her voice trembling as she replies, "Yeah. I'm okay."

Dust and dirt fly into the cabin as his boots hit the ground with a thud. The swirling storm of particles makes it nearly impossible to see where they are, the barren landscape enveloping them. Lace inhales sharply, choking on the gritty air.

"C'mon," Bo says, his voice steady as he opens her door, offering his hand. She takes it, finding comfort in the warmth radiating from his palm as she hops down, her feet hitting the ground with a soft thud. Tucking her under the right side of his jacket, Bo leads her a few yards away, out of the minor dust storm they've unwittingly created.

The ground beneath them splits at uneven intervals, suffering from hundreds of years of neglect. Lace squints through the haze, her heart pumping from the near-spinout, and that's when she spots it—a weathered church across the fence line, barely visible through the dust.

The once vibrant white paint has peeled away, exposing dark boards beneath, giving it a dismal appearance. Each plank looks to be bleached by the sun, warped and splintered, struggling to maintain the structure. The roof is a patchwork of faded shingles, some missing entirely. A weathered sign hangs precariously above the heavy wooden doors, swinging a smidge in the dry breeze. Bold, chipped, faded letters proclaim, "You Must Be Guilty." The message looming over anyone who dares to approach, like the church itself is both a refuge and a judgment.

Around the church, the ground litters with dried weeds and tufts of grass stubbornly pushing through the cracked earth, a reminder of life trying to exist in a desolate place. A rusty bell tower leans favoring the left side, the bell itself missing, leaving only a hollow sound whenever the wind whistles through. A cross sits crooked on the roof. Hanging on by a prayer.

"Huh," she says, tilting her head and squinting her eyes against the bright sun.

Bo follows her gaze, tilting his head in disbelief. "Well, ain't that ironic?"

Without a word, they make their way across the empty stretch of road, boots kicking up clouds of dirt as they approach the tiny church.

A haven in the middle of nowhere.

Inside, the air is cooler, thick with dust, as the light filters through narrow stained-glass windows, which have seen better days. It's simple—bare wood pews, a dinky altar at the front, and a few scattered unlit candles standing in the corner. Lace moves, her footsteps soft as she walks toward the front, her eyes on the cross suspended above the altar.

Bo lingers by the doorway, watching her. There's something different about her now—quiet, almost reverent. He's seen Lace tough, sharp-tongued, but never like this. She kneels at the altar, resting her hands on the worn wood, her head bowed. Bo settles into one pew, leaning back with his hands clasped behind his head with a lazy kind of ease, though his eyes never leave her. She looks fragile in such a way, but there's strength in how she kneels. Not asking for anything, but demanding it.

Lace closes her eyes, her lips moving in a whispering prayer. "Lord, I don't know what you want from me," she says, her voice raw and shaky. "I don't even know if you're there. I've tried to do the right thing. Tried to be good, but it's like I'm drowning out here. Everything keeps slipping away from me—my choices, my hope-." She pauses, her lips trembling. Her following words become softer, almost as if she's ashamed of the plea.

"I need a sign. Something to tell me I'm not lost forever. I need to know that there's something left for me—something worth fighting for, worth hoping for. I don't want to feel like I'm just fading away. Please, if you hear me—."

Bo shifts in the pew, the worn wood beneath groaning with the movement. He leans forward, resting his elbows on his knees.

"How raw are your knees? How often do you kneel to pray?"

Lace's eyes flutter open, her hands resting on the decrepit altar. She doesn't turn to face him immediately. Her gaze locks on the cross above her. His words slither through the quiet, coiling around her, tightening. Her body stiffens, muscles growing tense under his tone.

He leans back, the smirk on his face widening, more deliberate now. "Dance for me," he murmurs, his voice thick with a command, triggering the room to grow narrower, more stifling.

Calmly, almost cautiously, she turns her head. "Here?" Her voice comes out quieter than she intends.

Bo's grin deepens. He tilts his head, never breaking her gaze, playing a game of cat and mouse.

"Here."

Her heart thuds in her chest, an all-over-ish rhythm building as she rises to her feet, turning to face him fully. Her pulse races—not from excitement, but from—a sense of obligation.

Is he serious?

The question hangs in her mind, her lips pressing into a thin line as her unease grows. "No. I'm not dancing here."

Bo's posture remains relaxed, as if he has all the time in the world. He stretches out his legs, settling deeper into the pew, his smirk never faltering. "Why not?"

Lace's frustration flares, her hands gesturing toward the surrounding room. Toward the stained glass and the cracked wood. "Because we're in a church! Ain't that sacrilegious?" Her voice has more bite this time, but it doesn't suggest fazing him.

Bo shrugs, indifferent, his eyes gleaming. "Not to me. That's alright, darlin'. God's watchin', so give *Him* a good show."

She wants to refuse, but the expectation in Bo's gaze is palpable, pressing down on her like the stifling heat of the desert outside. She stands there, accepting the pull of his eyes as they roam over her, waiting, demanding. With a shaky breath, she glances back at the cross, its worn wood splintered and cracked.

Just like this place. Just like her resolve.

She takes a hesitant step back, reluctantly, and lets her arms fall to her sides, her body moving as if on autopilot.

Her movements are almost lethargic, like her limbs weigh a thousand pounds. Lace lifts her arms, her fingers trembling as they trace lazy arcs, not so much dancing as moving. Each motion is foreign to her, mechanical. She isn't in control of her own body.

Bo's eyes stay locked on her, his posture continuously relaxed, but his attention is intense and burning.

Her arms spread wider, almost mimicking the figure of the cross behind her, her wrists limp as her fingers extend outward. She doesn't know why she did it—whether to mock the moment or cling to some sense of meaning.

But as she keeps a grip on her position, arms stretching out, her body mirroring the sacred symbol behind her as if she was offering herself up to something greater—or perhaps to nothing at all.

Her body keeps moving, her arms rising and falling.

Caught in some silent prayer, some ritual she doesn't understand. She wants to feel something. Anything other than this hollow sense of compliance. But there's only the sound of her breathing and the faint creak of the floor.

"Keep going, Lace."

Her throat locks, a lump forming there, but she only does as she's told. Her arms float up again, this time with more weight. Surrendering to the inevitable. She stretches them wide, palms out, her fingers trembling as they hover. Despite being fully clothed, Lace has never felt so exposed, standing there as some sacrificial offering under his unrelenting gaze. She closes her eyes, trying to escape the moment's reality, but it's impossible. Bo's gaze is heavier than anything else, heavier than *Him*.

A puppet to its maker.

"Beautiful," Bo whispers, his voice dark and smooth, dead bees stuck on honey—the word twists, adding another brand to the ever-growing collection.

Lace's chest rises and falls with shallow breaths, her arms remaining outstretched, her body frozen in place as she waits for his following command.

Knowing it would come. Knowing she had no choice but to follow.

Knowing she secretly wanted it.

Forgive me Father.

24

Where The Wild Things Watch

ace leans her head back against the seat, watching the world slide by in soft, blurred colors. The silence is thick, punctuated only by the occasional voice of Richard Marx or Dwight Yoakam seeping through the static. Bo's presence beside her is nothing but solid and rough-edged, resembling the truck itself. His hands are steady on the wheel, veins bulging against sun-tanned skin.

"So... ranchin'," she says, glancing over at him.

Bo doesn't look at her right away, his jaw tightens like he's chewing on his answer. "It's hard to explain unless you've lived it."

Lace watches him, intrigued by this softer side. "What do you like about it?" she asks, her voice softer, almost cautiously.

He shrugs as though he's not sure he has the words. "There's a kind of... rhythm to it. Waking up, knowing exactly what has to be done every day. It's like the land tells you what it needs, and you listen. Some days,

I'd be out there in the fields, not another soul around, just me and the cattle and the wind. Feels like... I don't know, like the world makes sense out there." He shifts his grip on the steering wheel, his fingers tensing and relaxing. "And the animals... they got their own way of seeing things. They don't care about your past, what you've done, or who you've let down. They just... need you to be there."

"Who's takin' care of them now?"

Bo chuckles. "I got men."

She traces her fingers along the cracked leather of the seat, gathering her thoughts. "I don't know if I'd ever be able to stick with one thing like that," she admits.

Bo looks over. The softness in his eyes surprises her. "Maybe that's just how you're built, Lace. Some people are made to settle down and put roots in one place. Others..." He trails off, glancing at the cowboy's dreamland surrounding them.

She doesn't answer right away, letting his words sink in. "Sometimes I wonder what it'd be like," she murmurs. "To belong somewhere. To know that I'm... wanted, you know?"

Bo nods, the corner of his mouth lifting in a half-smile. "Maybe that's how you're meant to be," he says. "Some folks are like that—wind never lets 'em rest. Got a kind of freedom that way, not being tied down."

They fall silent again, each drifting down separate rivers.

"When I was a kid," she begins, "I used to go out back behind the trailer and stare up at the stars. Pretend I was somewhere else. Night was spread out, empty and hungry, like it was searching for someone to keep it company. Didn't matter where—just somewhere bigger, somewhere with more space to breathe. I'd close my eyes and pretend I was floating out there, just me and the stars. Didn't need anyone, didn't owe anyone anything. It was just me." She pauses, swallowing hard. "Sometimes I feel like that little girl's still out there, stuck under that sky, waiting for something to come along."

He clears his throat almost hesitantly. Trying to navigate his way through unfamiliar terrain. "You ever talk about your folks?" Surprised by the question, she tenses, but doesn't look away from the passing desert.

"Not much to say," she replies, her voice guarded. "My mom... she's still out there, probably sittin' in that same trailer. Ain't much has changed, as far as I know. And my daddy..." She trails off, her fingers tapping absently on the door.

"You ever close with her? Your mama?"

Lace lets out a humorless laugh. "Close? I dunno, maybe once. But I think I started remindin' her of all the things she'd given up. She'd look at me, and I'd feel like I was seein' every regret she ever had. And my dad—he was long gone before I had a chance to know him."

Bo's brows knit together. "He left when you were little?"

She shrugs, trying to mask the bitterness creeping into her voice. "Yeah. Guess he got tired of the whole family thing, leaving my mom high and dry. Heard he took up with someone else."

Bo watches her quietly, the depth of her words settling in. "Sounds like she was tryin' to make do, your mama. It ain't easy, raisin' a kid on her own."

"Yeah, well, maybe. But I can't help but feel like she didn't even try to hold on to me. Like she'd rather I just disappear and not remind her of every bad choice she ever made." She glances at him, her eyes dim. "I used to sit by the window, hoping he'd show up one day, come to take me away. Guess that's just kid stuff. Even though I ain't really know my daddy, I know. Deep down. That I am my father's daughter."

"Ain't no kid stuff about wantin' somethin' better, Lace. I reckon we all got dreams like that, somethin' to hold on to when life don't make a lick of sense."

She huffs, a smile flickering across her face for the first time. "Maybe. Just feels like I've been holdin' on too long, you know? Like everyone who was supposed to be there... just wasn't."

He rests a hand on her leg, giving her a brief, steady squeeze. "People leave, Lace. They got a way of doin' that. But it don't mean you gotta spend the rest of your life tryin' to fill that hole they left."

They fall into a thoughtful silence, each sitting with their memories and scars. After a while, Lace's eyes snare a flicker of motion on the ridge. A wild horse, its coat a deep inky black, drinking in the late-day sun. The animal stands motionless, silhouetted against the sky as if chiseled from the same rugged, ancient rock making up the ridge. Muscles ripple under its coat, sleek and powerful, each line elegant, fierce, and untamed. The wind lifts its mane in a delicate sweep, strands of hair in the style of molten silver.

Lace gasps, reaching out as though the gesture might hold the moment. "Look, Bo."

Bo halts the truck to a stop, both mesmerized by the creature. The horse stands there, proud and unmoving, its head held high, a guardian of the silver state's heart. The animal's gaze locks onto them.

No. Just *Lace*.

Heavy and intelligent, as though it's sizing her up.

Seeing right through her. There's a challenge in its stance, a refusal to bow to anything or anyone.

Her voice comes out barely above a whisper, full of awe and yearning. "That's what freedom looks like."

25

Mechelle Vinson

"Want me to grab you anything?" Bo inclines his head toward the convenience store. The building stands as a lone sentinel under the harsh afternoon sun, surrounded by miles of empty pure land. Waves of heat rise from the asphalt, making the edges shimmer and blur, as if the whole world might melt into the dust.

Lace shakes her head, her eyes already on the vending machine standing outside the store. "No, thank you. I'll just get something from there," she says.

Bo digs into his pocket, pulling out a few crumpled dollar bills and some loose quarters. "Here, take these," he offers.

But she waves him off, already halfway out of the truck. "I got it."

Before he can argue, she swings herself down onto the pavement and heads to the back of the truck, climbing over the edge of the bed with ease. Her canvas bag is wedged into a corner, dusty and worn. She digs through it, fingers sifting past aged receipts, a dog-eared magazine, and a rolled-up shirt before she finds what she's looking for—a handful of change mixed with dozens of bills. She shakes out a few quarters, tucking them into her palm.

Bo stands by the gas pump, filling up the truck, but he watches her fiddle with the money from the corner of his eye. Lace heads over to the vending machine, the ground beneath her cracked and uneven, weeds poking through here and there. The machine is the kind with metal buttons which stick when you press them.

She stands there. Fingers hovering over the buttons. Her eyes roaming over the rows of candy behind the scratched glass. There's a line of Now and Laters, their neon packaging warped from the desert heat, edges peeling. Below, a row of Whatchamacallit bars. The wrappers dulled to a tired yellow, untouched and forgotten. Next to them, a few packs of Big League Chew resting in a sloppy pile. Down at the bottom, almost hidden out of plain sight, a lone Ring Pop—red, plastic-wrapped gem, a piece of treasure waiting for someone brave enough to claim it.

She slips a quarter into the machine; the metal chinking as it slides in. The machine shudders, gears grinding as though it's stalling on purpose, ensnaring her choice hostage. She presses her fingers lightly against the glass, the cool surface biting her skin, the cogs vibrating faintly through her fingertips. From there, a low humming drifts across the empty lot. Lace's head turns, her hand pausing midair, as she finds herself drawn to the sound—a man's voice, gravelly and rough-edged, crooning out a tune. He's singing it to the dry goldfields itself.

"Early one morning, death comes knockin' on my wall," his voice is low, worn with age, buried under years of dust and miles of untouched

expanse. The man sits on the curb a few feet away, hunched over a string guitar, his fingers moving leisurely, each note coaxed out with care, as though he's crafting the song from the soul.

"Steps so slow, I barely hear it at all."

Lace can't look away. She stands frozen, each line carrying a strange, haunting familiarity both comforting and exploitative. The song is unfamiliar, but it sinks into her, winding around the raw, open parts of her.

She glances over his shoulder. The wall behind him, where someone, maybe years ago, scrawled a message in thick, jagged letters. "THE ROAD BREAKS THOSE WHO HESITATE." She stares at the words. Feeling them sink in. Cutting through her defenses similar to the man's song.

The man's voice lifts again, rough and haunting, spilling his voice into the land.

"It hums a tune, low and deep, like a mournful sigh."

The bell above the gas station door chimes, and Bo steps out, the heavy crunch of his boots echoing across the lot. She senses him there behind her. But she doesn't turn around. Remaining caught up in the song. Bo stops a few feet away, watching her.

The man's voice fades into silence, leaving the sky empty again. The words on the wall linger in her mind.

"Says, Pack your soul, it's time to say goodbye..."

The highway shifts from the endless, barren stretch of desert to the outskirts of an itty-bitty one-horse town. As they approach, Lace eyes the first few signs—bright, handmade posters plastered on street corners and rusted fences, each a shout against the mundane landscape.

"Support the Court," one of them reads. Another boldly declares, "Stand with Vinson," the letters scrawled in thick, pink paint.

"What's all this?" Lace asks, smacking her lips as she pops the Ring Pop out of her mouth. She leans forward in her seat, squinting at the growing cluster of signs as they roll by.

Bo frowns, his eyes narrowing. "Meritor Savings case. Been all over the news. Some court ruling about men harassing women in the workplace." He spits the words out like they leave a foul taste in his mouth. "People all up in arms about it."

As they delve deeper into the town, the protests become more visible—groups of people standing on street corners, some with megaphones, their voices rising and falling in waves. Others shout in passionate bursts. Their emotions are as vibrant as the signs they hold.

Lace reads more of the messages, the words becoming clearer: "End Hostile Workplaces," "Cowboys for Cowgirl Rights."

The scent of fried food wafts from a nearby diner, mingling with the stale smell of sweat and engine grease from the frail mechanic's shop across the street.

Lace shifts uncomfortably in her seat. The reality of the protest sinking in. She hasn't learned of the case until this moment. What else is happening in the world to which she isn't paying attention to?

But witnessing the fervor of the demonstrators stirs something in her—maybe anger, maybe confusion.

She stares out the window, eyes scanning the signs flashing by.

Women with raised fists. Faces fierce and proud, their voices cracking through the air with demands she struggles to understand.

Lace can almost hear their urgency vibrating against the glass, something solely beyond her grasp.

She questions if it's all about power.

About fighting back.

The things Madam Lottie would chew fat about late at night, sipping whiskey, calling it "a man's world."

Bo's grip on the steering wheel hardens. "World's changin' fast," he mutters under his breath. "It's like the fuckin' pink frontier out here."

Lace turns to him, watching the lines on his face deepen as he speaks.

He looks older at that moment.

26

Shoot First, Apologize Never

o mumbles something about needing bug juice over the loud static of the radio, his voice barely cutting through the crackle. The sun's already dropped behind the settler's view, leaving the great basin draped in a silver glow from the moon. Lace doesn't know exactly where they are—somewhere in south Nevada, she guesses. Maybe they've crossed into a different state? It's difficult to tell from looking at the same stretch of nothing for hours.

Vegas should've been closer, but she isn't worried. She doesn't mind the drive. The endless cracked earth, the way the desert stretches out forever with only the occasional tumbleweed or faded sign—it's actually comforting.

Up ahead, something flickers in the headlights. As they roll closer, the shape of a scant building comes into view. A bar squatting low against the flat land, its exterior beaten up by years of sun and sandstorms.

A dim neon sign flickers, casting a muted orange glow over the gravel lot. "Hussey's," it reads, the letters half burned out. Next to it is a strip club with a brighter pink sign blinking in uneven intervals, as if trying to outshine the bar beside it.

The truck crunches to a stop, and Lace spots a row of motorcycles lined up front. Chrome glints under the neon, their heavy frames leaning on kickstands. Clearly been frequent fliers since JFK became president. The scent of gasoline and dust hangs in the air.

Lace leans forward to get a better look at the place. She's never been in a bar before. The closest she ever came to places interchangeable to this was sneaking peeks at the TV when Darlene wasn't looking—scenes of dive bars and smoky rooms, but never in real life.

Now, here it is. Right in front of her. Real as anything.

Bo cuts the engine, and the truck rumbles into silence. He gets out, boots hitting the gravel with a thud, and walks around to her side. The door groans as he swings it open, holding out his hand. Lace takes it, stepping out of the truck. The night is thick, securing its breath, waiting for something to happen.

The door to Hussey's creaks open, and Lace steps inside, trailing behind Bo. She first smells stale beer, cigarettes, and sweat, all mixed in a way that suggests the place hasn't been aired out in years. The dim lighting doesn't help, either. To the left, a lone pool table sits in the corner. The green felt worn thin from years of use. A couple of balls lie scattered on the table. But no one's playing.

The sticks lean against the wall beside a broken neon Meister Brau sign; a company that ran its way to the ground ten years ago. The jukebox in the corner churns with life, though no music plays yet.

The bar stretches along the back wall, cracked wood and faded leather stools. The bottles lining the shelves behind the bartender glint faintly in the low light, their labels peeling and dusty. Only a few of the liquor choices appear to be drinkable. A couple of glass ashtrays sit scattered along the bar top, each overflowing with cigarette butts.

About ten older men sit hunched over their drinks throughout the bar, like they are part of the furniture. One man in the corner is nursing a beer, his weathered fingers drumming along to a beat only he can hear. Another sits by the jukebox, flipping through the songs without choosing one.

There's no energy here—only the quiet hum of men passing the time, waiting for something or someone to break up the monotony of their dreadful lives.

Vintage photos and posters of rodeos and honky-tonk bands from the 50s and 60s plaster the walls, faded to where the colors are barely recognizable. A ceiling fan spins lazily overhead, pushing the smoldering air around without cooling anything off.

She slides onto a stool, watching Bo order both their drinks, his voice low and gravelly. The bartender, an old-timer man with a thick white mustache and leathery skin, pours him two whiskeys without a word. He's seen men indistinguishable to Bo come through here a thousand times before.

Bo leans back against the bar, his hand wrapped around the glass, and looks at Lace. The tension from the drive easing off his shoulders now that they're in this quiet, forgotten corner of the world. Lace watches him, her fingers grazing her glass's cool, chipped surface.

The low hum of the jukebox swells as "Welcome to My World" by Jim Reeves fills the dim room with soft, swaying notes. Bo shifts on his feet, looking up, and Lace follows his gaze. Tied from the ceiling is a pocket-sized, tarnished disco ball, its surface chipped and dull, but it manages to hit the faint light from the bar, scattering flecks of silver. In a place like this—dusty, forgotten, and worn—a disco ball is out of place, a relic from when joy and celebration used to mean something here.

Bo holds out his hand. "Dance with me," he murmurs, his voice rough but gentle.

Lace hesitates before sliding her fingers into his, the warmth of his palm against hers. He pulls her close, his hand finding the small of her back, and their bodies fall into a rhythm matching the steady sway of the music. Lace rests her head against Bo's chest, listening to the steady beat of his heart beneath the fabric of his shirt. The room, the rodeo-worn men, the cracked bar—it all fades away as they move beneath the dull glow of the disco ball, caught in their world for a little while.

For minutes, there's only the music and the woeful pulse of the bar, the disco ball turning above them, and Lace lets herself drift into the moment, into the warmth of his touch.

But she senses something shift in Bo's body, a tension creeping back into his shoulders. He exhales, but Lace can taste the words before he speaks them.

"Lace," his voice hesitant. She pulls back enough to see his face, her brows knitting together in curiosity. His gaze flickers, unable to maintain hers for long. "There's something I've gotta tell you."

The way his voice dips makes her stomach tighten. She doesn't say anything; simply keeps swaying with him, waiting. "What happened with

Petal," he says, the name falling heavy between them, "it was a mistake."
Lace stiffens in his arms, her body tensing, but she doesn't pull away. She
keeps moving with him, though her mind is reeling.

Bo's grip on her waist tightens, his eyes tearing back to hers, searching
for some sign of how she's taking this. "It wasn't... I didn't plan it. Petal,
she came onto me." His words come out rushed, almost desperate. "I'm
not makin' excuses, Lace. I just need you to know—it wasn't about her.
It wasn't even about sex."

She looks up at him, her lips parting, her heart pounding in her chest.
The flecks of light from the disco ball glint off his face, painting his
features in shifting light patterns. "I don't want to lose you," he
murmurs, his voice raw. "You... you mean more to me than that."

Lace doesn't say anything for a long moment. Her mind is a swirl of
emotions—hurt, anger, confusion. But also something softer, something
dangerously close to forgiveness. She looks at him, at the way his jaw is
tight, his eyes pleading, and she knows he's telling the truth. Or at least
the truth, as he knows it.

The music plays on; the melody wrapping around them, the disco ball
turning lazily above their heads. She closes her eyes, letting the words sink
in, the warmth of his body against hers, the steadiness of his arms.

The betrayal lingers, but in this moment, it's distant, something
they've already begun to move past. Maybe they aren't there yet, but she
can see the possibility of it, the slow burn of understanding creeping in.

Bo leans his forehead against hers, his breath warm against her skin,
and Lace's heart softens enough to let him back in. The way he's
clutching her—the way his hands are steady, firm but not

overbearing—makes her believe that maybe, just maybe, this thing between them is worth holding onto.

God. I'm so fuckin' weak.

Without thinking, Lace leans in, her lips brushing against his in a kiss. Soft at first, almost hesitant. Testing the waters. But it deepens quickly.

His apology. His confession.

His arms tighten around her, pulling her closer, and Lace lets herself fall into it, into him. Lace's hands slide up the back of Bo's neck, her fingers tangling in his thick hair as the kiss intensifies, pulling them both deeper into the moment.

By the time they pull apart, breathless, the song has ended, leaving only the soft hum of the jukebox and the murmurs of the surrounding bar. Bo presses his forehead once more against hers, his breath shaky.

They stand there, wrapped in each other. The world outside may be waiting for them, full of uncertainty, but in this forgotten bar with its broken neon signs and dusty floors, it's only the two of them.

Moving in sync, finding something close to peace in each other's arms.

How much time they spent in the bar, drinking and dancing, Lace can't recall. The whiskey has blurred the edges of her memory. She knows she is about five drinks deep, and Bo has easily doubled that. As they stumble out of Hussey's, their laughter echoing into the empty plain. Lace struggles to keep her balance, her steps uneven as Bo slings his arm over her shoulder, dragging her down with each misstep.

"Bo—I don't think you can drive," Lace manages, between breathless giggles, her vision swimming.

Bo stops abruptly, his glassy eyes locking onto hers. He cups her chin in his rough hand, squishing her cheeks. "Baby," he slurs, his breath thick with whiskey, "there's no one in sight on this godforsaken road for miles. I won't hurt a thing."

He unhooks himself from her, stumbling forward—straight into the side of the building. Lace reaches out to steady him, but her movements are lagging, and she can only laugh as he tries to regain some resemblance of balance.

"Tell that badge-wearin' son of a gun if he wants me," Bo drawls, "he better saddle up and come fuckin' find me first."

But before Lace can respond, Bo lurches too far to the left and crashes into one of the motorcycles parked outside. The bike topples over with a heavy thud, its chrome gleaming under the pale light of the neon signs.

Lace's laughter dies in her throat as she watches the scene unfold. "Oh, fuck," she slurs, stumbling over to where Bo lies sprawled across the fallen bike.

The blood from a fresh cut on his arm mixes with the dirt, creating a muddy streak on his skin. His mumbling curses are barely coherent as he writhes on top of the bike, trying to push himself up.

"Bo, c'mon," Lace urges, her voice thick as she crouches down to help, though her hands are clumsy. "I got you. That's it, stand up."

As Bo pulls himself upright, two men leave the shadows, leaning against the wall adjacent to the bikes. Cigarettes dangle from their lips, glowing faintly in the nightshade. Lace recognizes them from the bar.

One of them flicks his cigarette to the ground and steps forward, his voice low and dangerous. "You just fucked with the wrong bike, cowboy."

Bo sways on his feet, wiping the blood from his chin with the back of his hand. "Ain't my fault your bike can't stand up on its own," he slurs, a smirk pulling at the corner of his mouth.

The men straighten, their eyes narrowing. "You think this is funny?" one of them growls, his fists curling at his sides.

Lace's heart pounds in her chest. The drunken haze isn't enough to dull the creeping sense of danger. She glances over at Bo, who looks far too amused for someone about to get into serious trouble.

"Bo, let's go," she whispers, tugging at his arm and pulling him toward the truck.

"Y'all better walk away before this gets ugly," Bo bites back, still staggering but defiant.

The tension snaps.

One man lunges at Bo, but Bo is swifter. With a grunt, he shoves Lace behind him and swings his fist, connecting with the man's jaw. The punch echoes in the quiet night, and the man stumbles back, but the others are already moving in, quickly closing the distance.

Bo grabs Lace's hand, dragging her to the truck. "Get in," he barks, but she hesitates as she sees one man following them, pulling a knife from his pocket. Before Lace can scream, Bo dives into the truck, reaching under his seat. When he returns, it isn't with any of his tools she expects—it's with her gun.

Her stomach drops as he pulls it from the seat and points it at the man approaching them, his hand steady despite the booze.

"Bo—" Lace's voice is little, almost drowned out by the pounding of her own heart. But Bo doesn't hesitate.

The gunshot cracks, a sharp, deafening sound. Lace freezes as the man drops to the ground, his body crumpling as a burdensome sack of potatoes in the dirt. For a split second, the world stands still. Bo standing over the body, the gun raised, chest heaving.

Lace can barely breathe. Choking on the scent of gunpowder.

She hears nothing but the sound of ringing.

The other men back off. Stunned into silence. The moment stretches on only long enough before Bo grabs her arm and yanks her back to the truck. "Get in the damn truck, Lace," he mutters, his voice hard as steel.

Her legs aren't connected to her brain. They're moving independently as she scrambles into the passenger seat, her hands shaking. Bo slides in beside her, slamming the door shut.

The truck roars to life, radio clicking as Johnny Cash bellows about a ring of fire.

They speed off into the desert night, leaving the turmoil—and the body—behind.

27
Face To Face

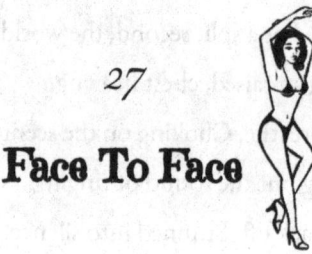

he silence in the car is suffocating. Neither Bo nor Lace makes any attempt to speak.

Bo just fucking shot someone.

Lace's chest tenses as she replays the moment over and over in her head as some broken reel of film stuck in the same horrifying frame. She can't shake the memory of Bo reaching over, his hand quick and sure as he yanked her gun from beneath the seat.

My fucking gun.

Lace can't believe it. She's never seen anyone shot point-blank before—let alone by someone she knows. They didn't stick around to see if the man happened to be okay. But Bo shot him in the chest. There's little to no chance he survived, but they didn't actually check. How could they?

Lace pulls her knees to her chest, curling herself up against the coolness of the car door as if she could melt right through and crawl into a tafoni. She turns delicately, enough to steal a glance at Bo. He grips the wheel with bone-white knuckles. Blood from his scratched forearm stains his shirt. He locks his jaw, and his hollow eyes remain fixed on the route ahead, unreadable and far too calm given recent events.

He isn't aware she's looking. Lace exhales, her breath fogging the window as she leans her forehead against the glass. The sliver of a crescent moon hangs high in the sky, almost too faint to see. She guesses it must be around three in the morning by its position.

Not that it matters. She has no fucking idea where they are.

She hasn't known for hours.

Bo hasn't bothered with a map. He hasn't asked for directions, hasn't pulled out a damn compass. They're driving blind, fueled by his half-baked confidence. She yawns, fatigue weighing heavily on her bones. The day—the week, the month, hell, her whole life—has been an endless blur, each hour dragging into the next without pause. Bo turns his head toward her, his eyes briefly on her as she yawns.

"We should find a motel," he mumbles, his voice startling her from her thoughts.

Lace doesn't lift her head from the window, her voice dripping with frustration.

"Where, Bo? There's fuckin' nothing out here if you haven't noticed. I don't even know where the hell we are. We should've been in Vegas ten hours ago."

She expects him to argue back, to snap at her, but he remains silent. The unsaid is crushing. Her eyes drift back to the window, watching the moon as it glows faintly in the dark sky. And from there, it launches.

Lace blinks, unsure if she's imagining it at first. The moon shouldn't be moving, at least not in said manner.

But it is. It drifts left, sliding across the horizon unnaturally hasty.

This is it. I've finally lost it.

She rubs her eyes, convinced she's hallucinating, but no—it's not her mind playing tricks. Bo jerks the wheel, the tires squealing against the dirt as the car swerves to the side. Tiny rocks spit up, hitting the car's underbelly as they skid to a stop in the middle of nowhere.

Without a word, Bo throws the door open and climbs out. The door slams shut behind him, the sharp sound jolting her bones. Lace swallows hard, her hands trembling as she grabs the door handle. She pushes it open, her legs unsteady as she steps out into the night, the chill biting at her skin. Bo stands a few feet away, his back to her, his shoulders tense as he stares at the vast stretch of nothingness ahead of them.

"Bo," Lace calls, her voice shakier than she wants it to be. He doesn't turn around, doesn't flinch. She takes a few hesitant steps toward him. "Bo, we need to talk about this. You just—you killed someone."

He lets out a low, bitter laugh, the sound rough and hollow. "You think I don't know that?" he mutters, finally turning to face her.

His eyes full of something Lace can't quite place—anger, guilt, something deeper. "You think I don't know what I did?"

She opens her mouth to respond, but the words get stuck. "You didn't have to shoot him," she finally manages, her voice trembling. "You didn't have to kill him. We could've—"

"Could've what, Lace?" Bo snaps, his voice rising. He takes a step toward her, his eyes burning with frustration. "Could've talked it out? Could've reasoned with a guy who was ready to gut me with a knife? Jesus Christ, Lace, wake up!"

Lace's eyes widen at his words, her hands shaking as she crosses her arms over her chest, trying to steady herself. "You didn't give me a chance to do anything! You just—" She stops, her voice breaking as the memory of the gunshot slices through her. "You grabbed my gun. Didn't even ask Bo. Just—shot him."

Bo takes another step closer, his face inches from hers now, his voice low and harsh. "What was I supposed to do? Let him stick a knife in my gut? Let him do God knows what to you?" His eyes search hers, the anger flickering with something else—something raw.

"I did what I had to do."

Lace shakes her head, her heart pounding in her chest. "No, Bo. You didn't have to do it like that. We could've run, we could've—"

"We did run," Bo cuts her off, his voice tight. "And if I hadn't shot him, we'd still be back there, dealing with whatever those bastards had planned for us. You think they were just gonna let us go? After I knocked one of 'em out? After I put their bike down?"

Lace stares at him, her mind reeling. She tries to find the right words, something which will make sense of all this, but nothing does. "We didn't even check if he was dead," she whispers. "We just... left him there."

Bo's jaw clenches, his hands balling into fists at his sides. "He was dead, Lace," he says, "Trust me. I don't miss." The chill in his voice sends a shiver down her spine.

Lace steps back, wrapping her arms tighter around herself as the reality of what he's saying sinks in. "I didn't sign up for this, Bo," she says, her voice shaking. "I didn't sign up to be a part of... this."

Bo's eyes narrow, a dangerous edge creeping into his voice. "What did you think this was, Lace? A joyride? A fairy tale? This is real life. Out here, it's kill or be killed."

"It's not the fuckin' Wild West anymore! You don't go around shootin' people in a fuckin' bar fight." Lace's stomach churns at his words, her mind spinning. "That's not who I am," she whispers, her voice breaking. "I'm not—I can't just—"

"Then what are you doing here?" Bo demands, stepping closer again. "What are you doing with me if you can't handle this? You wanted out of that brothel. You wanted a way out—well, this is it. But it ain't pretty, and it sure as hell ain't easy."

"I wanted out, but not like this," she whispers, her eyes burning with unshed tears. "I didn't want this."

Bo exhales sharply, his hands running through his hair in frustration. He looks away, staring out into the open again, his voice quieter now but no less tense.

"You think I wanted this?" he mutters, shaking his head. "You think I wanted to kill a man tonight? Think I don't know what I've done?" The vulnerability in his voice throws Lace off guard, but she doesn't know how to respond. The silence between them stretches on, heavy with all they cannot convey.

"I did what I had to do to keep us alive, Lace. You might hate me for it, but it's the truth."

Lace swallows hard, her throat tight as she stares at him. The tears she's been hanging onto finally spill over, her chest aching with all they've endured.

"I don't know how to live with this," she whispers, her voice barely audible. "I don't know how to be okay with what just happened."

Bo doesn't say anything, only looks at her with those haunted eyes. The space between them reflects a chasm, and Lace isn't sure if they can ever close it. The wind picks up, rustling through the sparse desert brush, carrying their silence into the night.

Bo steps toward her, his eyes locked on hers, his expression hard but conflicted. He reaches her, looming over Lace. His ragged breath, his chest rising and falling as if he's trying to keep something grimmer at bay.

In a single motion, Bo grabs her by the waist, pulling her hard against him. Lace gasps as her body collides with his, her mind spinning. His fingers dig into her skin, not enough to hurt, but enough to let her know he's holding on.

Trying to stake a claim on her. He's rough, his grip tight, and the next thing she knows, his lips are on hers, fierce and demanding, swallowing her breath.

Lace can barely keep up as Bo pushes her back into the truck, his hand already tangled in her hair, pulling her head back to expose her neck. His lips crash against her skin, his breath fiery, his movements far from gentle.

There's no softness here, no hesitation. He's taking her in a way that suggests he's trying to purge the anger, guilt, and desperation building up inside him.

"Bo—" she manages to breathe out, but her words are lost in the moment, drowned out by the rough way he handles her. Bo's hand moves to her chin, forcing her to look at him, his gaze searing into hers. There's no apology in his eyes—no regret, only raw, unfiltered want.

He doesn't ask for permission, doesn't need to, because Lace is already responding to him, her body leaning into his, her breath coming in shallow gasps. She knows what this is, what it's turning into, and part of her craves it simply as much as he does.

Bo's grip tightens on Lace as he pushes her against the side of the car, then down against the leather seat of the truck. Lace gasps as he pins her wrists behind her back, her heart pounding. His hand is firm as it moves over her mouth, muffling the diminutive, breathless sounds escaping her.

That's when her mind flashes to her former bedroom door at the ranch—the painting. The image burns into her brain: the tattooed man, his hand covering the woman's mouth, her hands bound behind her back, helpless. Lace becomes keenly aware as her body forces itself into the same shape. A wave of disbelief crashes over her.

This isn't how it was supposed to be with Bo.

It was supposed to be different—gentler, more romantic.

But here they are. Her body sinking into the position as if it's been waiting for this. She tries to reconcile the roughness of his hands with the tenderness she thought would be there, but it doesn't fit. Now, his grip is too tight, his body too heavy as he presses her down, covering her mouth.

The man in the painting. A part of her wants to fight, to push him off and tell him this isn't how she wanted it to happen, but another part of her—an older, more sullen part—stays still, allowing it. Conforming her body to mirror the painted woman's pose. She consciously keeps her expression open and inviting—or at least, what part of it isn't hidden by Bo's hand. Lace's mind spins, torn between the fantasy she has built up and what she's been conditioned to do, and it hits her with a sickening thud.

Maybe I was wrong.

Maybe there's no softness in Bo at all. Maybe this was always how it was going to be.

Each move he makes is rough, each thrust sending a jolt through her body. It's not love. It's not tenderness. It's something else.

She doesn't make a sound, her muffled gasps silenced by his hand, her wrists pinned behind her back, her mind trying to shut out the growing realization that this was never going to be the way she dreamed.

But as tears prick at her eyes, Lace sinks deeper into it, yielding to the weight of his body and the roughness of his touch. He doesn't meet her gaze, yet Lace maintains her inviting eyes, steady and unbroken.

Something in the intensity feels right, although it's all wrong.

Because who am I if not being sexualized?

28

About Fuckin' Time

he dream begins with a low, eerie undercurrent. Lace is back at the end of the brothel hallway. Only it's different now—longer, grimmer, more suffocating. The walls are close, too close, bending inward. Each door to the girl's rooms is open, light spilling out into the hallway floor in slanted, sickly shades of red. Lace walks soundlessly against the carpeted floor. Faceless men, hovering over the girl's beds in each room, standing stiff and lifeless.

Lace recognizes Gemma's tangled hair and Petal's slight frame curled beneath the covers. The men, faceless and looming, make no noise, but their presence is heavy and oppressive. The air clots and thickens, mist turning to molasses around her. She tries to move forward, but there are men in the hallway too—standing as solid as statues, watching her.

Lace hesitates, but there's no way around them.

As she passes, their hands reach out, fingers brushing her arms and around her waist. It begins with light touches, almost accidental. But the grip gathers strength.

They grab at her clothes, tugging, pulling, tearing. Lace tries to push through, but more hands appear, dragging her back. Ripping at her shirt. Her skirt. The fabric gives way, shredding under their grasp.

Lace stumbles, the hallway spinning, the men pressing closer. She gasps for air, her clothes torn away until there's nothing left. They've stripped her bare. She falls to her knees, the cold carpet beneath her skin. Desperate, she tries to crawl, but the hands keep coming—grabbing at her legs, her back, her hair—pulling her down. Her heart pounds, the walls closing in, the faceless men surrounding her, enclosing her in a cage of flesh.

A scream.

Perfectly raw, as it tears from her throat, echoing through the hallway in the nature of a thunderclap.

The men freeze.

The hallway detonates in flames.

Fire roars to life, racing up the walls, bursting from the floors, engulfing all in its path. The men's silhouettes flicker and twist in the firelight, consumed by the flames. The fire moves fast, too fast. It swallows the rooms, the beds, the girls, and it's coming for her.

She tries to scream again, but no sound comes out. Her throat constricts, the heat pressing down on her chest. The fire surges closer, showing no mercy to any in its path.

Lace stirs awake, blinking as the gauzy morning light seeps through the windshield. Muted ochres and dusty violets brush the surrounding wild; the cowboy's boundary, a delicate watercolor wash where land blurs into the sky.

She shifts, her senses grazing against the muted rustle of the desert—waiting with a fragile serenity.

The first thing she becomes aware of is the warmth of Bo's body pressing against her back. His sturdy legs provide an unexpected comfort as her head rests between them. His arms lie loosely at his sides, a relaxed pose hinting at a peaceful sleep. Lace's cheek presses against the rough fabric of his jeans, the faint smell of leather and sweat swirling around her—a scent both familiar and intoxicating.

She pushes herself up, careful not to wake him. Her movements are sluggish, her body sore and tired, yet she ignores the discomfort. It's only another morning, only more road, endless as ever. As she turns her head to glance at Bo's face, half hidden by the brim of his hat slipping down low, she can't help but study him.

His eyes are twitching as if they are secrets, pleading to be set free. He looks peaceful, breathing deep and steady, utterly unaware of her scrutiny.

Lace gently taps his knee. "Bo," her voice faint, as if it could rustle the leaves. When he doesn't respond, she nudges him a little harder this time. "Bo, wake up."

He stirs, moaning as he shifts in his seat. With a soft groan, he rubs a hand over his face, pushing his hat back into place. He leans over and presses his lips gently against her cheek, the warmth of the kiss sending a flutter through her stomach.

"Morning, baby," he breathes, his voice thick with sleep and affection.

For the tiniest moment, all the complexities of the night before fade away. It feels sweet and grounding—a simple connection reminding her of the layers between them. She meets his sleepy gaze and a slight smile tugs at the corners of her lips.

He glances at her with curiosity and recognition before reaching for the door handle and hopping out. "Hold that thought," he mutters, stepping into the crisp morning. He walks a few paces away, disappearing briefly behind the truck to take care of business. Lace watches through the windshield, the dry gulch at rest around them.

Bo gets back in the driver's seat, shifting into gear, tires crunching over the rocks as they pull back onto the highway, the arid West yawning ahead.

She doesn't feel the need to fill the silence between them. They both know where they're headed, and that is enough.

For *now*.

As the truck rumbles down the Old Las Vegas Highway in the pale light of mid-morning, the desert sprawling so vast and endless in all directions. Lace believes, at some point, they might drive off the edge of the world.

Lace squints against the brightness, her gaze locking on the horizon, where the faint glimmer of Las Vegas starts to come into view. The scratchy notes of Dean Martin's "Ain't That A Kick In The Head" cut through the radio's warbled fuzz. Both Bo and Lace exchange a knowing smile, the irony of the song hitting them just right.

The city sits like a mirage, shimmering in the distance, its neon lights dulled by the daylight but nonetheless standing against the barren landscape. From this far out, the buildings look almost too tiny to be real, their glittering facades lost in the heat waves rising off the desert floor. But as they get closer, the signs of life grow louder and more tangible. A distant hum of traffic finds their ears, the faintest echo of what awaits.

Lace can see the shape of the towers of MGM Grand and Caesar's Palace standing tall, their grandeur imposing from miles away. The infamous "Welcome to Fabulous Las Vegas" sign comes into focus, a beacon standing proudly against the scorched expanse surrounding it. The road ahead, long and straight, guides them, an arrow toward the city. It might as well have been painted yellow.

Mid-morning in Las Vegas isn't on par with anywhere else. The sky is a clean, cloudless blue, but the night's energy clings to the streets. The casinos loom in the distance, their towering facades plastered with larger-than-life marquees of magicians, dancers, and all the indulgences which await inside.

Lace glances at Bo, his face unreadable as they near their destination. The Strip lies before them, a waiting beast, its claws of temptation and excess hidden beneath glittering lights.

It's everything she has imagined—loud, extravagant, and pulsing with life—and yet strangely distant, as if she isn't ready to step into such a world. Just yet.

But there it is, undeniable and within reach. Bo's truck rolls onto the edge of the Las Vegas Strip, the tires crunching over the last bit of gravel before hitting smooth asphalt.

Without a word, Lace leans forward and pushes herself out of the truck's window. Bo peers at her, confusion flickering in his eyes.

"What the hell are you doin'?" he asks.

But Lace ignores him, determined, wriggling the rest of her body out until her legs are free. The wind, warm and dry, hits her full force as it rushes past, whipping her hair around her face. One by one, she throws each of her limbs over the side of the truck, her knees scraping against the rusted metal.

"Lace!" Bo yells again, louder this time, his voice edged with irritation. He looks back at her, one hand remaining on the wheel, the other hovering as if ready to pull her back in. "You tryin' to kill yourself?"

She finally makes it into the bed, straightening up as she sits on her knees, the full breadth of the wind pulling at her. From the bed of the truck, the Strip unfolds. Lace can see it all now—clearer than she could from the passenger seat. The first sight to greet them is Vegas Vic, the towering neon cowboy, his cheerful grin and wide-open arms welcoming all who pass. His red scarf fluttered in the warm breeze. She can almost hear him calling out, urging them to embrace the city's magic.

The truck bounces over a pothole, and Lace catches herself, laughing at the thrill of it all. "Get back in the damn truck," Bo hollers, though his grin betrays the scolding.

The vibrant colors of the Flamingo capture her attention. Its pink facade sparkling in the sunlight, while its lush gardens offer a tropical respite from the bustling city.

"Didn't I tell you I'd get you here!" Bo shouts, grinning as he navigates the truck through the lively streets.

A giant billboard featuring Elvis Presley proclaiming, "The King Lives!" stands tall. This is the Vegas she has dreamed of—the birthplace of legends, where magic and music intertwine. The photograph she has been staring at in her bedroom for her entire life is finally a reality.

"Look! There's Circus Circus!" she shouts, her voice bubbling over with excitement. She can already picture the acrobats soaring high above the crowd, the scent of popcorn and cotton candy filling patron's noses.

The Strip is loud and bright, even in the daylight, but it is beautiful in its own strange way. Lace has never encountered anything like it. She feels free as the truck carries her deeper into the neon world.

Bo's voice breaks through the noise. "You gonna stay up there or get your ass back in the truck?"

Lace laughs, "I think I'll stay."

The sound whips away by the wind as she crouches down, balancing herself on the edge of the truck bed. She doesn't want to get back in. Not yet. The city is pulling her in, calling her closer.

Lace runs her fingers through her wind-tangled hair. This is what they'd been driving toward all night—the city that promises it all and takes even more.

They are here.

Vegas is everything she thought it would be.

29

News Flash: Smoking = Bad!

ace stretches out across the worn bench seat of the truck, her legs dangling out the passenger window, the breeze gently whipping against her calves. Her head rests comfortably on Bo's thigh, and she lets her eyes flutter close. With a furrowed brow and clumsy hands, Bo tries his best to braid her hair. Lace endures the occasional tug at her scalp, his fingers fumbling with the strands like he's attempting to tame the wildness which always reluctantly escapes her. She doesn't need to see his handiwork to know it probably isn't her best look. His rough hands, more used to gripping reins or wrenches, struggle with the delicate task.

"Hell, I don't know if this is comin' out right," Bo says, his voice low and gruff, though there's a tenderness. His thumb accidentally brushes her scalp again, and Lace smiles faintly, eyes closed, comforted by his awkward efforts. She doesn't mind. There is something sweet in his attempt, regardless of whether he isn't quite getting it right.

Both of them are passing a cigarette from Lace's pack. They've stopped in the parking lot of a Chevron Station near Tropicana Avenue. She takes another drag of her cigarette before reaching her arm above her head, silently passing it to Bo.

He takes it in his free hand, speaking after he inhales, "Now, why in the hell we splittin' one cigarette? I can head right in and get us a whole pack if you're gonna be stingy like that." Bo flicks ash out of the window, "You really shouldn't be smoking these. They'll be the death of you."

"How many cigarettes have you gone through? You're puffing them down faster than I can count. And let's be honest—you're the older one, so if anyone's checking out first, it's gonna be you. Ever seen that like father, like son ad? I bet that old man was you." Lace replies lazily.

He gently cups the back of her neck and guides her to a sitting position before fully lifting her into his lap. His eyes widen at the sight of what he's done to Lace's hair, a wild tumble of curls framing her face. He takes one hand and brushes a loose strand behind her ear, his touch lingering.

"Where'd you see that commercial? Wasn't that back in the 60s?" he teases, a smirk tugging at the corners of his lips.

Lace's fingers drift to his chest, tracing delicate circles on his shirt. "Ah—so you do remember filming that, huh? What'd they pay you? One lucky penny?"

In one smooth motion, Bo leans forward and presses his lips against hers, igniting a fire deep within her. The taste of smoke lingers between them, intoxicating as he deepens the kiss, one hand sliding around her waist while the other tangles in her hair.

Lace feels herself getting lost in him. But as she's ready to dive deeper, Bo pulls away, his breath mingling with hers as he rests his forehead against hers.

"Stay put, will ya?" he says, between cheek kisses. "I'll be right back. You might wanna do something with that hair, though." His eyes give her a playful smirk, gesturing to her wild curls. "I'd hate to see you try to convince anyone that you're not the spittin' image of a desert drifter."

Lace laughs, a mix of warmth and embarrassment spreading across her chest. "Oh, real charmin'," she remarks.

"Don't go anywhere—and I'm not that old," he says, revealing a hint of seriousness beneath the humor. He slides Lace off his lap and climbs out of the truck, leaving her breathless as he walks toward the station's entrance.

"Yeah, maybe just thirty or so more years of wear and tear on me," Lace calls out.

As he strolls away, she can't help but admire how he carries himself, confident and relaxed. Her fingers lightly graze her lips, still warm from his kiss. But, Lace is drawn to the figure stepping out of a sleek Cadillac at the pump across from her. A woman, impossibly tall and glamorous, with a cascade of feathers and rhinestones shimmering in the sunlight.

It takes Lace a moment to realize she is staring at a real Vegas showgirl.

The woman's hair is piled high in a perfectly coiffed blonde beehive, strands glittering gold in the harsh daylight. Her makeup is impeccable, with bright red lipstick matching her towering heels and an iridescent leotard that sparkles with each movement.

Despite the mundane task of pumping gas, the woman carries herself as if walking across the stage at The Folies Bergere. Her gestures, from the way she flips her sunglasses down to the graceful arch of her arm pumping gas, are theatrical.

Lace can't look away. The feathers from her headdress—vivid blues and greens—sway in the breeze, giving her the look of a bird caught mid-dance. It's surreal, this intersection of fantasy and reality.

The line between the Strip's glamor and everyday life's grit doesn't exist in Vegas.

The woman glances up, briefly lingering on Lace and winks. A flush of heat rushes through her, unsure if it's from the sun or the jolt of being seen. Acknowledged by someone who lives in a world she can only imagine from afar. The show girl's smile is knowing, as if she sees something in Lace—an unspoken understanding of wanting more, of longing for a life of spectacle and lights.

That look—it's the same one Brandi gave her once. Same kind of gas station, same quiet weight in the air.

Every road leads back to her.

Bo returns, his hands full: a pack of cigarettes tucked under one arm and a six-pack of Coors balanced against his chest. He tosses the beer at Lace's feet and the pack of cigarettes in her lap.

Camels.

"Alright, rosebud," he says, a lopsided grin forming, "we need to figure out where we're gonna stay tonight. There's no fuckin' way I'm lettin' us sleep in this truck again."

Lace turns her head, the sight of him igniting a fire in her chest. "We should stay at the Flamingo," she suggests. "I think I fancy that one best."

Bo lets out a hearty laugh, "You're joking, right? We ain't got the cash for that. You wanna pay for it?" His tone is teasing, but the seriousness behind his words makes her heart sink.

"Come on, I got money we can use," she assures.

He raises an eyebrow, shaking his head as he chuckles. "No way, Lace. I'm not stayin' in a room bought with your sex money." His words settle heavily between them, a reminder of the realities they are both trying to escape.

"Seriously?" Lace pleads. "It's just money. I'm not ashamed of where mine comes from." Bo sighs, lifting his hat and running a rough hand through his hair, the kind that has seen the sun and the wind for too many long days. Lace continues, "did you forget a small portion of that came from you? Remember when you fuckin' paid me for sex?"

Bo chuckles, "*Small portion.* It ain't about that, Lace. I don't want you thinkin' that's the only way you're worth somethin'. We can find a place on the outskirts of the Strip. It'll be cheaper, and we can save that cash for somethin' better. And we never had sex that night. I paid you to talk."

"You really think I care where we stay? I just want to feel like I'm in Vegas."

He studies her, "I get that, but we gotta be smart about this. We're in a town that'll chew you up and spit you out if you let it. Let's not start off by throwin' away what little money we have on fancy hotels."

She opens her mouth to argue, but the glint in his eye tells her he isn't going to budge.

Instead, she leans back against the truck's dusty bench, letting out a sigh of resignation. "Alright, fine. But I still wanna see the inside of the Flamingo."

Bo chuckles. "We'll pass by it tonight. You can dream big while I keep my feet on the ground." His smile is infectious, and she can't help but smile back despite the lingering frustration.

"Deal," she replies.

30

Don't Feed The Desk Clerk

ace figures out they're heading north, but the only reason she knows is that Bo, for once, has no fucking clue where they're going. He stops to ask a disheveled man practically crawling across the corner of Las Vegas Blvd and Reno Dr, where the cheapest motel is. The man points north, mumbling about a place called The Tattered Tent Inn, before launching into a hysterical rant about Area 51, claiming he's the reincarnation of Benjamin "Bugsy" Siegel, despite clearly being under thirty and Siegel having died in 1947.

Bo slams on the gas before the man can say anything more.

The motel sits about twenty miles outside the Strip, undeniably a last stop for those who have been blacklisted from every hotel and casino in Las Vegas. As they drive through the bleak outskirts, Lace can't help but spot the strange sights flashing by.

A shack in the middle of the desert where you can enjoy a plate of ribs while browsing questionable Sasquatch *evidence*, including blurry photos and fur samples. Uncle Vern swears he's seen Bigfoot... over BBQ sauce.

She's never seen a drug deal happen right in front of her eyes, but in the last fifteen minutes, she's witnessed at least four, each more brazen than the previous. This desolate stretch of fringe, a magnet for desperation and poor decisions.

"This is some real hick shit," Lace remarks out loud as her eyes trail to a man in a full gorilla suit juggling bowling pins on the side of the road. A slim crowd gathers around him, cheering wildly.

"I don't understand why we can't just stay in the city. I got money, and you should too, Mr. I Own a *Ranch*."

Bo, lighting another cigarette with her pin-up lighter, exhales before replying, "I told you we aren't wasting no money on a damn room we barely will spend any time at."

He makes a sharp right turn, past a graveyard, and there it is.

The fucking Tattered Tent Inn.

The motel sits as if nothing more than a forgotten relic at the edge of nowhere, with peeling paint on its fading wooden siding. Above it, jagged mountains rise into a sky choked by low-hanging clouds, their tops shrouded in mist despite clear skies twenty minutes away. A chipping neon sign, half-lit, flickers weakly: "The Tattered Tent Inn." Below the fading letters, old-fashioned block signs promise "Cocktails," "Homemade Pie," and "Steak and Lobster," as if those words carry any magic.

A lone car's paint as yellowed as nicotine-stained fingers sits slumped in front of room 106. Rust crawls along its fenders, and its tires sink into the cracked earth, half swallowing the vehicle. Dirt stains creep up the motel's warped and dull, faded teal-numbered doors. Each room has its dusty window framed by ragged curtains that haven't seen a wash since Eisenhower graced us with his presence.

The air smells reminiscent of rain that has yet to come and never will, thick with dust and rotting wood. It's a place once part of the American dream but now waits to be erased by time, begging to be.

Clutching onto an era which has already slipped through its fingers.

Lace leans her head out the car window, taking it all in. The wind picks up, swirling around bits of debris scattered across the cracked pavement. Desolation seeps into her bones. A quiet reminder there's no one to save you out here.

Bo parks the truck, glancing at the sign with a grin. "This ain't that bad. Got character, huh," he says, his voice deep with sarcasm.

"Character's one way to put it," Lace replies, eyes lingering on the empty lot. It's the kind of place you get stuck in, where your dreams curl up and die.

Along with the neon glow of a broken sign.

Bo shoves open the door to the lobby, and it swings wide with a screech, a dying animal's last breath. Inside, the scene is a chaos of clashing colors and lousy taste, straight out of a nightmare—or an acid trip gone wrong. Mismatched wallpaper covers the walls; one side is floral, the other neon pink stripes. A giant lava lamp bubbles lazily on a shelf in the corner, glowing a radioactive green.

Racks of postcards stand awkwardly near the door, all depicting some dead-eyed cartoon cowboy grinning beneath the words, "Welcome to Paradise!" Except it's crossed out in thick marker, replaced with the phrase "Abandon." Above the postcards, a fake palm tree droops, its plastic fronds half-melted from what looks to be a long-forgotten electrical fire.

Bo and Lace step up to the front desk—or what's left of it. The counter is plastered with layers of stickers and graffiti, all faded.

One reads: "WHERE REALITY GOES TO DIE," and another: "FREE YOUR MIND—LEAVE YOUR BRAIN."

"Leave your brain? How the fuck they want me to do that?" Lace accidentally comments out loud.

The sight of a painting on the wall is something she wishes she could erase from her brain, Elvis riding a unicorn through outer space, surrounded by swirling galaxies.

She blinks.

Hard.

Behind the desk sits the strangest part, the desk clerk. His shirt is a loud explosion of neon leopard print, unbuttoned halfway to reveal a sweat-stained undershirt. He's got what appears to be swim goggles perched on his head and a name tag that reads "Bingo." A lit cigarette dangles from his lips, ash clinging for dear life to the end.

His eyes are hidden behind the thickest, ugliest pair of sunglasses Lace has ever seen, with lenses reflecting back twisted versions of her and Bo. He's got a Walkman clipped to his belt, headphones blaring what she believes may be a Kenny Loggins track, but warped as if it's been played one too many times.

"Checkin' in?" Bingo croaks, sounding quite thirsty. He doesn't bother taking the headphones off.

"Jesus fuck." Lace whispers.

Bo stares at him for a second, taking in the goggles, before dropping his elbows on the counter with a grin. "Yeah. One night. Maybe longer. We don't know yet."

Bingo's head bobs, catching in the last chorus of whatever's playing. He grabs a key from behind the desk, tossing it onto the counter with a dramatic flick of his wrist. The keychain is a hideous chunk of cactus plexiglass that most definitely glows in the dark.

"That'll be twenty bucks. Room 108," Bingo drones, "it's haunted, but you didn't hear that from me." He laughs, but it's the kind of laugh which kicks off low and builds into a cackle, his body shaking. Barely holding on to whatever reality he's in.

Bo snorts, picking up the key. "Haunted, huh?"

Bingo leans forward, lowering his sunglasses enough to reveal bloodshot, bulging eyes that might've seen a bit too much. His breath reeks of a combination of stale smoke and time-tested tequila. "The walls bleed, man. I've seen it. Like literal *blood*. And sometimes—" his voice drops to a whisper as if the walls are listening, "the TV turns itself on and shows you what you most fear. Some say it's connected to another dimension."

Lace raises an eyebrow at Bo. "Dimension of what? Bad taste?" She deadpans, glancing at the Elvis painting.

Bingo doesn't miss a beat, "Nah, sweetheart. The *real* deal. Parallel universe. You might wake up and be a lizard, for all I know. They showed me Madonna corrupting the youth. Some real scary shit."

"Comforting," Bo mutters. He signs the registry, which is more along the lines of a doodle pad from a mental institution, covered in illegible scrawl and weird symbols, and slaps two tens down.

He spots a note written in neon-pink marker that says, "THE MOON PEOPLE ARE WATCHING." He taps it with the pen and glances at Bingo. "You got Moon People here too?"

"Oh, yeah. They're mostly chill. But if they knock on your door at three a.m. Don't answer. That's when they want your soul. Or your socks. Depends on their mood."

Lace suppresses a laugh, but it slips out as a snort. Bingo's face breaks into a grin, his teeth stained purple from God knows what. He pulls a stack of business cards and slides one across the counter. It reads: "Bingo's Guided UFO Tours: See What the Government Hides! No Refunds if Abducted."

"UFO tours?" Lace asks, smirking.

"Oh, hell yeah," Bingo says, leaning back in his chair. "Roswell's got nothin' on us. We're the real fucking alien hot spot. They always come down, just checkin' things out, abductin' a few cows. Nothin' serious." He shrugs. Simply another day on the job.

Bo tucks the key into his pocket, clearly over it. "Well, thanks for the warning about the lizards and Moon People. We'll, uh, keep our socks on."

Bingo gives them a two-finger salute. "You do that, cowboy. And hey, if you hear Elvis singin' in the middle of the night, just roll with it. The King's still got it."

Lace and Bo exchange one last bewildered look before stepping out into the parking lot. A red-tailed hawk dives low, wings slicing through a low-hanging cloud, and lets a dead jackrabbit fall right at Bo and Lace's feet, the thud startling them as dust puffs up from the impact.

Lace can't help but laugh, "Are you ready to head back to the Flamingo now?"

Bo shakes his head. "Baby, we gotta see it through."

He glances back toward the lobby, where inside, the TV flickers with the *Like a Virgin* video, and just as Madonna steps off that damn boat, Bingo hurls a paperweight at the screen.

"Welcome to the dirty part of heaven," Lace murmurs.

31

There Goes Seven Years

s Bo pushes open the door to room 108. It creaks ominously, revealing a space considered anything but inviting. Grimy, green walls, speckled with mysterious, long-ignored stains, resist the dim lighting. A little mismatched table sits in one corner, its surface marred by rings from long-vanished drinks and a deep scratch telling a story of past frustration. CNN blares through the TV opposite the bed and the voice of a newscaster drones on.

"It's been nearly three months since the catastrophic explosion at the Chernobyl nuclear power plant, and the scale of the disaster is still being uncovered. Soviet officials report that the number of casualties remains uncertain. Still, new footage reveals a bleak landscape in the Ukrainian countryside, where radiation levels are too high for any form of life. Experts warn that the long-term impact of the fallout could be worse than initially feared, with radioactive contamination affecting areas hundreds of miles away."

The screen flickers, showing blurry images of deserted villages, rows of empty houses, and men in protective suits moving through fields turned barren. "The global community remains on edge, worried about the implications of this disaster," the newscaster continues, his voice as emotionless as the gray scenes on the screen.

Bo's eyes shift to the TV momentarily, but he only shakes his head. Lace, meanwhile, watches the images of empty playgrounds and stray animals wandering the streets, an uneasy feeling growing.

The world itself is falling apart in pieces, far beyond their control.

An unmade bed is the room's centerpiece, the floral bedspread a violent clash of colors—muted pinks and vibrant greens screaming for attention while being utterly unremarkable. Stained and well-loved, two flat pillows rest at the head, each wrangling the imprint of countless restless nights. Above the bed is a poorly framed print of a sunset nailed crookedly, its once-vibrant hues faded to a dull wash.

In the corner, an air conditioning unit buzzes, its vents coated in a fine layer of dust. As she steps further inside, Lace can't help but acknowledge the mix of amusement and dread. It's along the lines of a bad amateur porno, one not even the most extreme pervert would ever want to watch. Bo drops their bags on the bed, the thud echoing in the cramped space.

She crosses her arms, a half-smile forming on her lips. "Charmin', isn't it? I feel like we're in the backdrop for some horror movie."

"More like a cult classic," Bo says, glancing around with a playful smirk. "The kind where folks check-in, but they sure as hell don't check out."

Lace chuckles despite the odd chill creeping up her spine. "Well, let's hope we're not the next victims in whatever twisted plot unfolds here."

"Just stay close, darlin'. I'll keep the haints off your trail." He leans down to smother Lace in kisses. Lace rolls her eyes, but there's warmth in her heart. It's not the glamorous escape she had in mind, but it's real—and by curious means, that's enough.

The soft thud resonates in the room as Bo sets his worn cowboy hat on the bed. He heads toward the bathroom sink, and Lace watches him. The fluorescent light casts a harsh glow across his strong profile as he splashes cold water on his face.

"So," she begins, "how long do you think we'll be in Vegas? A few days, maybe? What comes next? Will I move to your ranch after this?"

Bo lifts his head, water dripping from his chin, and runs a hand through his damp hair, trying to shake off the unease creeping in.

"Lace, let's just take it easy," he replies, his voice low and measured, but the weariness lingers in his eyes.

But Lace presses on. "I mean. I think it'd be great, just us, the open land, your horses. What do you think?"

He grits his teeth, frustration building as her words swirl around him, "I think we should focus on today, alright? Not get too far ahead of ourselves."

Lace glances down at Bo's hat on the bed and registers something. A new tally mark scratched into the brim. There used to be nine. She's sure of it, and now there are ten. Gently. She picks up the hat.

"Bo, what are these tally marks?"

He freezes at the sink, his back to her, shoulders tensing as a coiled spring ready to launch. "It's not important," he mutters, but the edges of his voice are sharp, laced with irritation.

"It looks important," Lace presses, stepping closer, curiosity overtaking her initial concern. "There used to be nine back at the ranch. What does it mean?"

He raises his fist and punches the mirror with a sickening crack.

Glass shards explode outward.

She gasps. Frozen on the bed. He stands there, breathing heavily, blood seeping from his knuckles where he struck the mirror.

The distorted reflection. Shattered images of both of them mingling. She can see the raw pain etched on his face, his frustration bubbling over. "Damn it, Lace!" he shouts, his voice thick with emotion. "You don't get to pick the timeline of my life! I'm still figuring it out myself!"

Lace stares at him, her heart aching. "I just want to understand," she says softly, rising off the bed. "I didn't mean to overwhelm you. I thought we were on the same page." They stand in silence.

Bo's eyes soften, and the storm within him subsides as he looks at her. "I know." Bo takes a deep breath and turns to Lace with a steady gaze. "Get yourself ready. We're headin' out to the Strip, and for the love of God, put on some shoes." His voice carrying that rough Western timbre.

"I didn't bring any."

"Who doesn't own a pair of shoes?"

"Guess I didn't think we'd be here long enough for that," she mutters, her eyes darting away.

Bo only stares at Lace, his expression unreadable. "I'll be right back. Don't move," he says, grabbing his hat from the bed.

Left alone in the stark room, Lace glances at her reflection in the cracked mirror. She moves closer, the broken shards distorting her face, creating a mosaic. Lace opens her bag with trembling fingers. The clatter of her belongings spills into the sink filled with glass shards, a chaotic collection of cash, clothing, makeup, and a beat-up Polaroid camera Trish had given her.

Her heart sinks as she pulls out a tiny compact of powder, its surface worn but familiar. Brandi's name etched on the bottom, a fragile reminder of their once beloved friendship. She bites her lip; the tears start to well up, a bittersweet ache swelling within her. She can almost hear Brandi's laughter, the way it would warm a room.

A tear slips down her cheek, and she brushes it away angrily, not wanting to dwell on what she's lost. Yet, that single tear becomes a torrent, and she can't help but let her memories flood in.

With a shaky breath, she powders her skin, tilting her head to find a shard wide enough to avoid her shattered face.

I am good and loved.

I am good. I am loved.

32

Bear Necessities

he truck rolls to a halt in front of the Flamingo Hotel. Lace stands out in a zebra print dress, hugging her figure in all the right places. The dress has a plunging neckline, lifting her chest so high that if she tilted her head down, her chin would brush the top of her breasts. Giving her a borrowed confidence.

The hemline falls mid-thigh, letting her legs breathe, especially with the black kitten heels Bo bought her.

"Holy shit," she breathes, her smokey eyes widen as she takes it all in—the palm trees swaying gently under the glow of neon, reminiscent of a paradise crafted by artists with an eye for the absurd. "This place is amazing."

"Ready?" Bo asks, his voice low and steady, laced with an undeniable charm. He shifts in his seat, his hand resting casually on the gearshift, eyes gleaming.

"Ready."

She takes a deep breath, smoothing the fabric of her dress, and mentally prepares herself. As she steps out of the truck, the heel of her left shoe tugs on the pavement, and she stumbles, catching herself on the doorframe.

Bo watches, a grin playing at the corners of his lips. "Easy there, rosebud. Those things take a little getting used to."

"Yeah, well, I've never worn heels before," a hint of defiance in her voice. She straightens, trying to regain her balance both physically and metaphorically.

"Don't you fret none—you'll figure it out," he replies, stepping around her to the front of the truck to toss the keys to the valet boy. Bo turns back to Lace, his eyes searching hers as if gauging her confidence.

As they step into the vibrant chaos of the Flamingo Hotel, Bo wraps his arm around Lace, pulling her close to him. The warmth of his body against hers is comforting yet electrifying, a blend of possessiveness and affection. Bo looks effortlessly stylish in a crisp white linen button-down shirt, the fabric soft and barely rumpled, giving him a laid-back yet sophisticated appearance. The shirt is half-tucked into his sleek black pants, accentuating the strength of his physique. The contrast between the light shirt and inky pants makes him stand out in the sea of colorful guests milling about, his presence both commanding and reassuring.

Together, they weave through the throngs of people. Lace's eyes widen as they pass the gleaming slot machines, their bright lights flashing, beckoning her to try her luck. She leans into Bo, thankful for the sturdy support of his arm as they make their way deeper into the hotel.

Each step in her kitten heels feels precarious. She can't help but laugh nervously as she tries to keep her balance, her heels clicking on the glossy floor tiles.

Each light fixture sparkles as a cluster of diamonds, casting rainbows across the walls. The air is thick with the scent of fresh flowers mingling with the faint whiff of cigar smoke, and the soundtrack of chimes and bells from nearby slot machines creates an intoxicating symphony.

"Wow," she whispers, her voice almost drowned out by the sounds of laughter and the clang of coins spilling from machines.

She can't help but admire the flamboyant decor—tropical plants dot the room, and murals depicting island scenes bring a whimsical touch to the otherwise glamorous setting. Every corner supports something new and fascinating, pulling her deeper into this surreal world.

Am I on drugs?

"I've never seen anything like this," she admits, her voice filled with awe. "What do we do first? The slots? Roulette? Maybe blackjack? You're gonna have to teach me, though—I don't know a damn thing."

Bo grins, the corners of his mouth tugging upward as he watches her, arm firmly wrapped around her waist. "We'll start slow. No need to lose your dress first round."

Lace looks up at him, her gaze tracing the lines of his face, catching the faint shadow that sharpens his jaw under the fluorescent lighting. She leans up on her toes, carefully keeping her ankle from buckling. Her lips brush his cheek, a light, fleeting touch as she whispers, "You look handsome tonight."

Bo freezes, the grin slipping briefly, his surprise flickering beneath a steady, half-lidded gaze. "Enough of this," he says. "I have a better idea."

Before she can ask what he means, he pulls her toward the back of the casino, navigating through the crowd with purpose.

She sees the sign for the bathroom in the corner of her eye.

"Bo, what are you—"

"Trust me," he says, urgency threading through his tone as he pushes the door open and ushers her inside. The bathroom is unsurprisingly lavish, adorned with marble sinks and golden fixtures, giving the illusion they've stepped into a private oasis. The atmosphere shifts dramatically as the door clicks, locking them inside. He moves closer, eyes darkening with a mix of desire and urgency. Lace's breath falters, heart jolting as he steps into her space.

The Flamingo's bathroom is colder than Lace expects, the chill of the marble biting into her bare thighs as Bo sets her down on the counter. The fluorescent lights above flicker, making the room both too bright and too dull at once. Lace's gaze darts toward the mirror—eyes landing on her face, flushed beneath the zebra print of her dress, but it's not her.

She's looking at someone else.

Bo's hands are everywhere, the smell of his aftershave mingling with the faint scent of bleach is what she grabs onto. The barely dried blood on his knuckles smears into her blonde locks.

She wants to surrender to this, to share his passion for the moment. But something feels off—an itch beneath her skin, which she can't scratch. His fingers slip under her dress, hiking it up, and she flinches at his chill fingertips.

Bo doesn't realize. Or if he does, he doesn't care.

He presses his mouth to her collarbone, his lips trailing upward, grazing the side of her throat. She tilts her head back, releasing a modest gasp, but the sound leaves her throat *hollow*—something she's supposed to do, not something she believes.

The bathroom's too narrow.

The walls are too close.

Sounds of slot machines, muffled and distant through the heavy door, creep in. Lace shifts her weight, the unfamiliar tug of the heels nicking her thin skin. She'd stumbled getting out of the truck, her feet clumsy in shoes that are foreign, and now they dangle awkwardly off the counter.

"Lace," Bo whispers, his voice rough, sending a shiver down her spine. He pulls back enough to look at her, his pupils blown wide. "You have no idea what you do to me."

She blinks, her throat tightening, but she doesn't say anything. She can't. Her hands slide up his chest, focusing on the smooth fabric of his white linen shirt.

But there's no genuine connection.

It's just touch, just skin, just movement.

His words hang between them, and she wishes—for a second—that she could believe them.

Bo's lips crash against hers again, urgent now, almost desperate. Lace kisses him back, her body reacting out of habit, out of a need she doesn't fully understand. She recoils as his rough hands grip her hips, his thumb pressing against the tender branding. The cold stone digs into her skin, but it grounds her—keeps her from floating too far away.

"Bo..." she whispers, but her voice gets eaten by the kiss. She tries again, pressing her palms flat against his chest, pushing him back enough to breathe. "Here?"

"Why not?" His hand slides up her thigh, fingers pressing hard into her flesh. "I'm sure you've fucked other men in nastier places." His words land hard.

Lace almost wishes he would've slapped her instead. Would've hurt less. But she swallows the sting. Inside, though, something cracks. She blinks rapidly to keep the tears from spilling over. She can't let him see her like this. Not now. Not here. She's better than this—stronger than this.

Bo's hands are already moving again, his grip tight as he pulls her closer. Her body responds automatically, legs wrapping around his waist, her back arching off the counter. She lets him guide her. Lets him take control because that's what she knows. That's what she's good at. It's what she's learned to do—give him what he wants.

Because maybe, just maybe, that's how she keeps him.

But as his hands tug at her dress, pushing it further up her thighs, his lips trailing fire down her neck, leading to her breasts. Lace's mind drifts again. She looks at the ceiling tiles, her chest rising and falling with shallow breaths as she counts them in intervals of two.

Two.

Four.

Six.

Eight.

The world narrows to the sound of his breathing, the feel of his hands, the cold counter under her. Her pulse hammers in her ears, but it's not excitement—it's fear.

Fear that this is all she has to offer him.

Fear that this is all she'll ever be.

Her head turns to the side, her cheek resting against the cold glass, her eyes catching the mirror across the room.

She sees their reflection—distorted, broken, jagged pieces that don't fit together. Bo's breath is hot on her skin, his movements rough and urgent, but Lace is elsewhere. She's floating, disconnected, watching it all unfold. A scene in a movie she doesn't recognize. She bites her lip, her body arching under his, making the sounds she knows he wants to hear.

"What a beautiful day," she whispers, the words from the timeless rhyme, "We're Going on a Bear Hunt." Her whisper gets lost in Bo's grunting.

His fingernails dig into her hips. The words are a lifeline.

Something to cradle on to as she drifts further from the present. She used to sit on the worn-out couch in that outdated trailer, the TV flickering with *The Patty Duke Show*. Darlene would jump up, pretending to splash through imaginary water, her steps exaggerated and sloppy. She'd shift to marching through tall grass, lifting her knees high, grinning as she made Lace giggle so hard she'd fall sideways, rolling off the couch.

By the time they got to the scary part, her mom would throw up her hands, her voice triumphant as she shouted, "We're not scared!" Lace would squeal, clapping her hands, trying to mimic the movements as though no danger in the world could ever touch them.

Lace repeats softly, "I'm not scared."

When it's over, he pulls away, adjusting his shirt, running a hand through his hair. She stays where she is, legs dangling off the counter, her chest rising and falling with measured breaths.

Her skin too tight, too raw, the room too bright.

Bo leans down, pressing a kiss to her forehead, but it feels like nothing more than an afterthought. Lace closes her eyes, her throat tight.

She wants to say something—to tell him—how lost she is in the entirety of this. But she doesn't.

She only stays there, letting the silence wrap around her.

Because, in the end.

What else is there to say?

33
Sin City

ace sinks into the plush, red velvet seat at the roulette table. The wheel glimmers under the harsh lights, a beacon of chance and chaos, spinning tales of fortune and loss.

"Alright, baby, let's see what you've got," Bo hums, his voice a low rumble cutting through the cacophony. He leans over the table, his arms resting on each side of her, the warmth of his body pressing against her back.

"Should I bet on red or black?" Lace asks, her voice dripping with playful uncertainty, but she can't entirely hide the eagerness behind it.

She glances up at Bo, whose eyes glint with approval. The corner of his mouth curls into a charming smile.

"Go with your gut," he coos, his tone light, but there's a seriousness in his gaze. "It's all about instinct, darlin'." He presses a soft kiss on the right side of Lace's cheek.

With his encouragement, Lace places her bet, a sparse stack of chips precariously balanced on red, a grin spreading across her face.

The wheel spins. A chaotic symphony of clinking glasses, clattering chips, and raucous laughter seems to fade into the background, her focus narrowing as if time has slowed to a crawl.

A chill brushes against her skin, sending a shiver as she glances to her left. And there he is—the man Bo killed, sitting a few seats down, grinning with an eerie confidence that makes her stomach churn. A hollow, gaping hole in his chest cuts right through him, his face pale and haunting, a blend of familiarity and terror.

The sight grips her heart with icy fingers.

As the wheel spins, the world around her blurs, the casino chatter fading into nothing. He leans forward, cutting off her view of the table, his presence eclipsing all else. She's trapped in his gaze, the spinning colors of the wheel transforming into a surreal swirl of melancholy and light, each number a whispered taunt.

"Lace," she imagines him saying, his voice a sinister hiss. "You think this is a game?"

The wheel clacks to a stop, but she can't tear her eyes away from him.

"Excuse me, miss," a security guard approaches, a stern expression etched on his face. "How old are you?"

"Twenty-one," Bo interjects smoothly, stepping before Lace to shield her from the man's gaze.

"Let's see some ID," the guard replies, unflinching, his eyes darting between them with suspicion and authority.

Lace's heart drops. "I don't have any," she stammers. The dead man's grin echoes in her mind, taunting her as she realizes their precarious position. "I—I think I may have left it in our room," she lies.

I don't even have any form of ID. Any documentation that I even exist.

"Not having ID is a problem, sweetheart," the guard states, crossing his arms. "I can't let you gamble without proof of age."

"Look, officer, she's with me. We were just having a little fun," Bo says, his tone remaining charming but edged with impatience.

"Fun doesn't mean breaking the law," the guard retorts, his gaze unwavering.

Lace glances back at the roulette table, the chips scattered carelessly, mocking her.

"But she just won!" Bo argues, frustration creeping into his voice. "You can't just kick us out because she forgot her ID!"

"Rules are rules," the guard replies, an unyielding wall of authority.

The dead man's laughter rings in her ears as she grips the table's edge. "I swear I'm twenty-one," she pleads, desperation spilling from her lips. "I just—I didn't think..."

"Let's go, Lace," Bo says, taking her hand, yanking her out of her seat.

The guard shakes his head, backing away as if sensing the tension. "Sorry, but I'm going to have to ask you both to leave," he declares, his tone leaving no room for negotiation.

Bo squares off with the security guard, "What the hell's your problem? I told you she's with me. You got nothin' better to do than play hall monitor with a *goddamn* roulette table?"

The guard stands his ground, his jaw tightening, "Rules are rules. No ID, no gambling."

Bo's laugh is low, bitter. "Rules? Oh, give me a fuckin' break. You think this dump's about rules? Half these folks are probably cheating you blind, and you're picking on us?" He steps closer, his voice dropping to something sharper, more dangerous. "You like throwing your weight around, don't you? Makes you feel important?"

"You and your daughter are gonna have to leave," the guard says, his tone flat but dismissive.

Bo freezes for a split second but takes a step forward, his voice erupting like a gunshot. "Daughter?" he barks, his face twisting with fury. "What the fuck did you just say?"

The guard lifts his hands in mock surrender, already regretting his choice of words. "Hey, look, man, I didn't mean—"

"You didn't mean what?" Bo cuts him off, his voice rising with every word. "You calling me some old bastard, is that it? Or maybe you're just too dumb to know when to shut your mouth!" His hands twitch at his sides as if he's trying to stop himself from throwing a punch.

"Sir, I'm just doing my job," the guard stammers, his bravado cracking under Bo's glare.

"Your job? Your job is to run your mouth and insult paying customers? That what they pay you for, huh? Maybe I oughta find your boss and ask him what he thinks about his security calling folk's names!"

The guard takes a step back, his hand hovering near the radio on his belt. "Alright, that's enough. I'm not arguing with you. You both need to leave. Now."

Bo's eyes blaze, his fists clenching and unclenching, seconds from truly snapping. "Yeah, sure. Run away. Don't let me stop you. Coward."

Lace tugs on his arm, her voice barely above a whisper. "Bo, let's go. Please."

As they step away from the table, Lace's heart sinks. The excitement of the roulette wheel, the thrill of winning. It all dissipates.

"Stupid fuckin' casino," Bo grumbles.

As they push past the bustling crowd, the dead man flashes in her mind again, his lifeless eyes a reminder that there's no table they can sit at, no game they can win—not when they're dragging ghosts of their own making.

House never loses.

34

Ring In The Rearview

The valet throws Bo back the keys, and Lace tries to walk beside him, but her heels are already betraying her again. She barely takes three steps before she stumbles, her ankle twisting awkwardly as she nearly hits the pavement. Before she can process the fall, Bo is there, sweeping her off her feet without a second thought. His muscular arms cradling her, carrying her bridal style as if this remains all a part of his plan. "Christ. Those shoes givin' you more trouble than they're worth,"

"I didn't know they'd be this hard to walk in," she bellyaches, feeling nothing but embarrassment. He settles her into the truck, slamming the door as he climbs into the driver's seat.

"Damn casino, kicking us out like that," he fumes, irritation at the forefront as the truck roars to life. "Where do they get off? I swear, people ain't got no respect. We'll find somewhere that knows what they're doin'."

The radio clicks on as they pull into traffic, and the first notes drift out, soft, nostalgic. Lace barely registers the sound at first.

But as the guitar riff comes to life, Elvis's voice seeps through the speakers, smooth like honey, to the familiar croon of "It's Now or Never." Lace leans her head against the window, watching the lights flicker past.

The city is quickly becoming a place where time warps, reality bending just slightly, and anything slips out of reach the moment you try and stake claim. His presence suffocates the truck with a tension that has nothing to do with their earlier *spat*. Hand's grip on the wheel, knuckles pale, eyes straight ahead. She can see the minuscule vein in his temple pop out. Lace shifts in her seat, the heels relentlessly pinching her toes, the sequins on her dress peeling off, littering across the floor.

Elvis hums about tomorrow.

Tomorrow. Tomorrow, she can be anywhere.

She swallows, her hands twitching in her lap, unsure of what to do. Maybe she can ask Bo what is next. *Again*. But the thought makes her chest tighten even more. There is no *next* with Bo. There is only now.

And that's when he speaks. "Wanna get married?"

The question hits her. Knocking the breath right out of her lungs. Her head snaps toward him, heart thudding in her ears. Lace blinks, trying to process if he has given voice to what she thinks he did. Her mind spins, replaying his words in slow motion. She opens her mouth, but nothing comes out. "W-what?" she finally stammers, barely able to hear herself over the noise in her head.

Bo doesn't look at her. His eyes stay forward, his face unmoving, focused, as if he'd simply asked the most casual question in the world.

But she can see the tension in his jaw, the way his fingers flex faintly on the steering wheel. His words hang between them, suspended in the air, waiting to be kissed if it were a lone mistletoe.

"Wanna get married?" he reiterates, a bit softer this time. A dare.

Lace stares at him, her mind swirling with confusion and something else she can't quite name. Her heart races, hands trembling in her lap as she searches his face for some clue, some hint of a joke. But Bo's expression stays steady, unreadable. He isn't grinning, isn't laughing.

He looks—serious.

Is he serious?

They're in Vegas. Of course, this is happening. And Bo is—Bo. Of course, he would do something like this. Of course, he asks her this with a straight face in the middle of Elvis crooning through the speakers.

The truck bellows down the boulevard, weaving in and out of the madness, when Bo jerks the wheel hard to the right as if gripped by some reckless impulse. With a squeal of tires and a lurch, the truck swerves into the middle of the street, sending cars screeching to a halt, horns blaring from all directions. Lace gasps, clutching the door handle. The abrupt stop throws her against the seatbelt. Truck grounding to a halt right between Coin Castle and the Golden Goose. Cars zip past in a furious blur, people shouting.

The entire city becomes increasingly more rattled by Bo's disturbance.

Before she can keep up, Bo is out of the truck. The driver's side door slams shut, and he is already running around the front of the truck, his white linen shirt flaring out in the dry land wind. Lace sits frozen, her heart thundering in her chest, watching him with wide eyes.

Bo yanks her door open. He only stands there, looking at her with those intense brown eyes that always know more than they let on.

Without a word, he drops to one knee in the middle of The Strip. Cars swerve around them as if nothing had changed, but for Lace, everything has changed.

Oh fuck.

"Lace," he says, his voice low, steady. "Marry me."

Her heart skips a beat, unsure if she is hearing things right. But there he is, in the middle of the Strip, down on one knee, looking up at her as if this were the most natural thing in the world. She glances around, half expecting someone to pull them off the street, half expecting the earth to split and swallow them whole.

None of it appears natural. None of it matters.

"I don't have a ring," he gushes, his lips twitching into an all too familiar half-smile. "But I got this." He reaches to his left wrist, pulling off one of his turquoise gemstone bracelets. Bo's hand, rough and calloused, holds it up as if it's something precious. "I know it ain't much," he continues, still kneeling on the rough pavement, cars whizzing by, headlights flashing. "But I ain't got anything better. And I don't need to. Cause you know me, Lace. I'm not a man with fancy things. But I'm here now, and I'm askin', and I'm in love with you."

Her vision blurs, her heart pounding at the never-ending loop of his words, as surreal as the night itself.

A beat-up, rusted pickup truck careens down the Strip, swerving wildly as it barely misses Bo. The driver, a wild-eyed man with a ratty mullet that defies all laws on gravity, leans out of the window, a half-burnt joint jutting from his lips. "Hey! Get the fuck outta the road, you freakin' lunatics!"

The truck bounces violently over the potholes, the tires screeching, and the passenger, a woman draped in feathers and sequins, howls with laughter as she waves a half-eaten burrito out the window.

Lace's hands tremble as she stares at the bracelet. "Bo..." she whispers, barely able to find her voice.

What is she even doing here? The world is spinning out of control again, but this time. Bo is looking at her, waiting for an answer, his hand outstretched with the bracelet.

He doesn't say anything else. He doesn't have to.

His eyes, those piercing eyes, tell her all she needs to know. Lace swallows hard, her fingers twitching at her sides. With little consideration, she takes the bracelet from his hand.

"Yes," she hesitates over the noise of the Strip. "Yes."

Bo's grin spreads across his face. The kind telling her she has made the right choice—in spite of this possibly being the most reckless word she's ever uttered. As he rises to his feet, his smile transforms into something more sincere and vulnerable. Bo leans in, pulling her closer.

The world around them fades as he cups her face in his hands, his thumbs brushing her cheek. "You won't regret this," he proclaims, his breath warm against her lips.

He kisses her—hard, passionate.

A kiss speaking of everything they have been through and everything that lies ahead. Lace melts against him, her heart soaring as the chaos of the Strip continues to swirl around them.

35

The Gospel According To Joan And Michael

Bo climbs back into the driver's seat, his knuckles remaining white from gripping the wheel and bracelet, now draped around her wrist in place of a ring. The grin doesn't leave his face as he revs the engine.

"We're stoppin' at the first damn chapel we see," he states as he wraps his hand over Lace's thigh.

She glances at the bracelet. "You wanna get married now?"

Bo darts a glance at her, his grin softening, tender. "Of fuckin' course. No better time like now."

As they speed down the strip, the bright lights of Vegas burst around them, framing their reckless rush toward the future. The city buzzes with energy—tourists stumbling out of casinos, couples anchored in their grasp, strangers yelling at each other across streets.

"What's my last name gonna be?" Lace asks.

He gives her a sidelong glance, his brow arching in surprise. "You know what? You pick it. We're startin' fresh, so it should be somethin' that fits you."

"You don't want me to have your last name?"

He shrugs, his expression thoughtful. "It's not about me wantin' or not wantin'. It's about you gettin' a say in who you wanna be. We're makin' this life together, and that includes the name."

The Flamingo fades into the rearview, and soon, the iconic sign for the Little White Wedding Chapel comes into view, a spotlight screaming, "Hey, pick me!" Night presses in from all sides, but the chapel blazes against the darkness, a beacon for lost souls. But it's the couple outside that intrigues Lace's eye. They're posing under the garish lights. Two figures caught in the glow, looking straight out of a nightmare—or maybe some twisted, drug-fueled fantasy.

The man wears an oversized Hawaiian shirt, gaudy pink flamingos splashed across his chest, and his sunglasses are enormous and mirrored, reflecting the glow-like alien eyes. He grins wildly, his face slick with sweat, the tips of his greasy hair poking out from under a cowboy hat far too large for his head. He clamps down on a Polaroid camera, snapping shots as if he's documenting the end of the world.

Beside him, the woman is a spectacle of her own. Her yellow hair, teased into a rat's nest, spills down her shoulders. She's wearing a hot pink mini dress, so tight it looks painted on, and her lipstick smears as if she's been sloppily kissing someone—or maybe something—far too long. Her eyes are wide, pupils blown out. Without a doubt, she's riding the wave of something substantial, something illegal.

She twirls in front of the chapel, kicking her platform heels, laughing into the neon sky. Queen of this cracked, glittering wasteland.

The bold white lettering beneath the heart immortalizes Joan Collins and Michael Jordan, their names glowing as if to say, "if it's good enough for them, it's good enough for you." Lace stares at it, half-expecting a punchline to a dirty joke that hasn't landed yet.

The white picket fence curves into delicate heart shapes, illuminated by the pink and yellow lights. The gold crown marquee over the entrance shimmers under the neon as if promising a royal affair, though the chipped paint tells a different story. Off to the side, a massive Elvis figure towers high, spotlighted by a single pink neon tube, making his white jumpsuit glow as if he were some apparition.

Well, he might as well be now.

He's mid-swing with his guitar, frozen in time, his painted grin wide and mocking. The sign beside him reads "Walk Thru Wedding Chapel," the letters curling and twisting in a kitschy, exaggerated style as if marriage is purely another item on the Vegas checklist.

Bo makes a sharp turn right, heading toward the back of the chapel straight under the archway of *The World Famous Little White Chapel Tunnel of Love*, creeping along as they approach a painted pink Cadillac park's dead center. Its license plate reads "4 Elvis."

Lace straightens in her seat, her eyes widening as they roll forward. The ceiling above them swirls in a heavenly scene—a soft moon tucked into midnight blue skies, cherubs floating in the clouds, their round faces gleeful, golden curls framing their chubby cheeks. Scripted letters curve along the mural, proclaiming in bright white, "I Love You... I Need You."

"We really doin' this?" she asks, voice half-excited, half-unbelieving.

Bo gleams, squeezing Lace's thigh. "Fuck yeah."

As Bo puts the truck in park next to a gleaming Cadillac, Lace swings open the door. Her heels hit the pavement, landing squarely on a heart painted on the ground, bold letters reading, "I Thank God He Gave Me to You!" She glances down, momentarily taken aback by the sentiment.

Without a word, he comes up behind Lace, scooping her in his arms, cradling her once more as a bride on her way to the altar.

I am a bride-to-be.

She lets out a startled laugh, her heart fluttering as she wraps her arms around his neck.

As if the moment demands it, Bo leans in and kisses her, deep and passionate, the world outside fading away. Lace melts against him, surrendering to the wild thrill of it all.

With that, he strides through the arched door into the chapel, their laughter echoing off the walls, lined with cheesy decorations and unfortunate decisions.

36

I'll Take "Who Is Bo Walker?" for 500

A world plucked directly from a colorful fantasy immediately surrounds them as they enter the Little White Chapel. The lobby is snug but bursting with character, a carnival of kitsch.

Utterly overbearing scents of roses and something a smidge more artificial, reminiscent of plastic bouquets, violates their noses. To the right, a plush velvet couch sits. Its deep red fabric, worn but inviting, adorned with oversized heart-shaped pillows. Nearby, a record player sits atop a white wooden table, spinning "Forever Young" by Alphaville, echoing softly through the room.

An array of glittering trinkets on the table sparkle under the dim light—a collection of novelty wedding figurines, a few decorative ceramic lovebirds, and a gold-plated bell that reads, "Ring for a Kiss."

Lace's eyes widen as she takes in the scene. To the left, the wall displays framed photographs of couples who have married in this very chapel, inviting newcomers to leave their mark in this whimsical space.

The receptionist appears out of thin air. Dressed as a vintage Cupid, she is a vivid explosion of color—a riot of pinks, reds, and whites almost pulsating with energy. A nametag pinned to her frilly short skirt reads, "Lady Love Nugget." Her hair is a soft pastel pink, falling in waves shimmering with glitter, covered with tiny heart-shaped clips. On the one hand, she twirls a fake bow and arrow, the other gesturing wildly as if she were conducting a symphony of love, her enthusiasm contagious.

"Welcome, lovebirds!" she chirps, her voice a melodic trill bouncing off the walls. "You've come to seal your fate in the name of love, haven't you?"

Bo leans casually against the credenza, his trademark smirk appearing on his lips as he plays along. "Well, it looks like we've been struck by Cupid's arrow. What can you do for us?"

Lady Love Nugget's eyes sparkle with delight. "Oh, darlin', you've come to the right place! Here at the Little White Chapel, we specialize in spontaneous romance!" She points her bow dramatically at Bo and shoots a hot pink arrow, landing squarely in his chest. "Gotcha!" She giggles.

Lace stifles a laugh.

"So, what's next? We just sign on the dotted line, or do I gotta do a little dance first?" Bo cocks his head.

She spins around, gathering an assortment of glittering forms decorated with doodles of cherubs and hearts. "Just a bit of fun before you say I do!" She pulls out a plastic ring, "how about a complimentary ring for the occasion? It's practically begging to be worn."

Bo chuckles under his breath, shaking his head as Lace grips the gaudy plastic ring. The thing is ridiculous, something a kid would find in a quarter machine.

"Practically beggin', huh?" he says, crossing his arms, his smirk tugging higher. "Guess we can't say no to that kind of persuasion."

Lace slips the sparkling plastic ring onto her left hand, holding both out for him to admire. "Well? What do you think?" she asks, wiggling her fingers.

Bo reaches out, taking her hands in his. He inspects them as if he's making an important decision. "I think," he says gently, "you're about two steps away from lookin' like you robbed a gift shop."

Lace snorts, yanking her hands back, but she's smiling now, "C'mon, it's festive. You only get hitched once, right?"

With a flourish, Lace picks up the pen, her heart thumping as she signs her name. She hands the pen to Bo, who signs his name next to hers as Bo Walker.

Walker. Huh.

Lady Love Nugget claps her hands, practically bouncing in place. "Now. We need to get you in a wedding dress!"

37

I Do?

An illusion, dripping with velvet and gold. A mirage pulling from the strangest corner of Lace's mind. Lace steps forward, her bare feet sinking into the plush crimson carpet, muffling the path before her. Each step stretches into eternity, the soft rug brushing against her soles, the world around her tapering off, every detail magnified.

Her gown features a dramatic high neckline adorned with delicate lace, and sleeves flowing gracefully down the arms full of intricate patterns. A fitted bodice flaring into a flowing, layered skirt. Ornate lace detailing and sparkling beading reflect in the right light.

Halfway down the aisle, Lady Love Nugget rushes up to her, stopping before Lace, presenting a single red rose with a theatrical flourish. She takes the rose, her fingers brushing the soft petals. Clutching the flower as her makeshift bouquet, the sweetness of the moment strangely grounding her.

Light pours from crystal chandeliers, their glinting pendants sending scattered rainbows across the mirrored walls. Large gilded frames hang at even intervals, reflecting pieces of the scene—each mirror capturing a glimpse of red velvet, faux flowers, and Lace herself, creating an infinite loop of her image. A garish mural paints the back wall—rolling fields of lavender beneath an impossibly blue sky, creating an absurd backdrop which could be a child's idea of paradise.

Plastic floral arrangements sit on tall urns in each corner, the bright colors almost blinding under the chandelier light, their petals too perfect, too glossy, waxy facsimiles of the real thing.

Bo's waiting at the end, his pale blue tux just this side of ridiculous. Lace takes him in, her gaze drifting over the shiny fabric, the crooked bowtie.

It's almost laughable—but for some reason, he makes it work.

He makes it charming.

The cowboy hat persistently sits on his head, high enough to show his entire face. Lace pictures Bo with a sewing needle in hand, his jaw clenched as he threads it through his scalp, fastening the cowboy hat to his head forever, as though he'd fall apart without it.

He grins at her as she gets closer. His fingers are tapping a rhythm against his leg, each tap distinct. Ticking of a clock marking the seconds as they drag by—nervous or excited, she can't tell.

She sees a man sitting alone in one of the red velvet chairs. He slouches, his eyes obscured by tinted aviators, the lenses reflecting distorted images of the room. His skin glistens with a layer of sweat, each droplet making a soft plopping sound as it hits the floor. Muttering to himself, the words too soft to make out. His fingers twist in strange, almost ritualistic movements, each twist and curl exaggerated in the stretched-out time of the moment. Lace can't tell if he's blessing them or casting some kind of hex.

Elvis stands at the altar covered in sequins, swaying from the heat or whatever he's taken to keep his hips that loose. His voice—soft, crooning, with the languid, deliberate tempo of a Vegas Elvis—floats over the room, the words stretching out, echoing in her ears as if they were coming from underwater.

"Welcome y'all," he says, almost hypnotic as if moving through molasses.

"Please Love Me Forever" by Bobby Vinton spins on the record player. The record praying to be put down after being played a thousand times before, each note warbling as if struggling to break free from the grooves of the vinyl. Lace takes a breath, her chest rising and falling. She looks at Bo, and the corners of her mouth twitch as he gives her a wink.

She steps closer, her fingers brushing against the fabric of her dress, feeling every texture, every crease as if for the first time. The world narrows down to this moment—the record spinning, Elvis swaying, Bo waiting, the stranger muttering, and the smell of roses. It all drags on, suspended in time, moving through a dream, and Lace isn't sure if she wants to wake up or stay here forever.

Lace reaches the altar, and Bo's smile softens, his eyes meeting hers with warmth, making her heart skip. He takes her hand gently, his fingers wrapping around hers in a comforting squeeze.

"You look beautiful, darlin'," he whispers, his voice low and intimate, meant only for her. Lace blushes, her heart swelling as she looks up at him.

Elvis is already off on some tangent, his words drifting in and out of coherence. "Love is like... like a rhinestone, y'know? Shiny, tough, but you gotta keep polishing it..." he says, his hands gesturing wildly, his eyes half-closed as if channeling some divine wisdom. Lace can't help but stifle a giggle, her eyes flicking up to Bo's.

She leans closer, whispering, "Who is that strange man sitting in front of Lady Love Nugget?" She nods subtly toward the slouched man with tinted aviators.

Bo glances over. "We needed a witness, baby," he says, leaning in conspiratorially. "Grabbed him off the street, slipped him a five-dollar bill. Figured he'd do just fine." Lace bites her lip to keep from laughing, shaking her head.

Elvis clears his throat dramatically, bringing their attention back to him. "Now, if y'all are ready to make history here today..." He drawls, his voice filled with the sincerity of a man who has performed this ceremony two thousand times. Elvis smiles broadly, raising his hand. "Let's hear some vows. Sir, why don't you start us off?"

Bo takes a deep breath, his eyes never leaving Lace's.

He gives her hand a reassuring squeeze.

"I reckon this here is about as true as I ever felt. Lace, darlin', when I look at you, I see every sunset I ever watched on the range, every morning mist that rolled in over the mountains. I see the kind of freedom I've been chasing my whole life but never knew had a name until I met you. You make me wanna pull my hat off and stay a while, make me wanna be a better man."

"You got that kind of fire that lights up the darkest nights. You're the wild and the gentle, the storm and the calm after. I wanna spend my days riding beside you, my nights holding you close."

"I'll love you like the land loves the sky—forever reaching, never letting go, even when it seems like they're miles in between. I swear on every star over the desert, on every trail I've wandered, that I'll love you—through dust storms, dead ends, and whatever else the world throws at us. It's just you and me, rosebud, against the wind. And I wouldn't have it any other way."

Lace's heart swells, the words sinking deep into the roots of her soul. She opens her mouth to speak, but before she can muster a response, Lady Love Nugget, sitting in the audience, sobs loudly.

Elvis turns to him, his expression impressed. "Well, hot damn, son! Looks like you've been 'round this block before, ain'tcha?" He turns to Lace, "And now you, baby."

She takes a shaky breath, her eyes clinging desperately to Bo's. "Bo," she begins, her voice cracking under all she's kept buried. "I don't know what the future looks like for us. I don't know if we'll make it through the rough parts. But I swear to you, I'll love you with every broken piece of me. I'll be there, even when it's hard, even if it falls apart. You're the only one who's ever made me feel like I'm not just... disappearing. You make me feel like I'm finally here, like I matter. And I promise you'll always have me no matter where you go or what you do. I love you."

Her voice breaks, a tear slipping free as she forces a smile, fragile but real.

Elvis grins, turning to Bo with an unmistakable twinkle in his eye. "Well now, Bo, do you take this fine-lookin' gal to be your lawfully wedded wife? To hold 'er close, cherish 'er sweet, and love 'er true, whether you're high-rollin' in the casino or just kickin' up dust in the desert? From now 'til the lights dim and the glitz is gone, hound dog?"

Bo locks his eyes on Lace's, his smile warm and tender. He gives her hand a gentle squeeze and nods. "I do, baby. More than anything," he says.

Elvis gives a little wink and turns his gaze to Lace, his voice smooth as ever. "And how 'bout you, sunshine? Do you take this here, cowboy, to be your husband? To ride by his side through thick and thin, through the bright lights of the Strip and the dusty trails, all the way down the line 'til the road runs out, sugar?"

Lace swallows, her eyes fixed on Bo's. She takes a deep breath, her voice barely above a whisper. "I do," she says, her head and heart on opposing sides.

Elvis claps his hands together, flashing his signature grin. "Well, ain't that just the sweetest thing I ever did see!" He raises his hands high, his voice echoing with a flair of showmanship. "By the power vested in me by this here chapel, the great state of Nevada, and yours truly, the King of Rock 'n' Roll, I now pronounce y'all husband and wife. Bo, go on and kiss your bride!"

Bo grabs Lace's waist, leaning in, his lips brushing against Lace's as he cups her cheek gently. The kiss is soft and lingering. Lady Love Nugget stands up from her seat, clapping her hands together, tears streaming down her cheeks as she cheers for them. The man fumbles with a needle, his hands shaking as he tries to tie a rubber band tight around his bicep with his teeth, oblivious to the ceremony.

A loud crash echoes through the chapel as one of the gilded columns topples over, sending the fake ivy and colorful bouquets across the floor. The chandelier above sways dangerously, its crystals clinking together.

Lace pulls back from Bo, her eyes widening in shock as Elvis stumbles backward, his sequined cape snaring on a chair.

The strange man barely reacts, remaining *focused* on his task, but Lady Love Nugget shrieks, firing an accidental arrow. The arrow flies across the room, hitting its mark on the side of Elvis's temple, sending him crashing into the lavender mural.

With a deep breath, Bo pulls her close again, and they kiss—this time not exclusively for show but as a promise to each other.

38

Filthy Liar

Hand in hand, they step out of the chapel, a shared smile lingering between them. Nothing but smitten. Bo lifts Lace's hand to his lips to press a soft kiss on her knuckles. "Didn't think I'd be the marrying kind," Bo says, a chuckle in his voice, his eyes crinkling at the corners as he looks at her.

"Guess I must've changed your mind," Lace replies, her voice teasing but heart lighter than it's ever been. She never thought she'd be here, not in a million different lifetimes. And yet, here she is, married.

The door to the chapel bursts open behind them, and Lady Love Nugget comes rushing out, her hair bobbing with each hurried step. "Wait! Wait just a minute!" She calls, her voice full of exaggerated urgency as if she were conducting a love emergency. Bo and Lace turn, confusion written on their faces.

Lady Love Nugget's cheeks flush, her pastel pink hair shimmering with glitter as she waves a clipboard in the air as if it were Cupid's scepter, her other hand clinging to the twirling plastic bow. "It's—it's about your marriage certificate," she pants, looking between them, her expression a mix of regret and awkwardness. "According to public records... well, sugarplums, it's just not valid."

"What?" Bo's voice drops, his hand instinctively tightening around Lace's.

Lady Love Nugget bites her lip, her eyes wide with exaggerated sympathy as she looks at Bo. "It's just that... darlin', you're already married. Right here in the system, plain as glitter on a Cupid's bow." She taps the clipboard for emphasis, her gaze apologetic. "I'm afraid that means this one can't be official."

Lace's heart comes to a screeching halt, her eyes widening as she looks at Bo. "Already married?" she whispers, the words barely making it past her lips.

Are you fuckin' kidding me?

Lace blinks, her heart pounding, a mix of emotions washing over her—anger, fear, disbelief. She steps back, pulling her hand free from Bo's grasp.

"Bo, what is this?" she demands, her voice trembling. Lady Love Nugget stands awkwardly to the side. She twirls her bow absentmindedly, clearly regretting her part in this revelation.

Bo takes a quick breath, his eyes desperate as they lock onto Lace's. "It's not what you think. I was married a long time ago, but it's over. I thought it was all done. I didn't know it was still..."

Lace shakes her head, taking another step back. "How could you not know?" she whispers, her voice breaking.

The dreamlike haze of the day shatters, replaced by a cold, hard reality. Her chest tight, her stomach in knots. "How could you bring me here? Are you fuckin' serious?"

Bo stretches for her, his grip firm as he tries to pull her back, his voice urgent. "Lace, come on. Let's get out of here. We'll talk about this again at the motel. Please, rosebud." He tries to guide her away, his eyes pleading, but she yanks her hand free, her eyes filling with tears. "Lace, please, let me explain. I love you. This doesn't change that."

But Lace turns away, her heart aching, her vision blurring with tears. "It changes everything, Bo," she cracks. She turns and walks away, her feet carrying her across the pavement—the world around her spinning out of control. *What's fuckin' new?*

Bo stands there, watching her go. But he takes a deep breath, jogging after her, catching up quickly, his hand trying to find hers. "Lace, please," he says, his voice soft but urgent. "Come with me. Let's just get back to the car. Get out of here. We can talk about this back at the motel."

Lace hesitates, her eyes brimming with tears, but the pleading look in Bo's eyes locks her in place. After a long pause, she nods, her shoulders slumping in exhaustion. "Fine," she whispers.

As they reach the car, Lady Love Nugget comes rushing over again. "Oh, lovebirds! Hold up a moment!" she calls, her voice still ringing a melodic trill, her clipboard clutched tightly to her chest.

Bo sighs as he whips around to face her. "What now? Spit it out."

She gives them both a broad, sympathetic smile, "Now, don't you two fret too much! If you, cowboy, just get yourself a proper divorce, you can come right back here, and we can do this all over again! Better and shinier, I promise! I mean, love deserves a proper celebration, don't you think?"

Bo brushes past Lady Love Nugget to the car door.

Lace stares, her emotions too tangled to find words, her heart forever heavy. Lady Love Nugget winks at her as if to say it'll all work out and spins around, skipping back toward the chapel, her wings fluttering.

39

All's Fair In Love and War

he Tattered Tent Inn's attached diner sits in a quiet corner, bathed in the low, muted glow of a few stained-glass lamps. Lace and Bo are already sitting in one of the green vinyl booths, still in their wedding attire—Lace in her crumpled white dress and Bo in his pale blue tuxedo, the brim of his hat casting a shadow over his eyes. Years of use have thoroughly torn the cushion beneath them. It's a puny place, almost timeless, that hasn't changed in decades.

The warm but dim light gives the whole nine yards a honeyed hue—the counter lined with worn stools, each topped with cracked brown leather, and the bleak wooden booths dividing the diner into cozy pockets of privacy. Simple photographs and a couple of dusty vintage signs cover the walls. A lone ceiling fan spins lazily above, its chain clicking every so often, the only sound breaking the quiet hum of the place.

Bo leans back, his arm resting along the back of the booth, but there's no comfort in his posture. His eyes are on Lace, desperate to gauge her feelings, but all he finds is the icy wall she's put up between them. She stares at the worn tabletop, tracing one of the many scratches carved into its surface with her fingers.

The waitress—a woman in her fifties with a weary smile and a nametag reading "Shirley"—walks over, pad in hand. Her eyes widen as she takes in their attire, her smile brightening. "Oh my goodness, y'all just got married, didn't ya?" she exclaims, her voice carrying the warmth of someone who's worked long hours but continues to find time for kindness. "What'll it be? It's on the house!"

Bo glances at Lace, waiting for her to say something, but she only shrugs. Her eyes remain downcast. Shirley's words are a punch to the gut, reminding her of what they've lost, what *Lace* lost.

He clears his throat, offering Shirley a smile. "Two coffees, honey. And maybe a couple of slices of that pie," he says, flicking his hand toward the glass case on the counter.

Shirley nods, jotting it down. "Comin' right up," she says, and with a practiced spin, she heads back to the counter.

Bo turns his attention back to Lace. He shifts closer, his voice lowering, dripping with an almost deliberate softness. "Rosebud—" he says, his fingers brushing against hers as if trying to reestablish their connection.

Lace finally looks up at him, her eyes wet, the hurt plain on her face. "Tell me about her, Bo. Your ex. How old was she?" She takes a deep breath, her gaze hardening. "Was she my age?"

Bo's thumb moves in tight circles over her knuckles, his eyes narrowing. He hesitates and leans in, his voice dropping to a whisper, edged with frustration. "You should be grateful you have someone who sees past the ranch. Someone willing to fight for you. I'm what you've got, and that's more than you'd get from anyone else. You want a life, you want something real? It's with me, or it's nothing."

Lace's voice trembles, fury and heartbreak tangled together as she stares him down. "This whole thing has been some kind of sick, twisted emotional whiplash! One minute, you're here, and the next, you're a million miles away. You're damn near fifty, and what do you have to show for it? A mysterious so-called wife, no kids—hell, I don't even know if that's true 'cause you never tell me a goddamn thing about yourself!" Lace blinks, tears slipping down her cheeks.

Lace's voice shakes, raw and furious. "You were at the ranch too, Bo. That's where we fucking met—don't you get that? What the fuck were you even doing there in the first place? How many times had you fucked one of my friends before I showed up? Petal. For sure, Trish. Hell, probably Madam Lottie while we're at it! You think you can just stroll in, belt buckle shining like you're some fuckin' saint, and judge me? Judge the same fuckin' person you keep coming back to?"

Bo's jaw clenches, his hand squeezing hers hard enough to hurt. He leans in closer. "Don't put that on me, Lace. You think I came there looking for someone like you? You were just a girl in a line of faces, just another pretty thing at the ranch. I didn't make you choose this. Hell, I didn't even notice you at first. You're the one who couldn't stay away, who kept coming back like I was some kind of *goddamn salvation*. So don't act like I'm the one who turned this into something it wasn't."

Lace's voice rises, trembling with anger as she snatches her hand from Bo's grasp. "You think you're better than me, Bo? Just because you weren't wearing a dress and heels when we met?" Her eyes are burning, the hurt behind them turning to fury. "Well, fuck you for thinking you get to judge me while you're sittin' here like you're above it all."

Bo's knuckles go white. "I ain't judging you, Lace, but if you're so fuckin' ashamed of where we met, maybe you should think about why you stayed."

"Stayed?" Lace's voice cracks like a whip. "Stayed! You think I had a choice? What was I supposed to do, huh? Just walk out the door and find some neat little nine-to-five? Don't you understand? You're supposed to be my home now." Her voice is louder now, drawing glances from the one other diner. "Not all of us get to ride off and play cowboy when life gets too fuckin' complicated."

Bo's eyes flash dangerously, his voice a low growl. "You could've left any time. If you're so hell-bent on blaming someone for the way things turned out, then maybe you should take a good, long look in the mirror."

Lace's face pales, flushing with fiery rage. "You son of a bitch," she spits, sliding out of the booth. She shoves the table aside, the silverware rattling as she storms toward the exit. A silver star bell loudly rings as she pushes open the door.

Shirley steps back to the table, lugging two steaming cups of coffee. Her eyes follow Lace, who's stomping toward the open expanse.

She looks down at Bo. "You better go get her."

Bo tosses a few crumpled bills onto the table and shoves past Shirley, his long strides eating up the distance between him and Lace as he bursts out of the diner.

★

"Don't you walk away from me," he shouts, voice cracking with something desperate, almost pleading. Almost. "You think you're gonna just run off and pretend like none of this ever happened?"

Lace whirls around, her hair flying as a whip, eyes glistening. "Maybe I am!" she screams back. "Maybe it'd be better than sittin' here, lettin' you tear me apart every time you open your stupid fuckin' mouth!" Lace continues to stride past the motel into the nearby graveyard.

Bo trails behind her, his expression hardening. "You're so quick to blame me for everything, but you're the one who keeps runnin'. You're the one who doesn't know what the hell you want."

"I wanted you!" Her words suspend above them, raw and jagged. "I wanted you to be different, but you're just like the rest of them. All your pretty words, your bullshit promises—you never meant a goddamn thing!"

Bo's face contorts, anger twisting. "You don't know what you're talkin' about."

"You don't get it, do you?" she cries, her voice splintering. "I wanted you to be different, Bo. I needed you to be different. Not like all the others who just looked at me and saw... saw something to use." Her voice cracks, and she wipes at her eyes furiously as if frustrated with herself for breaking down.

Bo's expression falters, a flicker of something softer crossing his face. "Lace, don't—" he starts, but she cuts him off.

"No, you don't get to talk now," she snaps, her chest heaving. "You looked at me like I was just... something to hold on to until you got bored. But I needed you to see me—really see me—for who I am, not just what you could take. I wanted you to want me for more than what I can give you."

Her knees threaten to buckle as the truth spills out, and she takes a step back, her arms wrapping around herself, trying to hold her insides together. "I know I'm not perfect, Bo. I know I'm a mess. I'm scared and don't know how to be loved." Her voice drops to a whisper, almost a plea. "But just 'cause I've learned to live on little doesn't mean my worth is measured in scraps."

Bo's throat tightens as he steps toward her, his hand reaching out instinctively. "I never said that—Lace, I—"

"Don't," she chokes out, stumbling back another step, her eyes brimming with tears now flowing freely down her cheeks. "Don't tell me you care, not when you never bothered to look past the ranch." Her voice shakes, laced with bitterness and heartbreak. "I wasn't some girl to pick up, Bo. I'm not just a body you can crawl into when you're lonely. I wanted you to slowly learn every curve instead of rushing to the finish line." She trembles as she speaks, every inch of her being laid bare, leaving her vulnerable. "I wanted more," she admits, her voice dropping to a fragile whisper. "I wanted to be enough for you to love me. For you to see something worth saving. But you didn't. You just—didn't."

Bo's eyes widen, "That's not fair, Lace. You're not givin' me a chance—"

"A chance?" Lace's voice rises, breaking on the last word. "How many chances have I given you to be different, Bo? But every time I try to open up, you push me back into the same damn box everyone else puts me in." Her voice falters, the last of her strength crumbling. "I can't do it anymore. I can't keep letting you hurt me."

A slight gust of wind sweeps across the open land, kicking up dust. It grabs ahold of Bo's cowboy hat, knocking it off his head and sending it tumbling across the cracked dirt.

It lands near Lace's feet, and she stares at it as the hat rolls to a stop, the inside facing up. Her gaze locks on the ten tally marks scratched into the lining. Deep and rough carvings mark each one. A scar.

She crouches down and picks up the hat, her fingers trembling as she stares at the crude etchings. Lace lifts her head with great care, eyes glistening with anger.

"What are these? What the fuck do these marks mean, Bo?" She demands.

He doesn't answer right away. His mouth opens, his jaw working as if struggling to find the right words. But when he speaks, it's barely a whisper, his eyes refusing to meet hers.

"You know," he says, the words almost getting lost in the wind.

Lace's hand stiffens around the hat's brim, her heart sinking. "Tell me," she chokes out, her voice shaking with a desperate need for him to deny what she already suspects. "Say it, Bo. Just fuckin' say it."

But he merely stands there, his face hollowed out by the gambler's wasteland, silence stretching between them as a chasm. And in that moment, Lace knows—deep down. She's always known—what those marks mean. What they count.

I knew it. I fuckin' knew it. Little scratches, each one a record of a girl he's used and tossed aside. I'm just another number to him, another notch on a brim that holds his twisted sense of pride.

Lace drops the hat like it's crawling with disease.

She takes one last shuddering breath. Turning and stumbling toward the open desert, her steps uneven and hurried as if trying to outrun the pain. "Lace, don't go!" Bo shouts after her, his voice desperate, but she keeps moving, her sobs echoing in the night.

"I wanted that person to be *you*," she whispers as she walks away, her heart breaking with each step.

40

Mine.

'm dragging myself through the dust, stumbling over my feet, like the whole world's pulling me down into the dirt. The sky's bruised and fading, and I'm this tiny, worthless thing caught in the middle, shrinking smaller with each step. There's a lump in my throat so thick I can't swallow it down, and Bo's voice is there, circling in my head like a vulture. *"You know."* Like that's supposed to explain everything! Like I'm supposed just to accept that the truth was always right in front of me. I wasn't too stupid not to see it. I actively chose to ignore it.

The motel is behind me now, a flicker of neon in the distance, barely a pinprick of light on the outer limits. I keep moving forward because stopping would mean feeling it all—the pieces of what's breaking inside me.

So I keep stumbling over rocks and dirt, my feet aching with each step. The desert stretches forever like it's trying to devour me whole.

And maybe that's what I want—maybe I want to disappear out here, let the sand and wind scrape away the pieces of me that hurt, the pieces I've never known what to do with. It's like my body's already given up, already decided there's nothing worth fighting for.

But the thoughts keep coming, crashing like a wave that knocks my breath out of my chest. Out here, there's no noise to drown out the truth, no distractions to keep me from seeing what's staring me in the face. I'm nothing more than a body that's been used up and discarded. That's all I've ever been. I reach down to yank off the bracelet and ring, chucking it as far as I can into the darkness.

I keep pushing forward, my legs barely hoisting me up anymore. A sharp rock pinches at my foot.

I have to keep moving.

If I stop now, I'll sink into the ground and never get back up.

The parched wilderness is vast and unforgiving, stretching out in all directions, an endless reminder of how tiny I am. How insignificant it all is. The sky above me pulsates with heat lighting, and a chill is setting in, but I keep walking because there's nothing else I know how to do. I wanted so badly for Bo to be different. I needed him to see something in me that wasn't only skin-deep, to look at me like I was worth loving and not just touching.

But he didn't.

He never did.

I was just another pretty face, another warm body. I was never Lace to him, not really—just a girl he could lose himself in until the lights went out. Until the thrill was gone.

And I let him. God, I let him.

But it was never about me. It was never about anything more than what I could give or do to make him hang around a little longer.

Pathetic.

The wind surrounds me, stinging my skin and blowing through my hair.

I stumble over the hem of the stupid dress, nearly going face-first into the dirt. The silky fabric tangles around my legs like it's trying to drag me down.

I finally snap. "God fuckin' damn it!" I scream into the night, my voice echoing back at me from the emptiness.

I claw at the dress, yanking and tearing at the fabric with trembling hands. It's suffocating me, pulling me down with every step, and I can't stand it for another second.

I grab the neckline and rip it down the middle. The dress falls to the floor in a crumpled mess of white silk streaked with dirt, leaving me standing in nothing but pink briefs. The wrong day of the week stamped across my backside.

Tuesday. Actually, I don't even know what fuckin' day it is.

The brisk night air bites at my skin. I shiver, the desert's chill sinking into me as I drop to my knees. My hands hit the ground hard, the rough rock scraping against my palms, and I let out a ragged sob. I can't stop it—don't even try to anymore. I fall forward, curling up on the cold earth, pressing my forehead to the dirt like it's the only solid thing left in this godforsaken place.

The tears come hard and blistering, pouring out of me in broken cries that tear at my throat. I claw at the ground, my fingers digging into the dry, cracked earth as if I could hold on to something.

Anything. But there's nothing here.

There's only emptiness, stretching on and on, just like the feeling I can't escape in my chest.

I'm sobbing so hard now, choking on nothing but my thoughts, my body shaking with the effort of trying to let go of a hurt that's been living inside me for as long as I can remember.

The wind kicks up around me, stinging my exposed skin, carrying my cries off into the night. I press my forehead deeper to the ground, my tears mixing with the dust, my body sinking into the earth as if it's the only place to take me now. The devil didn't bother takin' me. He just lit me up with all this want and left me nowhere to pour it.

I stay there, curled up and shaking, letting the lawless sands swallow my sobs whole because there's no one else left to hear them.

There never was.

41

stumble back to the motel, each step as if I'm dragging the weight of a thousand failures behind me. The neon sign buzzes louder with each inch closer, that sickly yellow glow flickering above me like it's struggling just as hard to stay alive. But I keep moving, although each step drains any remaining strength. I don't know what else to do. There's nowhere else to go.

Consequently, I see the parking lot, and when I see that empty space—it's like someone punched me in the gut.

No.

Shot in the chest.

Left for dead.

I stop. The breath knocked out of me, my whole body sagging.

His car's gone. It's just a patch of bare asphalt but to me. It has all been erased. Like the ground's been yanked out from under me, and I'm free-falling into some dark pit with no end. I keep walking, even though my legs are shaking, even though my lungs burn with each ragged breath I take. I stumble closer to the door, and it's wide open, swinging on its rusty hinges, letting the night crawl inside just to die. It sways back and forth with each gust as if mocking me, taunting me with the truth.

The whole damn place a cruel joke. The universe is in on something, and I'm just now laughing at the punchline.

My body steps over the threshold, shuddering as I lean against the doorframe for support. My fingers dig into the wood, gripping tight as if trying to keep myself from crumbling. But there's nothing to restrain me. There's no sign of him, no trace of his life left behind.

The room is just—empty.

Still, it's like he vanished into thin air and slipped out of my life as easily as he came in, leaving nothing but the coldness already filling the space where he used to be. The bed is a mess, the sheets twisted and tangled. They're cold to the touch when I graze them. As if he was never here at all. There's nothing left behind—nothing that smells like him, nothing that proves he was real, that any of this was real.

Just emptiness. Just silence so loud it presses against my ears, against my chest, squeezing tighter and tighter until I can barely breathe.

I see my bag thrown open on the floor, its contents scattered. Panic rises as I drop to my knees, my hands trembling as I reach for it. I scramble through the mess—clothes, makeup, Trish's Polaroid camera—but the cash envelope is gone. He took it. Every last bit of it. Every dollar I'd saved, every bit of hope I had for starting over, gone. My throat tightens, and my vision blurs as the realization settles in, heavy and suffocating.

It wasn't much—Madam Lottie took most of it. But it was my life savings. My literal life's work.

He stole my chance.

My escape.

The betrayal crashes over me.

I sink to the floor slowly, my back pressing against the bed, and I draw my knees up to my chest. It's like time is stretching. Like I'm caught in some endless loop where seconds are drawn out into minutes and minutes into hours. The tears gather again, blurring my vision, and I try to fight them back, try to swallow down the sobs that are clawing their way up my throat, but it's no use. It's like wrangling back a flood with nothing but my bare hands.

I bury my face against my knees, my arms wrapped tight around myself in a futile attempt to hold the pieces together. Like I can keep myself from fully unraveling. But I'm falling apart, piece by piece, and I can't stop it. The sobs tear out of me, harsh and ragged, my body shaking with the force of it.

Maybe love isn't soft or kind. Maybe it's just the prettiest lie we can tell ourselves to survive the nights we're too scared to be alone.

The wind blows through the open door, and I let it. I let the cold seep in, let it sting my skin because at least it's something. I curl up tighter, my body trembling as the tears keep coming.

The motel room closes in on me, the walls pressing as the first light breaks over the horizon, and I ask if this is all I'll ever be—just a girl sitting alone in a cheap room, crying over someone who was never mine.

I ask if I'll ever find a way to be more than this. If I'll ever find a way to be seen for who I am and not just for what I can give.

Because right now, all I feel is emptiness.

The ache in my chest that won't go away, the cold that's seeped into my bones. It seems like the harder I try to be someone worth latching onto, the more I turn into someone you can't keep your grip on. I'm the kind of woman you think you want—until you have to keep.

Now, I'm left with nothing but the sound of my sobs and the chill of the wind creeping through the open door.

And I'm still here, waiting for someone who will never return.

42

wo weeks later, I'm standing on the side of a lonely highway with just my duffle bag, my thumb outstretched as cars whiz by, their taillights disappearing into the end of the trail. I don't know where I am anymore. Whenever I manage a ride, they ask where I'm heading. I tell them it doesn't matter where they take me. I always end up somewhere else, somewhere new, like the road keeps spitting me out wherever it feels like, just to watch me stumble.

The sky is an endless stretch of blue, the kind of blue that's too bright—too harsh, like it has no business existing when everything inside me is bruised and aching. The sun beats relentlessly and sweat trickles down my back, sticking my shirt to my skin.

My legs are tired, my feet sore from walking miles and miles, and my body hollow, worn out. Nothing left but the bones hanging on for dear life.

I watch the cars squinting against the glare, and I think about if any of them see me. If anyone sees the girl on the side of the highway, her torn shorts and hair tangled in the wind. I contemplate if they see the desperation in my eyes, the hope that someone will stop and be kind. But they keep driving, speeding past me, leaving nothing but dust in their wake.

The sun sinks lower in the sky, and I keep my thumb out, my feet planted firmly in the gravel. The cars pass one by one, and I don't let myself cry.

Not anymore.

I only embrace the numbness, which I've realized just comes with the curse of being a woman. A pickup truck slows down, gravel crunching beneath the tires as it pulls off to the side. I take a deep breath, wiping the sweat from my forehead, pick up my bag, and walk toward it. The driver leans out, a man with an angry face and a pensive stare. I muster a smile, hoping it's enough to convince him. He asks where I'm headed, and I tell him nowhere in particular.

He nods and gestures for me to hop in. I climb into the passenger seat, the worn leather warm beneath me, and close the door. He shifts the truck back into gear, and we roll down the highway, the wind whipping through the open windows, carrying back some of the dust and dirt to its rightful owner.

I lean back, watching the world blur by, grateful for the distance between Vegas and me inch further apart.

Five minutes into the drive, the man glances at me, his eyes lingering just a little too long. His lips curl into a crooked smile, showing yellowed, uneven teeth. The truck smells like stale cigarettes and sweat, and his voice grates against my ears like gravel when he finally speaks, "So, girl, how much for a blowjob?"

My stomach turns, but I don't flinch. I don't bother looking at him. I just stare out the window, watching the mountains blur by, and I can sense the hole burning in my side, waiting.

I sigh, a slow, tired exhale, and for a second, I consider telling him to fuck off. Consider opening the door and throwing myself out of this truck just to get away from him.

But I don't. I need the money.

And men like him, they'll always pay. I turn to look at him, my face expressionless, my voice hollow. "Twenty bucks," I say, and he grins, a sick, satisfied grin that makes my skin crawl. He pulls off to the side, the truck coming to a stop with a shudder, and I feel nothing.

No fear, no anger, no shame.

Just emptiness. Just the cold, hard truth of what I've become.

I move toward him, and he unzips his pants. His breath already quick, coming in shallow gasps. I close my eyes and let myself drift away, letting my mind go.

I make a mental list of what I now kick myself for over-romanticizing.

Sex. (all of it)

Music. (especially the good)

Praise. (God never listened to me anyway)

I try to let go of the facade that it could've been different.

Should've been different.

43

An hour later, he clears his throat, mumbling something under his breath. His eyes stay forward, his voice rough as he says, "You're gonna have to get out here, girl. I'm making a turn up ahead, heading out to California. Week-long retreat at Salvation Mountain."

Sounds like a place I should look into.

I sit up straighter, glancing out the window, and my heart sinks. I recognize the place as we get closer—the old as dirt bar where Bo and I had stopped during our road trip.

Hussy's.

The bar looms up from the desert haze, a wreckage of memories wrapped in peeling wood. The man pulls to a stop, dust clouding around the wheels like a sigh. I climb out, but he doesn't say goodbye or good luck.

He just drives off. The sun is fading, warm like a secret whispered against your skin. I step toward the bar—the door hangs slightly ajar, and inside, it's empty except for a few souls lost in their own regrets.

I hear the clinking of glasses, a jukebox warbling "Crazy" by Patsy Cline, something that makes me ache. The last time I was here, Bo was beside me, laughing, tipping his hat like he could charm the whole damn world. I remember the way we danced, the way the air crackled with danger and lust, like a match waiting to be struck.

The floorboards creak under my feet as I walk in. No one looks up.

I make my way to the bar, and the bartender, a woman with lines around her eyes, raises her brows in acknowledgment. Her eyes are softer than I expect—like she knows. I order whiskey, and she pours without a word, sliding it across the bar. I take a sip, and it burns, but it's the kind of pain that makes me feel something, anything. I close my eyes, and the memories flood back—Bo's hand on my waist, the way he spun me around and pulled me close like he would never let go. The flash of violence, the bike, the gun, the man lying still on the ground. He was just a broken, selfish man who took what he wanted.

I open my eyes, and the bar is regrettably still here, the jukebox regrettably still playing Patsy Cline. Looking around, I see myself in every woman here—eyes hollowed out, dreams crumpled and stuffed into the back pocket of a pair of ripped jeans.

I'm not the first girl to end up here, and I won't be the last.

And for a moment, I hate him.

I hate Bo for leaving me, for making me think I was something more, something special. But the hate fades, and all that's left is the emptiness. The bartender watches me, her eyes knowing, and she reaches out, touching my hand for just a second. "You'll be alright, sweetheart," she says, her voice soft, like she's speaking to a wounded animal.

And maybe she is. I tip my head in false agreement.

I finish the whiskey and look at the bartender. She's watching me. I clear my throat, and my voice comes out rougher than intended. "Did you ever love someone like that? Someone who made you forget yourself?"

The bartender pauses, her hand wiping a glass. "Yeah, sweetheart. I think most of us have." She sets the glass down and leans on the bar, her eyes locking on mine. "But you learn, eventually."

I nod, biting my lip, my eyes stinging. "How'd you do it? How'd you get out?"

She smiles, but it's sad, like a memory that will forever roam. "Time. And a lot of nights just like this one. You keep waking up, keep putting one foot in front of the other, until one day, you realize you ain't thinking about them as much anymore. And then, eventually, you stop thinking about them at all." She leans her forearms across the bar, stopping a few inches from my face. Her breath smells like tobacco. "Just cause you got a soft spot for the mountains don't mean you need to freeze up there," she whispers.

I look down at my empty glass, running my finger over the rim. "I don't know if I can do that."

"Honey, I don't think you need me to tell you that that's all a crock of shit."

I nod again, a shaky breath escaping my lips. I push myself off the stool, my legs feeling like they could give out any moment, and I walk over to the jukebox. My fingers hover over the buttons, my vision blurring as I scroll through the songs. I find it, "Welcome to My World." I press the button. Jim's voice blooms into song, slow and soft, filling the space. I close my eyes and let the melody wrap around me, pulling me back to that night. I sway, my arms wrapped around myself, gripping tight like I could keep the pieces of me from falling apart.

I don't even know if Bo ever really happened or if I am so lonely, so starved for love, that I imagined it all.

Nothing left—no photograph, letter, or keepsake to prove he was once here. There's not even a smell lingering on my clothes.

Not a mark on my skin. Just empty memories that are more like dreams, like something my desperate heart conjured up because it couldn't bear the emptiness any longer. I spin slowly, my feet shuffling against the worn floorboards, and the tears come again, hot and heavy, sliding down my cheeks as the room blurs around me.

The music plays on, and I let it take me, let it break me apart piece by piece. I think of the way Bo looked at me that night, the way he smiled like I was his whole world. It physically pains me to know it was all a lie.

I think of everything I wanted—love, safety, belonging—and I realize that maybe those things were never meant for me.

Perhaps I was always meant to be alone, to wander without a place to rest, without a hand to hold.

I think about Jean and that note I left her. Swore it on every star I could count, whispered it like a prayer. *"I will find the dirty parts of heaven,"* I said. *"And when I do... I will find you."*

But I won't. I can't. Some lessons come wrapped in razor wire, and I wouldn't wish mine on anyone, least of all her. She's better off without me, dreaming of something pure, something I can't touch anymore.

She'll hate me for breaking that promise, but at least she'll never wear this same weight.

I'll carry it for both of us.

I whisper to God.

"Cut off my chest. Take my hair. Shave down my ass. Peel this hairless skin away from me. Take the curves that bend me, the marks that tell the world I'm a woman. Leave me bare—flat, raw, unrecognizable. Let me become something harder, sharper—just bone and muscle, nothing for anyone to touch or take."

"Let me live as a man."

"Let me walk without their eyes tracing me, their hands carving pieces of me that were never theirs to hold."

"Let me be free of the softness they mold, the sweetness they swallow, the body they use to keep me bound. I don't want it—I never did. I never asked for this. If giving it all up, every inch of what they call a woman, means I can finally exist in peace, then take it."

"Take my chest. Take my hair. Take the skin, the curves, the softness."

"Take all of it. Take it all. Just let me be."

44

stay in that bar until the sun threatens to rise, dancing, crying, and drinking until it all gets too pathetic to watch. With pity etched across her tired face, the bartender finally kicks me out at sunrise.

"Go on, sweetheart," she says, her voice a mix of exhaustion and gentleness, "You can't stay here forever."

And so, I find myself on the side of the bare stretch, the rusted horizon stretching before me, unending and indifferent. I sit there, knees pulled up, arms wrapped around them, the sky glowing faintly with the dawn. I feel like the world has moved on without me, and I'm just a relic left behind—something that no one knows what to do with anymore. My eyes are swollen, my throat raw from crying.

I have nothing, not even the strength to stand up.

That's when I hear the rumble of an engine, a busted truck pulling up in front of me, a dull roar in the placid morning. The truck door creaks open, and a man steps out.

He's handsome. It looks like he's in his forties, bald, with a sun-weathered face, no different than every other man baked under Nevada's wrath. He's got a blade of grass between his teeth, eyes squinting against the rising sun. He looks at me, and there's something almost familiar in his gaze—like I've seen it before in another life. "Howdy, darlin'," he says, carrying that western lilt. "Need a ride?"

I stare at him for a long moment, and the thought crosses my mind. But deep down, I know the truth. I know it in the way he stands there. By the way, his smile doesn't quite reach his eyes. He's simply another version of Bo. Another stranger with empty promises and a heart that won't ever have room for me.

I could get up.

I could climb in that truck and drive until the desert runs out.

But what's the point? What's the point of climbing back up when I know I'll just be thrown down again, left to pick up the shattered pieces of myself—alone?

Suddenly, the unmistakable roar of another engine probes my ears. I squint at the growing cloud of dust in the distance, and I can see the silhouette of an Audi Quattro hurtling toward me.

My heart skips a beat. A name slips into my memories.

Gemma?

No, it can't be.

She skids to a stop right there in the middle of the byway, dust flying in all directions. She sees me. Sees me sitting there with that man standing over me—and I see the heartbreak on her face.

She stays in the car, her hands gripping the steering wheel, her eyes wide and filled with disbelief, pain, and something a little close to fear.

Fear that she's too late.

With dawn creeping closer, painting the pink frontier in a soft, cruel light.

He waits.

Gemma waits.

I sit there, the weight of every choice I've ever made pressing down on me. Love is the cruelest gamble of all, isn't it? We always forget the sharp sting of that first heartbreak, the way it carves us open just because someone new shows us a flicker of kindness. How many times can we climb back up, knowing the fall is inevitable, only to avoid being alone?

He shifts. A lone tumbleweed meanders lazily behind him. Nowhere to go but everywhere to be.

Gemma parts her lips as if on the verge of speaking, but the words never come. It's almost as if the entire world retains its breath. I close my eyes, embracing the sun's warmth, beginning to touch my skin.

I could leave.

I could stay.

I could try again.

I could let it all end *here*, on this lonely stretch of land.

I don't move. Heaven's shallow curve blurs, tears spilling all over again, and all I can do is sit there and wonder—if I have it in me to get up one more time.

Mechelle Vinson in front of the Supreme Court in 1986 after the justices heard her sex discrimination case. (Photo *via* Washington Post)

"I didn't know what to do," she told The Post. "This is a man that I believed in. All the while he was nice to me, he was saying he was going to help me. I just felt sick, like, you know, why is this happening to me? … And he kept saying to me I was a big girl now and he wasn't going to hurt me, and to take my clothes off."

Mechelle Vinson to the Washington Post

Acknowledgments

I'd like to thank my parents, Jennifer and Robert, for not laughing in my face when I said I wanted to go to art school. Lubomir Kocka and Greg Viens, thank you for believing in my skills as a storyteller. All my peers at SCAD who pushed me to become a stronger writer. Johnny Cash, Nancy Sinatra, Dolly Parton, Rod Stewart, Dire Straits, and Elvis Presley for keeping me company, as I wrote. My friends, for listening to my insufferable rants about this story. To you, my beautiful readers. The great state of Nevada, which upon visiting, was everything I thought it would be and more. And finally, a big hug to the little girl put into a special program for kids who had difficulty reading.

Funny how things work out.